'⸺ ⸺ ⸺ ⸺ ⸺ ⸺ ⸺ ⸺ back my

⸺ ⸺ only a few hours of daylight left to warm me.

'No,' she says, her eyes meeting mine for the first time. There's something peculiar about them. The color, so dark as if her pupils are melting, swirling, then shifting again, and the way her gaze remains steady. They seem to reach within me, prodding. 'She's probably with Victor anyway. They fight a lot.'

'I doubt she'd be very happy if she knew you played in a funeral home.'

Even as I say the words, I know they aren't true. Trecie has the aura of the neglected: silently desperate, unnaturally composed. And there's something else I recognize, though I can't be sure what it is: the turn of her nose, the natural arch of her eyebrows, or that sense of aloneness even when in the company of others. Now it's clear she would never cry if her mother pulled a comb through a snarl.

Amy MacKinnon is a former congressional aide and freelance writer. She lives outside Boston, Massachusetts with her husband and their three young children. Visit her website at www.AmyMacKinnon.com.

TETHERED

AMY MacKINNON

An Orion paperback

First published in Great Britain in 2008
by Orion
This paperback edition published in 2009
by Orion Books Ltd,
Orion House, 5 Upper St Martin's Lane,
London WC2H 9EA

An Hachette UK company

1 3 5 7 9 10 8 6 4 2

A CIP catalogue record for this book
is available from the British Library.

ISBN 978-0-7528-8398-4

Printed and bound in Great Britain by
Clays Ltd, St Ives plc

The Orion Publishing Group's policy is to use papers
that are natural, renewable and recyclable products and
made from wood grown in sustainable forests. The logging
and manufacturing processes are expected to conform to
the environmental regulations of the country of origin.

www.orionbooks.co.uk

To Erica Michelle Maria Green
and all the other children
who were never loved enough

CHAPTER ONE

I plunge my thumb between the folds of the incision, then hook my forefinger deep into her neck. Unlike most of the bloodlines, which offer perfunctory resistance, the carotid artery doesn't surrender itself willingly. Tethered between the heart and head, the sinewy tube is often weighted with years of plaque, thickening its resolve to stay. More so now that rigor mortis has settled deep within the old woman.

Each time I tug on that vessel, I think of my mother. I imagine other daughters are reminded of their dead parents whenever they hear the refrain from an old song, or feel the heft of a treasured bedtime story resting on their own child's nightstand. My trigger is the transformation of a battered corpse back to someone familiar. I was too young when she died to remember her scent, and I have no memory of her voice. But her wake – like the accident – plays in my head like a movie reel, some frames taut and crisp, others brittle, fluttery things. Though always her face is clear: before, after, and then after again at the funeral.

I remember my grandmother's friends clustered near the Easter lilies, whispering their doubts about my mother's eternal salvation. My grandmother, her frayed black slip hanging just beyond the hem of her dress, bringing me to kneel on road-burned knees before the casket (*don't look!*) and then hurrying me along, leaving me alone in the family room. I remember holding fast to my doll, a gift from one of my mother's many boyfriends. He said he chose her because she resembled me. Even then I knew better. The doll was elegant and slight, with porcelain cheeks and delicate lashes, lips like my mother's and eyes that clicked shut when I laid her beside me at night. She wore a red flamenco dress, gold earrings I once tried to pierce through my own lobes, and a parchment calling card tied to her wrist, her name in curvy script: *Patrice*. But what I remember best of all from that day was Mr. Mulrey, the undertaker. The mourners huddled in an adjoining room, their fingers clinging to rosary beads, their souls lashed to prayers, their drumbeat-chants vibrating within me. I ran from that room, desperate to escape, and rushed headlong into Mr. Mulrey. He was standing in the doorway of my mother's room, filling it, appearing as bewildered as I felt. I clutched at his suit coat and he turned to me, hands worrying at his own set of beads. All of him stooped as if to avoid a raised hand: shoulders sunk, chin nearly resting on his chest, eyes buried deep beneath a low, dark brow meeting mine.

'I want to go home,' I said. I told him about my

grandmother's house, a place much like the funeral parlor with its heavy drapes and multitude of crucifixes, with long silences interrupted only by longer prayers. The way she pressed me to her bosom, suffocating with her old lady smell, vowing to protect me from my mother's fate. I fingered the thick gauze that bound my head and asked if he'd take me to where my mother was.

He pocketed his beads then and folded my hand inside his enormous one. We walked away from the hum of mourners and stopped within a few feet of where my mother lay tucked in a lit alcove at the far end of the room. She appeared pink and rested. Her usual red lips were softened with the palest shade of coral, her pillowy bosom hidden beneath a lace collar. But there she was. With candles casting hypnotic shadows against my mother's face, the room seemed kinder than the one I'd left earlier.

'Don't be afraid,' said Mr. Mulrey, ushering me over to the coffin. He allowed me to touch my mother for the first time since the accident. I stroked her hand, but it was hard and cold. So instead my fingers sought the fabric of her dress, knitting through her lace cuff as I spoke.

'I was sleeping when we crashed,' I said. 'Then I was shaking her and shaking her, but she wouldn't wake up.'

He let me go on like that; at least I don't recall him telling me to hush. He simply knelt beside me, alongside my mother, listening. When I finished, he remained quiet.

'Mommy,' I whined, poking her arm, clutching Patrice to me, her doll's eyes fluttering with each jostle. 'I want to go home.' I wanted to sleep in my own bed, not in Grandma's with her musty blankets and sharp toenails, with bedtime stories about mothers passing on to eternal damnation.

That's when Mr. Mulrey again took my hand in his. 'She's dead.' He brushed aside a lovely curl that flipped over my mother's brow where the worst gash had been to reveal the precise row of stitches he'd made with thread to match her flesh.

'Where's all the blood?' I asked, but he misunderstood. I'd meant the blood that concealed her face in our final moments together as we lay in the street. He tugged open her collar to expose three neat stitches in her neck, telling me how he drained her blood from the carotid artery and replaced it with formaldehyde that then hardened inside of her. In spite of myself, I was awed by his ability to erase the wounds, to help me see my mother again.

I kissed my doll's cheek and settled her against my mother, watching until Patrice's eyes trembled closed. I almost snatched her back. I wanted to. Instead, I unraveled the calling card twined to her tiny wrist and hid it at the very bottom of my dress pocket. It would be the only memento I had of my mother. When I started to cry, fingering the three stitches (*one-two-three, one-two-three, one-two-three, breathe*), Mr. Mulrey placed a hand on my shoulder and whispered, 'Never mind what the others say. We're all sinners and all sinners are welcomed by God.'

But I wasn't comforted by a god who couldn't give me back my mother; I found salvation in the undertaker who could. I suppose that's why I became one.

MY FINGER FINDS the carotid artery in the old woman's neck and plucks it through the throat. Against my powdered glove, her tissue appears more gray than it actually is. Cancer does that; it drains the color from a person's body as it drains the life, leaving the once vital carotid grizzled. Taking my scalpel once again, I slice the artery to empty it and turn my attention to what I imagine had once been a shapely thigh. I massage it before penetrating the slack skin with the syringe pump, straight into her femoral artery. A vibrant pink formaldehyde will restore the luster to her skin. Her sunken cheeks will need plumping, so I ready those syringes as well. Glancing at the bulletin board to a photograph her son gave me, I begin planning how I'll sculpt her face. It'll comfort her loved ones to be reminded of the woman she was before the cancer devoured her.

As her blood flows out and the embalming fluid flows in, I suture her mouth. People almost always die with their mouths open. Linus, the funeral director here, once said he thought it was because a person's soul was expelled with the last breath. I'm often reminded of that while threading the needle through my clients' lips. It seems a naive sentiment for a man who's lived as much as Linus. Most people in the town of Whitman and in the adjacent city of Brockton trust Linus to lead them to their next world because his is a sincere belief. I used to think it was an ideal born of good business sense. Looking up at the golden-hued portrait of Jesus gazing out over a moonlit village, and beyond to the woman lying before me, I realize I should have known better. Linus hung the painting in this workspace when he opened his funeral parlor more than forty years ago. The artist, whose signature I've not been able to decipher these past twelve years, christened it *The Shepherd*. When Linus showed me around my first day, he said it reminded him that he and the dead were not alone. For me, it was never the case. I've always known I'm alone with the dead.

I remove my glove and take an ivory taper and a gardening book from a box I keep hidden in a nearby cabinet. After I check the dog-eared page, I return the book to its spot. I don't know why I keep these items hidden, except perhaps that Linus would misinterpret them as instruments of faith, evidence of my conversion. I fit the candle into its holder, strike a match, and then allow Mozart's Violin Concerto no. 5 to lift the dreariness of my basement workspace. The candle appears to flicker in time to the strings being plucked. This is the only time I listen to music.

As with all trades, there's a routine to mine. It's during this interlude, as the bloodletting begins but before the cleansing commences, that I perform this ritual of sorts. While Linus has his prayers to purge the soul, I bathe the body with music and candlelight. What with the clinical stainless-steel worktable, angled for maximum drainage, fluorescent lights, and frigid concrete floor, it seems only proper that there be some softening of the moment, some recognition of the life lived. It's not meant to be a send-off into another world, more a farewell from this one. Yes, a good-bye. A trip to where I don't know, the ground usually. Most times the deceased leave the embalming room propped in a somber coffin with satin pillows to comfort the bereaved. Then off to the freshly dug earth or, occasionally, a fired oven. Few go straight from the deathbed to the flame.

Though I would prefer to use a warm washcloth and sudsy water the way a mother would when welcoming a newborn at the beginning of life, the law requires I use an approved antiseptic and disposable sponge for this last bath. The gore of the blood draining and the odor of deterioration make this process difficult, but I simply recall the tenderness of that first bath and try to honor it.

As Piano Concerto no. 26 cues, I finish washing the old woman. I remove my gloves, turn off the music, blow out the candle. More gloves and a cotton mask – sterile formalities in this most intimate of times – and then I lift the trocar from its hook on the wall. I insert the instrument into the small incision in her abdomen, just above the navel, and then turn on the suction. It's important for the aesthetics of the wake that all bodily fluids and soft organs be removed.

I wash her again with only the humming water pipes as an accompaniment this time, then cover her body in a sheet. She'll have to wait for her dress and pumps. Her son forgot to bring them when he dropped off her photograph. Though there's an armoire just outside this room filled with clothes to adorn the dead – high-collared dresses with modest hemlines and easy-access snaps, dark suits with starched shirts and Velcro back seams – most people prefer to dress their loved ones in something familiar. Though sometimes a daughter will shop a better department store for a demure dress that will rot in the ground, often with price tags still attached.

With the bathing finished, I plug in the rollers and fetch the makeup box and hair dryer from the closet. People tend to overlook this aspect of the preparation, but it's oftentimes what mourners remember best. Somehow it soothes them to know the dead are well coiffed. (I've never been able to wear makeup myself.) With her hair damp, I begin applying her makeup: thick layers of foundation to cover the few cancer ulcers on her forehead and chin, the spray of broken blood vessels along her nose, blush to liven her cheeks, and a shade of tangerine lipstick I found on her chest of drawers. Her scalp – pink again – runs like ribbons through her fine hair. The photograph shows a woman who preferred a few well-placed bangs along her forehead, the rest teased up and away to cover the bare spots toward the crown. I smooth the ends with hair wax, spray it all with extra-hold formula bought in bulk from the salon down the street, and then reach for my stylist's shears. I've learned over the years that a little more layering will add much more fullness.

Her preparation nearly complete, I turn to my instrument tray and remove the bouquet of morning glories from their wax paper and transfer them to a jug of water. Years ago when I started my own garden, the book I turned to was *Nature's Bounty: The Care, Keeping, and Meaning of Flowers*. In addition to advising the novice gardener about natural compost and the buoyancy of evergreens in winter, it listed a variety of plants and their significance. So for the old woman, morning glories (*affection upon departure*). It seems an appropriate choice given her family's devotion.

I wash my hands a final time before turning off the lights; she won't mind the darkness. I take the stairs up to ground level, where the bodies are waked, leaving behind concrete slabs and glaring lights for ambient rooms filled with leather sofas and demure tissue boxes. It's a purgatory of sorts for the grief-stricken to gather and whisper their regrets to the dead and each other.

It will be empty now. Linus buried a middle-aged father of three this morning, and the old woman isn't to be waked until tomorrow afternoon. I begin to imagine the cup of tea I'll make in the cottage Linus leases me, hidden behind the wisteria-covered (*cordial welcome*) trellis that divides my life from this Victorian funeral parlor. Linus lives even closer. He and Alma share the two floors above the business; they have no trellis, no desire to keep away the dead. Looking around the parlor's sitting room, I sense something odd. But there's nothing amiss here; it's all the familiar colors from the palette Alma chose for their own living quarters: chocolate leather sofas, burgundy wingbacks, and creamy wainscoting peppered with brushed brass switch plates. I suppose it makes sense, their living among the dead.

I head to the entrance door and place my hand on the knob, eager for natural light upon my face, but stop when I notice something startle behind an abundance of calla lilies (*modesty*) on the foyer table. It's a little girl.

She runs one finger along the end table, a wisp of hair hiding her eyes. She's no more than eight, slight, and alone.

'Hello?' I say.

She flinches, looks toward me, but doesn't speak.

'Where's your father?' I ask.

She pauses and then raises a finger tucked beneath a faded pink sleeve, pressing it to her chest. 'Me?'

I check to see if anyone else is in the room. 'Are you here with your father? Did he bring your grandmother's dress?'

She glances around before shaking her head.

'Who are you with?'

She gives me her back and begins to walk away. I'm reminded of the dozens of children who've passed through here, too stunned by events to be coherent, to be mindful of their elders – sins my grandmother would have forgiven with her boar's-hair brush.

'Wait,' I call.

The girl becomes motionless. I peer around the corner to Linus's office, but the door at the end of the hall is closed. 'Is your family talking to Mr. Bartholomew?'

'The big guy?' She looks off as she says this. Her profile is quite lovely and I wonder what it's like, to be pretty.

'Yes,' I answer. There's a slight shift in her expression – a sense of relief, of recognition? I can't be certain. Her eyes dart in and out behind those wisps.

'He always wears sweaters?'

Her skin appears oddly yellow under these forty-watt bulbs, or maybe it's lost the sun-kissed luster of summer, become sallow the way mine does during New England's waning autumn months and then blanched a dusky hue in the endless stretch of winter. Even her legs, bare beneath a denim skirt, have an odd pallor. When she speaks, I can't help but stare at the gap between her two front teeth, the way her tongue catches in that space. Her hair, dark and fine, hangs in long curly spirals to her waist. I wonder if she cries when her mother combs it.

'So you know Mr. Bartholomew?'

'Linus lets me play here.'

I suddenly remember the single mother who moved into one of the rentals down the street. Most nights I see the woman shuffling along the sidewalk with a child, both heading toward Tedeschi's corner store on the next block. Sometimes I'll catch the woman blessing herself as she passes the cemetery across the street from here, motioning her child away from the edge of the sidewalk, away from the only busy street in town. They walk in all weather, a cigarette dangling from the woman's lips, head bent, while her little girl skips ahead. The girl doesn't appear to know she's dancing alongside the dead. This must be her, the daughter.

I start to approach the child, then stop. 'My name is Clara. Clara Marsh.' She raises a hand near her mouth to nibble at her cuticles. 'What's your name?' I ask.

'Trecie,' she says. With her other hand, she fingers a day lily (*coquetry*).

'Trecie?'

'Patrice, but everyone calls me Trecie.'

A name, it's only a name. It means nothing.

'Does your mother know you're here, Trecie?' I check my watch. I have only a few hours of daylight left to warm me.

'No,' she says, her eyes meeting mine for the first time. There's something peculiar about them. The color, so dark as if her pupils are melting, swirling, then shifting again, and the way her gaze remains steady. They seem to reach within me, prodding. 'She's probably with Victor anyway. They fight a lot.'

'I doubt she'd be very happy if she knew you played in a funeral home.'

Even as I say the words, I know they aren't true. Trecie has the aura of the neglected: silently desperate, unnaturally composed. And there's something else I recognize, though I can't be sure what it is: the turn of her nose, the natural arch of her eyebrows, or that sense of aloneness even when in the company of others. Now it's clear she would never cry if her mother pulled a comb through a snarl.

I look to see if Linus's door is still closed, if he's meeting with a distraught family and can't be interrupted for something as innocuous as a forgotten child. I heard voices in there earlier.

'Are you sure Mr. Bartholomew lets you play here? Wouldn't you rather go to the playground with the other children? It's just down the block from Tedeschi's.'

She shakes her bowed head, tucking back stray bits of hair that have come loose from behind either ear. 'Nobody ever yells here.' She jerks her head, suddenly beaming as she casts about the room. 'I like the candles and the flowers and the chairs.' She stops, then smiles again, revealing those teeth. 'I think you like it too.'

It's time to shoo her on, make her go home, but my beeper vibrates against my hip and my focus turns to the next tragedy. It's the medical examiner. Instead of the cup of tea I long for, there's a body waiting for me.

I glance at the girl before walking down the hall to Linus's office, wondering if it's safe to leave a wayward child there alone, what might be missing when I return. Pressing my ear against the door, listening for voices, there's only the scratch of writing. A brush of my knuckles against the oak panel and he calls out.

Linus is sitting at his desk, fountain pen poised over a sheaf of papers, and for a moment his mind remains with his work. His skin is a vivid shade of black, smooth and unlined, as if his has been a life untouched by tragedy. At an age when others begin to wither and fold, everything about Linus is lush and full: his cheeks, lips, and especially his belly, always plump from Alma's cooking. He's saved from appearing obese by his impressive height and excellent carriage. Still, he's a big man. His hair – gone gray now, though his mustache retains some of its color – is clipped close, his limbs are long and beginning to bend, gnarled at the fingers, and one must imagine the toes, from arthritis: osteo. I assume even in his youth his gestures were languid, intentional, backed by a remarkable physical strength. I've seen him lift bodies the size of tree trunks with little effort. It's easy to stand in his shadow. When he raises his bowed head, his face softens into a smile, catching me in his circle of warmth. I take a step back.

'You didn't work right through lunch again, did you now? Lord, look at you, all skin and bones. Go on upstairs, Alma has some of that leftover turkey pot pie with that homemade cranberry sauce of hers.'

'Linus, the M.E. called.'

He drops his chin and mumbles a brief prayer before he speaks. 'You call if you need me.'

'I will,' I say, though I never do. I turn to go, but the child. 'There's a girl out in the mourning room. Trecie?'

'Trecie?' His face twists and he appears confused.

'Yes, about seven or eight, with long dark hair,' I say. 'She said you let her play here.'

Linus's pen, a good one, is caught in midair and then twitches in his hand. It spasms there until he drops it and begins to massage the knotted joints of his fingers, his eyes never wavering. I wonder if he thinks I've lost my mind, but then he speaks. 'She was paying me a visit just a little bit ago. She still here?'

I nod. 'So it's all right, then?'

'Oh, yes,' Linus says, his jowls lifting into a smile.

I close Linus's door and hear his chair creak as the latch tumbles into place. He begins to hum and then his bass drifts into song. Softly, for only his ears, but for mine, too, *Was blind, but now I see . . .'*

For all the years I've known Linus, there's still much about him that confounds me. In our work, we're privy to the underside of humanity: the bludgeoned grandfathers with generous wills; the strangled girlfriends with dead babies nestled deep within their wombs; the many shaken infants. Yet again and again he seeks the humanity in people, though again and again he must be disappointed.

I head back to the room where Trecie is standing next to a silver candy dish brimming with peppermints in cellophane twists. I don't expect either the candies or the dish to be there when I return.

'You may have one,' I say. 'Just one.'

Trecie doesn't respond, just shakes her head. She

walks toward the empty room where the bodies are waked, where the old woman will soon lie. Her funeral bouquets have already been arranged, and the upholstered folding chairs line the walls, set to receive her mourners. Trecie nears the space reserved for caskets, then abruptly plops down, cross-legged, her fingers encircling her naked ankles, her tiny feet hidden inside once white sneakers with faded cartoon characters.

'I like your hair. It looks like mine,' she says.

My hand goes to my head, grasping the hair pulled back in its elastic. It's a thicket of wiry brown coils, *woolly,* my grandmother called it, not at all something to be admired. It hangs nearly to my waist, since salons aren't a part of my routine. I haven't worn it loose since the day of my senior-year portrait.

Trecie gathers her own between her hands to form a ponytail. 'How do I look?'

'Pretty.'

She drops her hair and cups her chin in her hand as she regards me. 'When you were a girl, did you wear your hair down?'

There's a sore just above the nape of my neck, raw and sweet, obscured by the elastic. Without intending to, my finger goes there.

'Whenever it was long enough, I wore it up,' I say. She couldn't know; it's simply an innocent question. She continues to watch me, unblinking. 'I have to leave now, so you should probably go.'

She hesitates, unraveling her legs, and then lifts

herself, slowly. Trecie wanders back toward the foyer, her fingers skimming the funeral bouquets along the way; the flowers wave as she retreats. Then she stops. Pointing to the room we've just left, Trecie says, 'Where do they go when you're done with them?'

I must leave; I need to bring home the dead. And I don't know how to speak to children, especially of such things. 'To the cemetery, like the one across the street.'

She nods, though she doesn't move. 'But where do they all *go*?' Her right hand finds its way back to her hair and she begins to twirl a section near the crown.

I'm mesmerized by the motion, distracted. I wonder what she means, and then I understand. True, this is a place that inspires such questions, and each time a child passes through here, inevitably he or she asks Linus or a family member. No one has ever thought to ask me. 'Some people believe that after they die, they go to heaven.'

She stops twisting her hair, her forehead wrinkled and mouth open. I've confused her. How to explain such a thing?

'Like perennials.' I point to a lavender flower in one of the old woman's arrangements. 'Irises lie buried during the coldest part of the year until they blossom in May. By late spring their flowers fall away, and the leaves die in the fall. All winter they lie dormant under the ground until the next spring. Then they come back to life and bloom again.'

Trecie tilts her head and looks at the stained-glass

window casting garnet speckles across the far wall. She resumes her twisting. 'Is that what will happen to all those people in the cemetery?'

'No.' I've made things worse. I try to imagine a world that would appeal to a child, a beautiful lie, and try again. 'Do you have a favorite place?'

'Here.'

'Isn't there someplace else? Somewhere special?'

'Victor took me to the Marshfield Fair once. I had cotton candy and got to see the whole town from the top of the Ferris wheel.'

'Well, heaven's like that. You go there.'

I brace myself for more questions I can't answer, preparing excuses and a quick exit, but she laughs, wrenching her hand free of her hair, taking several strands with it. 'You're lying!'

I start backing out of the room, my beeper vibrating against my hip with each step. 'No.'

'Yes, you are. You die' – she smiles, snapping her fingers – 'just like that.'

I say the only words I know to say. 'That's what some people believe.'

Trecie looks at me again, and I'm reminded of Mr. Mulrey, of being seen for the first time. 'Isn't that what you believe?'

I feel in my pants pocket for the car keys, in my blazer for my cell phone. 'You may stay here, but don't go downstairs. That's private. Only Mr. Bartholomew and I are allowed there. Do you understand?'

She catches herself before a smile parts her lips, and nods instead. It occurs to me as I hurry toward the hearse that Trecie knows this already. She knows because she's been downstairs.

CHAPTER TWO

Death has its own aura. Whether I'm picking up a body from some downtrodden hospital morgue or a pastel hospice, its presence makes itself known before any of my five senses are alerted. If I believed in such things, I would say death tickles the sixth sense. But it's simply instinct. Humans – all animals, really – are born to seek life and avoid death. I suppose I'm an anomaly.

I know without checking the address the M.E. gave me; I'm drawn to the triple-decker. Sun-bleached aqua paint hanging in long strips and a limp rose of Sharon, its few remaining leaves crackling in the wind, are all that distinguish this apartment building from the others. Most everything is covered in a filmy grit. It collects in one's ears and eyes, in one's spit. It's as if it rains only dust here in Brockton. The cars on blocks, the overflowing Dumpsters tucked between buildings, even the people, all appear to be some shade of gray. There are no open spaces for gardening, almost nowhere to put an Adirondack chair – almost nothing lovely to look upon if even there were, fading architecture being the exception.

Though this is a city of neighborhoods – Haitians, Brazilians, Cape Verdeans, the few remaining Irish, elderly mostly, and a handful of Danes and Puerto Ricans – the young toughs and the drugs they sell make it so almost no one who lives here can afford to be neighborly. It's said the life seeped out of them, of this city, when the shoe factories closed. All that's left of the mills is pulverized brick and mortar, as if cremated by years of bombing raids, their remains carried off by the winds as war refugees scavenge among the rubble for meth and heroin, shaking free yet more dust.

Through the torn screen door, I spot the patrolman shuffling about the foyer, hands dug deep into shallow pants pockets, waiting for me to arrive so he can leave. Before I reach the first step, the policeman, Ryan O'Leary, pushes open the door. I hear other voices coming from down the narrow hall, voices of authority. I look toward the street and see a Crown Vic parked across from a patrol car.

'Vic-tor-y for the missus,' whispers Ryan, letting the screen door slam behind him.

'Pardon?'

'Bitch killed him.'

'Should I leave? Is the medical examiner investigating?' I ask. I didn't see his car.

'Nah, M.E. left,' says Ryan. 'Said it's a heart attack, but bitch killed 'im for sure.'

I watch Ryan twitch and jump, slide his jaw back and forth until there's an audible pop. He arrived home last month from a yearlong National Guard rotation, eager to assimilate, the other cops eager to overlook his strain. He'd been on the department just a few years when he was called up, returning more jittery than before. He still wears a military buzz close against his scalp. His constant movement must be the reason for his wiry frame, the bulge of veins along his forearms. Though he bears the scars of childhood acne, his face is always shaved close, the scent of Polo clinging to it. Hands back in his pockets, his balance sure, he dribbles a ragged tennis ball between his feet. Ryan would do better on street patrol than on attendings. I imagine car chases and B&Es during the night are more to his liking. My eyes stray to the gun holstered at his hip. This must be torture.

'Is it down the hall here?' I ask, feeling around my jacket pocket for a calling card to leave the family. In their grief, they may forget which funeral home they've chosen, or in this case, the one the M.E. chose for them. It wouldn't be the first time. If there's more than one person around, I'll leave a card with the family member most composed and another on the kitchen table.

'I been to this house a hundred times on domestics,' says Ryan, seemingly unaware of the *thwack-thwack-thwack* of the ball now against the house. 'He used to beat the shit outta her. Hey, that's street justice for you. Can't say I blame her.'

'Where's the body?' I ask.

Ryan catches the ball under the arch of his foot. 'You got one guess.'

I don't mean to sigh but do. Ryan dribbles the ball between his feet and then kicks it into the street. It smacks against his patrol car before disappearing. He pulls open the screen door, holding it for me, and I walk past him toward the voices at the end of the hall. Along the way is a living room on the left, dotted with rumpled newspapers and crushed beer cans; a cramped dining room to the right that serves as a storage room for tired Christmas decorations and rabbit-eared televisions; and two bedrooms farther down on the left, both with unmade beds and clutter-strewn bureaus. I know better than to expect the body to be waiting for me in any of these rooms. Gastrointestinal distress usually precedes a heart attack.

At the end of the hall is the kitchen and beyond that the bathroom, door slightly ajar, a varicosed foot propping it open.

There are two plainclothes detectives, Mike Sullivan and Jorge Gonzalez, talking to a fifty-something woman in worn slippers and robe, her mutton face ringed by frayed platinum curls. She's sitting at a Formica table, picking at a hole in her vinyl-upholstered chair, dropping yellow foam onto a pile of crumbs and dirt collecting at her feet. She appears to be crying. When she presses a crumpled paper napkin to her nose, I notice her cheeks are as dry as her hair.

Mike Sullivan's eyes race across her face. There's a hardness to Mike that coarsens the softness of his Irish features. His tall frame carries only lean muscle, each fiber rigid and flexed. His hair is fixed in place and his skin is forever pale. His lips are too full for a man's and, when he isn't speaking, usually pressed closed. There's a constant furrow about his brow; lines stream from the corners of his eyes as if dried riverbeds. Only his eyes seem bound to this world. An opaque blue, they're always seeking the story from others, never revealing their own depths. Mike has endless questions. He's often quizzed me about some body I've prepared, usually after the M.E.'s autopsy. From the tone of his voice, I expect he'll be by the funeral home later.

'The neighbor upstairs said she heard you and Mr. MacDonnell arguing earlier. Said she almost called us it was so bad. Did he hit you today?' Mike asks Mrs. Mac-Donnell.

Her fingers leave the foam to loosen a pocket of her robe, caught beneath a thick radial of flesh, pulling free a pack of cigarettes. She fumbles with the Newports, passing a lighter to her other hand as she tugs one from the box. When she lights the cigarette, deep ravines pool around her lips. She inhales again before answering. 'Yeah, he hit me.'

'Why didn't you call us?' asks the other detective, Jorge Gonzalez. He's a soft touch, but then he hasn't lived, or died, as much as Mike Sullivan.

Mrs. MacDonnell shrugs, continues to smoke, wiping at nonexistent tears.

I want to get on with collecting the body, but I know better than to interrupt now. Under the layers of burning tobacco and days-old trash is an even worse stench coming from the bathroom. My hope is the dead man made it to the toilet in time to evacuate his system before cardiac arrest seized him. I look again to the bathroom door, but it's impossible to tell from the angle of the foot whether the body is sprawled on the floor or seated.

'You said your husband had high blood pressure,' Mike says. 'Was he on any medication?'

Mrs. MacDonnell heaves herself up and shuffles over to the cabinet above the sink. She searches among the scattered bottles of cough syrup and vials, then pulls out two prescriptions. She squints at them before raising the glasses that hang from her neck onto her crooked nose. As she reads, I notice three blue smudges just above her collar. A darker, lumpy bruise, as colorful as an oil spill, seems to throb just below her right ear.

'Here,' says Mrs. MacDonnell, holding out the bottles to Mike before replacing her heft onto the seat. 'Lipitor and the nitroglycerin that doctor gave him last month when we was at the emergency room. It's for angina.'

'Which hospital was that?' asks Mike.

'Brockton City,' snorts Mrs. MacDonnell. 'Did you think we'd go to some fancy Boston hospital?'

Jorge turns to Mike, his expression imploring Mike to end the questions, but I can tell from Mike's utter stillness he has more.

'One more thing, Mrs. MacDonnell,' Mike says as the woman reaches for another cigarette to light off of the dying one. 'Did Mr. MacDonnell ever do any drugs, say coke, methamphetamines? Something that might affect his heart?'

She stops puffing, her eyes flicking to Mike's face. I don't want to be here any longer. I don't care to see the vagaries of another's drama play itself out, but I understand the unspoken rules of the scene and don't move; only my eyes to see Mike tense, ready to pounce on Mrs. MacDonnell.

Reaching for another napkin, she says, 'I don't know.'

Mike bends to meet her head-on. 'So if I ordered a test, a toxicology test to check his blood for drugs, I wouldn't find anything there?'

Mrs. MacDonnell's fingers seek the hole in the chair again and rapidly pluck out large tufts of foam. 'How the hell should I know?'

'Mike,' says Jorge. 'Can I talk to you a minute?'

'You stay,' says Mrs. MacDonnell, pushing on the table to rise to her feet. 'I got to go to the john.' Looking sideways to the foot that protrudes from her own bathroom, she says, 'I'll be next door if you need me.'

They wait until the screen door slams before speaking.

'Mikey, look,' says Jorge, stepping in close to his partner. 'Case closed. He was on meds, the M.E. called it. I talked to his doctor for chrissake, it's a heart attack. What the hell you doing?'

'Come on.' Mike's fingers rake his hair. 'How many

times have the police been called out here? How many times did they threaten to kill each other?' Lowering his voice – I can barely hear him: 'If we look around, I guar-an*tee* you we'll find some powder. We ask the dealers, they'll tell you sweet Mrs. MacDonnell was out trolling for meth. I guarantee it.'

I want to slip through the doorway, out to where Ryan is still pacing in the foyer. His company is better than this. But the tension freezes me in place. Other people's anger does that.

Jorge presses still closer. 'Now you want to get a fuck-ing search warrant? Case closed, Mikey. Case closed.'

'Let's just run a tox test.'

'It'll take the crime lab months before they turn something like that around. You know how backlogged they are, and this ain't exactly a priority. Then what? Prove she put the drugs in his morning coffee? Even if she did kill him, all the evidence will be gone.' Jorge throws his hands in the air as if to toss confetti. 'Gone.'

He walks away from Mike, whose eyes remain locked on Mr. MacDonnell's foot, and says, 'Let it go.'

'She gets away with murder?'

Jorge rests a hand on Mike's shoulder. 'Mikey, he beat the shit out of her. Is it such a great loss?'

Mike's face is stricken, and I shrink back into the wall, afraid of what's to come. 'So she gets away with murder?'

Jorge sighs. 'What happened to you, Mikey, to Jenny, that was wrong. That kid should have been put away for the rest of his life, what he did. But this is different. There's no evidence a crime even took place.'

Mike continues to stare off as Jorge gives his shoulder an affectionate shake. 'You know, maybe you should listen to the chief, take some time off, talk to that doctor – '

'For chrissake, Jorge – '

'Mikey, what do you want me to say? You're seeing things that aren't there again.'

I think I've melted into the nicotined wallpaper; I'm no longer aware of myself, and it seems they aren't either. There've been many times when this has worked, when no one in the room is aware of my presence.

But then Jorge starts. 'Jesus, Clara, where did you come from?'

'I'm here to retrieve the body. The M.E. called me.'

'How long you been standing there?' he asks.

Mike looks past me to the hallway, where Ryan's footsteps smack toward us along the hardwood.

'The body's in here?' I gesture toward the bathroom.

'Yeah, on the pot, like I told you,' says Ryan, stepping into the kitchen. He nods in the general direction, rolling back and forth from his heels to the balls of his feet.

The bathroom is only a few steps away, and as I walk toward it I'm suddenly awash in relief, eager to be rid of the tension over there. All is forgotten when I push open the door.

'Oh.'

Ryan peers over my shoulder, the awe or disgust settling him until he whispers, 'Now that's what I call a Big Mac Attack.'

It's true; Mr. MacDonnell is a very large man. He sits slightly askew, his head slumped against the shower stall. There is no bath. He's wearing only a white tank top, coffee splotches dribbled along the front, and faded boxers around his ankles. Curly red and gray hairs cover every surface of his exposed body, a ruddy contrast to the bluish tint his lips have taken on. While his flesh isn't soft and rolling, it is densely packed, an indication of enormous weight. His eyes are bulging slightly, a startling blue, unfocused and mute. His dignity is somewhat preserved by this morning's edition of the *Boston Herald*, open to the sports section, covering his genitals.

I stand in the bathroom doorway, assessing the particulars of this removal. If I were the praying sort, I'd give thanks he's sitting on the toilet. Yet his mass is such that he'll need to be removed sideways – a lot of lifting, since I won't be able to wheel the gurney alongside the body and roll it into the body bag. This is one of those instances when I'll need to page one of several removers Linus employs on a freelance basis. They're usually young, work as landscapers in the spring and fall, drive plows in the winter, and assist in removals as necessary throughout the year. Linus may even hire one to drive a limousine if we have a particularly large funeral: a desirable position considering the pay and tips, but only a few are so privileged; not many of the young men own suits.

'Why don't you give her a hand, Ryan,' says Jorge.

'I ain't touching that!' Ryan shudders.

'That's all right, I can do it,' I say without turning. 'Please keep the family outside while I remove the body.'

'Jorge, I'll meet you at the station,' Mike says. 'I'm going to stay here and help Clara. I'll catch a ride back with Ryan.'

I almost face them. 'Thank you, but it won't be necessary.'

Mike waves me off. I notice he's still holding the prescription bottles and realize his motives aren't altogether altruistic.

'C'mon, Mikey, my shift ends at four. The wife's expecting me with Chinese food in an hour,' says Ryan.

'I need you to stay at the front door in case Mrs. MacDonnell or anybody else wants to get in,' says Mike. 'It's going to be ugly trying to get him out of here.'

'I'd prefer to do it alone.' In spite of the cool autumn afternoon, I can feel the heat creep upward along my spine. Droplets form at the base of my neck and then bead down my back.

Jorge glances at me and then over to the body. 'Okay, Mikey, you stay here, but promise me no games. Remember, case closed.'

As Ryan and Jorge walk to the porch, Mike heads into the bathroom. I check my pockets and then leave to fetch my things from the hearse. They don't hear my approach, so make no effort to lower their voices.

'Imagine hitting that?' Ryan says.

'C'mon,' says Jorge. 'Mikey's got to start some -where.'

'Like the playground?'

A sound like muffled laughter escapes Jorge. 'Oh, mierda – '

'Look, I know it's been a while for Mikey, but Jesus, she has the body of a twelve-year-old boy.' Ryan's hands press flat against his chest. 'And since when has he been into black chicks?'

'She's not black, man,' says Jorge. 'She's a little bit of this, a little bit of that.'

'Whatever. Is he that desperate, he'll help remove a fat dead guy? I couldn't get it up just thinking about where her hands have been, and that hair – '

'Excuse me,' I say, and keep my gaze steady on the rose of Sharon just beyond them as I walk onto the porch. Still, I can't close my ears as Ryan mutters and Jorge swears when I pass. Finally, I reach the hearse and busy myself, finding relief in the slamming of the detective's car door and the roar of the Crown Vic as he pulls away.

From the hearse, I remove two pairs of gloves, one small, the other large, along with the gurney, body bag, and my case. Ryan ignores me when I return to the house and struggle up the stairs. His teeth nimbly work over raw cuticles, reminding me of a man I once saw eating chicken wings, the way he splayed the tips from the drums, snapping them apart and then cleaning each bone until it gleamed white. Without glancing my way, still gnawing, Ryan holds open the door.

Mike is standing in the kitchen now, holding fast to the prescription bottles, lost in thought. He's shaking them: *ka-ta, ka-ta, ka-ta*. The percussive rattle of the pills startles me back to my childhood, to an outdoor concert I once attended with my mother. A glimpse of her whirling in a peasant skirt, long, wavy hair flying about her shoulders, and I see myself, or my hand at least, shaking an improvised tambourine made of a soda can and sunflower seeds, dancing with Patrice in my arms (*that's it, Baby Doll*). Like my mother's, my own hair long – though darker, thicker – hovers at my waist. A flash of her red smile and then she's gone. *Ka-ta*.

'Ready?' I say. It's been a long day and fatigue suddenly overwhelms me.

'Hear that?' Mike asks, still rattling the bottles.

I lay his gloves on the kitchen table and lean my business card against the napkin holder. Mike places one of the bottles next to it, continuing to shake the other. I'm grateful for the sudden quiet.

'Hear that?' Mike asks again. 'There's hardly anything in here. She said he got the nitro last month, but there's hardly any pills left in the bottle.'

'You think he OD'd on nitroglycerin?' I snap the small gloves on, watching puffs of talc waft about them.

'No, I think *she* OD'd him on nitro,' says Mike. 'They fill these bottles to the top, but you're not supposed to take more than two or three when you're feeling chest pains. It can cause cardiac arrest. She said he hasn't been to the hospital in a month, and the bottle's nearly empty.'

'Should I remove the body or are you going to call the M.E.?' I imagine the time we'll spend wrestling Mr. MacDonnell's body out of here and then, alone, the hours I'll spend filling his body with gallon after gallon of formaldehyde. And still I have the old woman to dress. It will be a long night in the basement. Perhaps the M.E. will intervene after all.

Mike looks at the bottle a long while. I watch him, waiting for his answer. He's motionless, impossibly still. 'No,' he finally says. 'Case closed.'

Mike rests the bottle alongside the other and turns his back to me, removing his suit coat and then folding it over the back of the chair. I notice the erectness of his shoulders and the pant loop his belt missed, the tarnished handcuffs clasped to his left hip and the gun holstered on his right. The outline of a wallet is visible in the bulge of his back pocket, where his body curves full, and I wonder if he carries in it pictures of his long-ago wife. Jenny. Without realizing, I reach for a strand of my hair, nearly pull it free of the elastic before catching myself.

He turns and takes the gloves I left for him on the table. He's lost in thought as he slides first the right and then the left glove on, covering a dulled wedding band in the process. I find myself staring at that spot on his finger, trying to see the ring through the film. Then the cell phone tucked in his other rear pocket begins to wail.

'Sullivan.'

The room is too small not to listen, so instead I busy myself with adjusting the stretcher to its lowest setting in the space just outside the bathroom. I pull several alcohol wipes from my satchel. Though Mr. MacDonnell is resting on the toilet, he may need to be cleaned a bit once he's lifted. The odor will certainly be worse. When I hold the mostly empty jar of Vicks VapoRub to Mike, he doesn't notice, too consumed with his conversation. On my way here, I tried to stop at the Whitman CVS to buy more, but there were no parking spots in the rear lot. Seniors tend to frequent the pharmacy there, mothers of ill children too. I try to run my errands at night, when the hearse can be shielded; most of the stores I shop are the twenty-four-hour kind.

'Yes, Reverend,' I hear Mike sigh. 'I'm working my way through them.'

A pause and then, 'When did he call? Did he a leave a name or number?'

Another sigh, then Mike says, 'Let me call you when I get back to the station. I got to take care of something first.'

Mike replaces his cell phone and turns to me. 'Okay, ready. I'll get under his shoulders, you get the feet.'

It's a struggle simply for Mike to squirm his way into the snug bathroom and position his hands under the body's arms. While I pull at the ankles just outside the door, Mike lifts and turns, pushes and grunts. As our

34

efforts grow louder, Mike slips and falls against me, almost on top of Mr. MacDonnell. Our heads knock together, not hard. He waits a moment too long, his nose presses into my hair, his cheek brushes my forehead. He inhales. Surely it's my imagination. Before he pulls away, I notice he smells of peppermint and stale coffee.

'Sorry.'

I try to shrug. Holding on to the door frame with one hand, I reach across the body to slide Mr. MacDonnell's lids closed. It's been several hours and one eye has already hardened, refusing to cooperate. Mike is breathing through his mouth as he stretches behind Mr. MacDonnell to flush the toilet. The stench is getting worse, but Mike doesn't ask for the Vicks. He leans against the wall, perspiration gathering about his brow. 'That was Reverend Greene calling about the Precious Doe case.'

No, I don't want to hear. Instead I look down at Mr. MacDonnell. His tank top is rolled up along his chest now, exposing a kettle-drum belly; his underpants are hooked around only one ankle, dangerously close to slipping off; the newspaper lies askew on the floor. It's too late, I'm already returned to thoughts of Precious Doe.

I remember the hundreds of stitches I wove, the layers of makeup, a shiny brown wig of human hair donated by another girl who'd read of Precious Doe in the newspapers, a little girl who said her alopecia seemed a small thing when compared to Precious Doe's fate. The long layers of hair were a perfect shield for the sutures that crisscrossed Doe's skull, a perfect headdress to replace the strands that had been shorn away. It was a closed casket.

The girl's body, left in a strip of woods stretching between Brockton and Whitman, was discovered by a man and his dog while out for a New Year's Day walk. The dog picked up the scent of the shallow grave in spite of the scattered coffee grounds buried with her. A deep freeze left her remains mostly intact, though her fingertips had been burned away. No child fitting her description had been reported missing; no one stepped forward to claim her. Her head was found a day later, concealed some yards back in a trash bag, her eyes still open, the whites sprinkled with the dust that invades this city. Usually in such a case, a body would remain in the medical examiner's office until the next of kin signed a release; it could take years. But this was different.

Reverend Greene took it upon himself to convince the district attorney, a longtime friend and parishioner, to seek a court order releasing the girl's remains to the Baptist congregation. No one could bear the thought of her body languishing in the medical examiner's office.

In his eulogy, it was Reverend Greene who christened her Precious Doe:

'Lord, this child who lies here before us today is known to You and You alone. But she is no Jane Doe. This child may not have been cherished by her mother, she may not have been cherished by her father, by an aunt, an uncle, or a grandfather. But, Lord, her life was no less precious because

they did not abide by her. Yes, Lord, we here today, all of the hundreds gathered from Whitman and Brockton and beyond, we Baptists and Catholics, we Protestants and Jews, we people of faith and even the faithless, are here to cherish this little girl, our Precious Doe.'

Linus donated his funeral services and a white coffin with pink satin lining and matching tufted pillow. He opened the doors to the Bartholomew Funeral Home for two full days to accommodate all of the people who came to pay their respects. An anonymous donor bought her a cemetery plot in Colebrook Cemetery, just across the street from the funeral home; another donated a gravestone. For now, the marker identifies her simply as Precious Doe; the headstone still waits to be engraved with her true identity. Alma made her a white high-collared nightgown and I arranged a bed of daisies to lay her on within the coffin. Fine white Shasta daisies (*innocence*).

For a while, some of those who crowded her wake would visit her grave and leave an assortment of mementos: velveteen teddy bears holding cutout hearts, a cacophony of helium balloons that would droop piti-fully after a morning's dew, and, once, a tattered baby blanket with faded carousel horses.

But I am done with that body; I don't have any desire to know more. I'm not caught three years in the past. I'm here with Mr. MacDonnell's body now, and soon with the old woman waiting for me at the funeral home. I try to envision the promise of chrysanthemums (*cheerfulness*) and burning bush (*wisdom*) blossoming in my garden, my patio chaise, the down comforter, and a pot of tea. Tomorrow. For now, Mike forces me back to yesterday.

'Clara, you listening?'

'Yes?'

'I lost you there for a minute. Something you want to share?'

'No, nothing.'

He doesn't let go of Mr. MacDonnell's body; he barely moves at all. I recognize that utter stillness – it's for my benefit this time. Silence is the better option.

'Do you have some free time tomorrow? I want to ask you a few more questions about Precious Doe. Maybe you'll remember something, you know, shake something loose.'

'I've told you everything I remember.'

'You never know. Sometimes talking it over jogs something in the memory. Even the smallest detail could help.'

There's no dissuading him now; if not tomorrow, then the next day or the day after that. Now that he has me in his sights, he won't stop until I agree. Better to avoid the barrage of calls, but first there's Mr. MacDonnell.

After a half hour's struggle, we maneuver him into the body bag. Mike helps me down the front stairs while Ryan holds the door. He speaks on his cell phone, peeling strips of paint from the clapboards; a particularly long one is caught in a weed patch below the porch. 'I know, baby, I'll be home as soon as I can.'

As we wheel the body across the city street, neighbors stand with arms folded in the doorways of their own triple-deckers, watching our progress. An old man with an oxygen tank beside him sits on his front porch, his forearms leaning on a walker, a cigarette dangling from his left hand. His eyes never leave the body bag, even when he flicks the cigarette in an impressive arc onto the crumbling sidewalk. In the distance, a subway horn wails its departure. Mrs. MacDonnell does not come out to say a final good-bye; perhaps at the funeral home she will. After securing her husband's body, I close the hearse's rear gate, waiting for the inevitable. Mike's voice doesn't fail me.

'So, tomorrow? About three all right?'

'Yes,' I say, pulling my keys from my pants pocket. 'I expect I'll be in the basement' – I gesture to the back of the hearse – 'so let yourself in.'

'I'll see you then.' Though I don't look at him full-on, I can sense Mike staring past me to the apartment we've just left. He starts to cross the street and then turns. I could pretend I don't notice, just get in the car and close the door. It's already open.

'The reverend said the anonymous caller contacted him today.'

I wish Mike would listen to his partner Jorge, understand the finality of death: *case closed*. No loved one ever stepped forward to claim the unidentified girl. I imagine to her mother, to her father she was only a splinter, an irritating nuisance picked at and squeezed until all life was expunged in a moment of boil and pus. She's dead, nothing else matters now. *Case closed*.

I nod as I get into the hearse.

But Mike persists. 'The man said something about a birthmark. You remember anything about a birthmark?'

I don't answer Mike, I can't say why. I don't know if I'll tell him about the perfect pink star I found at the nape of her neck as I stitched her. For now, I simply close the door and drive away.

CHAPTER THREE

The granite arch at the entrance to Colebrook Cemetery sparkles under the glaze of ice, the first frost of the season. It's as if the moon and crystals have conspired to train a klieg light on the inscription there: *I AM THE RESURRECTION AND LIFE.* I suppose loved ones need the reassurance of a world beyond the one they have before they can go farther into this place.

It's after midnight, the only safe time to be here except if I need to scout a plot for a client. Even now I step lightly, my footfalls a whisper in this most quiet place. In daylight, wandering along these paths, there's always the risk of being spotted by the family of a client. Some want nothing more than to turn their heads in polite revulsion; others long to share stories of their loved ones whose bodies now lie here instead of in the bed next to them or in the room down the hall. It's better I come at night.

Most of the sites here are simple. There are no towering family monuments, the kind one would expect to find in a neighboring town such as Hingham or Cohasset. The people of Whitman are plumbers and housewives, firefighters and administrative assistants; the ordinariness of their gravesites reflects the lives they've lived. The only exceptions are the various war memorials scattered throughout. All are meticulously kept, the flags never allowed to fade, with veteran wreaths laid each May and November without fail by an honor guard of old men wearing uniforms they can no longer button. A fair number of townspeople come to these ceremonies before lining Washington Street for the parades. All carry their own flags.

I pull my wool coat tight, nearly twice around me, and tuck my hands under my arms, a slim flashlight at the ready. In the distance, toward the rear of the grounds, twin spots of light appear. I step off the path, become one with the shadows, careful to quiet everything about me. Though this area is dense with trees, I can't risk the flashlight; I know these paths well. Teenagers won't be here now. In late spring and through the summer though, I often see them testing each other's will with blindfolds and beer. Other nights, young lovers can be seen straddling someone's gravestone and each other, professing their eternal love. They might hear the occasional scuff of my shoe or sense my presence, but they always attribute it to the ghost of whomever they set out to disturb. During these evening rounds, I check in on those gravesites that aren't tended by family or friends. Headstones may need to be realigned, litter and weeds cleared; it's the job of the groundskeeper, true, but it's my duty. Not everyone has a loved one.

Moonlight sluices through the naked limbs of the grand oaks that shield this place, dappling the concrete pathway with both gloom and shafts of light; plenty enough for me to make my way toward the far boundary of the graveyard. As I near the rear entrance, not twenty feet from Precious Doe's grave and just to the right of the weeping willow, there are the headlights from a car parked in the back lot. The engine's off. There's the soft thud of footsteps on wet turf, the snapping of twigs. I slow my approach, and then his figure emerges from the dark, a loping shadow in the car's beams. I know whose burial plot is head to toe with Doe's. It must be him.

Ducking behind the town's war memorial, an enormous slab of granite with a rough-hewn top, like a page torn from death's own ledger, I flatten myself there, become smaller, translucent. Mike stops one row forward. I'm mindful of my breath (*one-two-three, breathe*) so he won't see the rise of vaporous puffs above me, a ghostly image.

He shuffles his feet through the layers of leaves that have gathered against the mound that's his wife's grave. Time has softened its features; it's now a gentle rise of grass instead of scarred earth. Doe's appears the same. Of course it does.

Time drifts by – five minutes? Ten? My breathing's finally slowed. My thighs ache from crouching so long, my hands have grown numb. When I reach to steady myself, each blade of grass is an icy spike, a thousand pinpricks of cold. He must feel it. Every so often I check on him, but Mike has barely shifted. Tracing the letters engraved within this memorial helps return the flow of blood to my fingers. Though there isn't enough light to see the words, my fingertip can read them. *DEATH CANNOT KILL THEIR NAMES.* I already know the image carved into the top, two red roses (*adoration*). It's a thoughtful gesture by the town to memorialize the soldiers, but they're wrong: death ends everything. Precious Doe's name died with her. Her story, too. Wishful thinking and a granite stone cannot revive a life.

Her headstone is unlike most of the children's here. It's a standard upright, Colonial Rose granite – no hearts or angels etched into its face. No whimsy at all. The only adornments are the words *Precious Doe* in curvy script across the top, a poem by Emily Dickinson below that. I don't need to trace the letters with my fingers to read them:

> *So has a Daisy vanished*
> *From the fields today–*
> *Blooming–tripping–flowing*
> *Are ye then with God?*

It still seems fitting.

In the next instant, the wind picks up, creating mini funnel clouds of detritus; leaves scrape along various headstones and then rest against them when the breeze stops. All's quiet again until a terrific crackling breaks the silence that smothers this place. I peer around the edge of the monument and watch as Mike swipes at the dead leaves with his foot.

'Jesus, they're everywhere,' he says.

His gaze settles on Precious Doe's headstone, just beyond Jenny's, filled just weeks after hers. His shoulders sag, his head bows. He's caught in a beam of moonlight with the spindly branches of the willow drooping over him, a million fingers reaching to pluck him away.

'God,' he cries, lifting his head toward the skies, 'they're everywhere!'

He turns his attention back to his wife's site, his gestures becoming frantic. He falls to his knees, and his hands are claws, tearing the leaves from Jenny's grave; then he crawls to Doe's, raking at the earth until only jaundiced grass is visible. His breath comes in great heaving gulps, rapid and unsteady.

I wonder what it would cost each of us if I were to reveal myself. But he can't see me – he's no longer here anyway.

I pull back, crouching lower against the ground; I don't want to know any more. He inhales, quick and ragged, strangled gasps, and then nothing. It's a hateful sound. The crisp air is pungent; his efforts have churned the scent of wet earth and rotting compost. I concentrate on that and not the reason for the sudden quiet. If only I were Linus, I could step out and tell him everything would be fine, just fine – and he might believe me. My fingers weave themselves into my hair, twist around and around, until relief descends.

A few minutes go by, a rustling of clothing, and then a flash of blue sirens and more headlights pour in from the back lot. A car door opens. A man's voice calls, 'Is that you, Mikey?'

Mike fumbles getting to his feet. I can't help but look as he rubs his temple. 'Who's that?'

The man makes his way toward us, toward Mike, his flashlight burning into Mike's face. Mike raises his arm to shield his eyes and turns in my direction. His forehead is smeared with dirt and there's a scrap of leaf in his hair. I want to wipe both away so the cop won't see them. Not everyone knows this side of life.

'It's me. Bully.' He walks the few yards to where Mike is standing, the patrolman's thumbs hooked into his belt, his bulky chest overwhelming his too short legs. What height he has is in an extended torso; his face droops with loose cheeks and fleshy eyelids befitting his nickname. 'Saw a car in the lot and wanted to make sure it wasn't those teenagers tipping gravestones again. You okay?'

'Fine.' Mike's voice is steady, his head bent. 'I was driving by and thought I saw some kids myself.'

Bully adjusts his belt lower along his gut; the leather chafes audibly against a jangle of metal. He looks off to where the rest of the graveyard is obscured by darkness. 'You should have called us. It's out of your jurisdiction.'

They settle into an awkward pause with only the thrum of the cruiser's running engine and the occasional static of the police radio to fill the night. I watch as the cop's gaze wanders over to the headstone. He looks to where his own feet are planted and then stumbles back, off of the mound. 'Coming up on three years, huh?'

Even in the half-light, I can sense Mike stiffen.

'You're sure you're okay? You need a ride home to-night?' Bully leans in and sniffs the air.

Mike shakes his head. The cop steps forward, lifting a stunted leg, and then remembers to survey his footing. He stays rooted, reaching instead to grip Mike's shoulder; thinks better of it. 'Hey, we're still playing poker at Jimmy's. Every Friday. You should come by, have a beer. He TiVos the Patriots.'

'Yeah.'

Bully waits a moment too long, looking to Mike for guidance. 'Okay, then.'

We both watch him get into his cruiser and drive away. Mike's shadow, thrown by his car lights, is within my reach. I could touch it. Stretch and reach. Instead, I release a fistful of hair to the wind blowing in his direc-tion. My foot slips from under me, sending a wayward acorn skittering, and Mike whips his head around. Both of us freeze an instant, wait. Then he clears his throat and heads back to his car. It isn't until he turns the cor-ner, his sedan's lights casting shadows elsewhere, that I can breathe again.

CHAPTER FOUR

I hear them walking along creaking floorboards upstairs while I finish Mr. MacDonnell's makeup. The sensible shoes of those milling outside are visible through the basement window, small mountains of cigarette butts and crumpled paper cups gathering at their feet.

They're here for the old woman; she has a two-day wake. Long ago, not really I suppose, a person could get an afternoon off from work to pay his respects to the dead, and then a full day to attend the funeral. In the last decade or so, wakes have been confined to one day, with funerals held the next. The standard hours for wakes were two in the afternoon until four, a two-hour interval so loved ones could gather their bearings, and then six until eight to accommodate those who slipped out of work early. But now, families are requesting four-hour marathons. I've heard Linus try to dissuade them, explain the sheer physical and emotional exhaustion that comes with standing in receiving lines for hours –

they seldom end promptly – greeting familiar faces from the present and confronting ghosts from the past. There usually isn't time for even a humid roast beef sandwich.

The old woman is from a different generation, though, a period when a life and a death were honored. It helps that most of the mourners are elderly themselves and therefore able to attend afternoon showings, eager for a chance to gather with friends, whatever the circumstances.

Turning back to the body before me, I wonder about the paradox of Mrs. MacDonnell, her bruises still visible when she met with Linus to discuss the arrangements, choosing one of the more expensive coffins for her husband. A new Velcro suit, too. I imagine Mr. MacDonnell didn't own many, if any at all.

I flip through the pages of *Nature's Bounty* for something appropriate to bury with Mr. MacDonnell: Adonis (*sad memories*), foxglove (*insincerity*), or perhaps a simple pine bough (*pity*)? No, marigolds (*cruelty in love*) would be best. Though the marigolds' fragrance can smart, I don't worry that someone will detect them. The funeral bouquets will more than overwhelm one small clump.

I brush his eyebrows, wiry and unruly, snipping stray bits I'd missed earlier. With his shave and trim, I'm able to glimpse the man Mrs. MacDonnell met before their lives together led them down the same beaten path I imagine their parents walked before them.

As I comb his hair one more time, there's a knock at

the door. It's precisely three. When Mike opens it, he hesitates before stepping in. I'm a rubber band curled around a child's finger ready to spring, but he doesn't notice. He's wearing his usual uniform of a jacket and tie, gun at his hip, and badge clipped to the front of his slacks. Above the cloud of formaldehyde, I can smell his soap, crisp and sensible. I use the same. My fingers itch to touch my hair. My eyes seek the spot on his temple where the smudge of dirt was, but it's free of the earth he disturbed last night. He's carrying a tattered manila folder, bound with several elastics. His eyes stray to the worktables, lost and unfocused. I don't interrupt; it will be a moment or two before he returns to the present.

There are few bereaved family members Linus allows into this room. Without exception they're immediate family, and only if preparations haven't yet begun on the body. That day, Linus accompanied Mike when his wife lay atop my worktable. As Linus guided him over, Mike remained stoic, never even reaching out a hand to caress his wife's cheek. Linus stood a step behind Mike, one hand at the small of Mike's back. With the other, he cupped the crown of Jenny's head, stroking her matted hair, disregarding the blood, and then he spoke in that low rumble: 'It's okay, she can hear you. They both can. Let it out now, let it out.'

I didn't see Mike's face — I slipped out of the room without looking — but I still remember his keening as I hurried down the hall.

'Nice coffin,' Mike finally says, his eyes lingering

over Mr. MacDonnell, two fingers scratching at a spot on his own stomach. 'Guess we'll never know if love or guilt bought it.'

I unclip the paper bib from around Mr. MacDonnell's neck and discard it along with my gloves. I'm finished with this body.

Walking over to the counter, I open Precious Doe's file box. There are before and after photos, a guest book, a funeral card, and a bit of hair. Linus says he keeps these mementos in case someone steps forward and cares to have a record of the deceased's passing. It's without a complete lock, though. Her killer left only a few sparse strands, bits I shaved away when I stitched her. It was then, with her hair gone and complexion blanched by death, that I saw the birthmark. If the M.E. had taken the time, had not been distracted by temperamental refrigerators and leaky roofs, an impending OSHA review of workplace safety, he would have found the birthmark first. Shame no one ever takes the time anymore. Not even for a murdered little girl.

'As you can see, there's nothing new in here,' I say, but still Mike wanders over, removing each article, studying them as if for the first time.

'Do you have any photos of her lying on her stomach or sides?'

The M.E. determined her body had been in the woods for two icy days, exposed to the elements, though remarkably untouched by vermin. 'Just this.'

Hands at his hips, lips pursed. I know I must be careful.

I've attended some pickups where Mike is still there, speaking with a lover or friend of the deceased. He has a way of encircling someone with questions, slowly, quietly, until a grief-stricken boyfriend suddenly becomes wild-eyed, ensnared in the noose Mike's tightened around his neck. More than once, I've been sent away and the medical examiner's been called back.

'Mind if I show you the autopsy photos again? Like I said, it might jog something free.' Mike is already pulling the elastics from around the folder, but his eyes never leave me.

He spreads a series of photographs along the counter. There are fifteen, all of little girl Doe damaged beyond recognition. The pictures are taken from various angles, some revealing her more pronounced injuries. In others, one could be forgiven for mistaking her for a castoff doll. The most haunting pictures are the ones that show the simple gold stud in her left ear, a gesture some adult made to enrich her life. Her right lobe was too damaged by the attack to have held on to something as fragile as an earring. In my peripheral vision, I can see Mike watching me, studying me, as I view the M.E.'s photomontage.

I wait for Mike to speak. He surveys the pictures, shuffling them around, moving one on top of another, then settles on a photo of a back view. Finally, he begins. 'I think I told you our anonymous caller contacted Reverend Greene again. He hadn't called in over a year, but he's all we've got. The FBI pretty much left it to us. They've got bigger problems, I guess.'

He pauses again to scan my face, though I continue my silence, looking beyond him to Mr. MacDonnell. I notice a lick of hair on the dead man's forehead, sprung from its place. My fingers begin to twitch, needing to comb it down, but I dare not move.

Mike taps the photo. 'The caller said there was a birthmark on the back of Precious Doe's neck, a very distinctive shape. I don't see anything in the photos, but maybe we missed it.'

He still hasn't asked me a question, so I don't answer.

'So?' he says.

'What do you want to know?'

'Why don't you tell me?'

I won't tell him – he can't understand. He doesn't know what it is to be invisible, to be discarded and dismissed. Whereas the world saw only Precious Doe's body, I know what lay beneath the flesh, the layers hidden under the welts and bruises. She felt more than just pain, though. I know. They ignored her in life; they haven't the right to claim her in death. That's my job. Too, I won't remind Mike that Precious Doe was found barely a week before his wife was killed by a chronic drunk driver. That he lost his mind when he lost his Jenny and he couldn't have heard me anyway. I don't want to tell him what I know from working with the dead: they can't come back, they're gone forever; that there's no justice in death.

Mike's breathing is audible in this echo chamber, heavy as if he were gasping for air instead of grasping at straws. When he speaks, his words are slow to come.

'This girl was murdered, probably by her father or her mother's boyfriend. Some animal who threw away a child. If you're withholding evidence, I could charge you with obstruction of justice or, or hindering a police investigation. Why won't you help me?' He waits. 'Clara?'

Mike won't stop, I know he won't. So this is it. 'It was a stork bite in the shape of a star.'

He whirls to face Mr. MacDonnell, raising a fist to cover his mouth. His rage presses against me, smothering. In spite of it, I walk past him and retrieve the black comb from my instrument tray. Without gloves, I begin fixing the dead man's cowlick.

Mike crosses the room to stand beside me, too close now. My lungs constrict, unable to fill themselves. It sounds as if his teeth are clenched, his full lips thinned and blanched. I can't look, and wish I couldn't feel his breath against my ear, smell the bile when he speaks. 'Jesus Christ, why didn't you tell me this three years ago?'

My hand pauses before pushing back the unruly curl, but it flops aside. Pulling on the drawer that holds my grooming accessories, I reach for the gel. Across the room the mourners' feet continue to mill outside, and I imagine reaching for the basement window latch, if it would open.

Instead, my hand squeezes the tube and gel explodes onto the concrete floor. 'Let the dead be dead.'

Mike looks to Mr. MacDonnell before turning his attention to me. 'The dead are never dead.'

He continues staring at me, but I fix on the blob of gel oozing along the angled floor, edging toward the drain. The familiar creep of heat rolls from my chest to my throat, heading toward my cheeks in earnest. I want to press myself against these cinder-block walls and fade. Before I can take a backward step, he gathers his folder and snaps the rubber bands around it. He slams the door behind him, an explosion in this concrete bunker. I try again and Mr. MacDonnell's hair is finally in place. Walking to the sink, I wash my hands, ignoring the tremble. A damp paper towel pressed to my neck cools the flush; my fingers are desperate to entwine a patch of curls, then tug, sharp and brilliant. I can breathe again. The evidence goes in my pocket. I consider my outstretched hand, pressing it against the wall. Another breath and it melts away; another and I will disappear with it. There is no time for this; I must prepare Mr. MacDonnell's mourning room. His wife has chosen a two-stage wake for tomorrow, followed by the funeral on Friday.

I make my way up the stairs, unnoticed by the old woman's mourners, and then enter the back hallway. There are two wings to this funeral home so Linus has the option of simultaneous wakes, something he reserves only for family members who share the unfortunate experience of dying together.

As I enter the waking room, I notice Linus has already placed several arrangements of flowers on the end tables and pulled the rack of leather folding chairs from the closet. I don't turn on the lights, preferring instead the dim glow from the hallway and the lone scented candle – vanilla – as I set several chairs along the wall. Mike's words fill my head; I drop to the chair, my legs unsteady.

I'm not afraid of his threats to prosecute me. Though . . . no, it's not that. Mike seemed so certain, and I suppose for him it's true: The dead are never dead. His wife's ghost swirls and shifts about him, palpable even to those nearby. Or maybe what we're sensing is that he's dead too. I remind myself that these are Alma's superstitions, shake myself free of them, and rise to my feet. There's work to be done.

When I stand, I notice a small figure gazing out at me from the shadows. There on the far side of the room is Trecie. I reach for the back of my chair, wanting to smile, knowing I can't.

'What are you doing here?' I ask.

She walks over to one of the arrangements, a red, white, and blue VFW wreath, and fingers one of the carnations (*fidelity*), then moves in front of a large mixed bouquet adjacent to it. 'These are pretty.'

I want to be the sort of person who would go to her, wrap an arm around her frail shoulders, my jacket, too, and take her to my kitchen. Feed her cookies I baked myself, along with hot cocoa and a toasted cheese sandwich. I would hum as she purged her story, consoling her in all the right places. I would very much like to be that person, but no one ever showed me how.

'Trecie, I'm sorry, but you need to leave right now. There's a wake going on in the next room.'

'I know,' she says. 'I was there.'

'I'm going to have to tell Mr. Bartholomew.'

She turns and gives me the smile I couldn't muster. I've forgotten how lovely she is, and I feel a pang from deep within. Still, I can't force the simplest gesture. She fingers a yellow rose (*jealousy*) and then a daisy until they come loose from the florist's sturdy foam, the rose tumbling to the floor.

'What are these?' Her voice is high and sweet. Ever so childlike.

My mind flits about. I can't seem to steady it. Surely there is no intended meaning with this funeral bouquet – it's just the sixty-dollar special.

'The yellow one is a rose and the other is a daisy. Please put them back, they're for Mr. MacDonnell.'

She returns the rose, leaving it slightly askew, unanchored amid the arrangement. It will wither in a few hours without access to its moist base. Trecie glides to the other side of the room, twirling the other blossom between her fingers. Her back is to me now, the candlelight catching a naked spot on the crown of her head. How I'd like to cover that space, a mirror image of mine. I hurry to the bouquet and push the rose back into its sponge, nearly restoring symmetry to the design. 'Can I have this flower?' she asks.

I nod, hoping it will quicken her departure.

Trecie settles herself on the floor in the space where

Mr. MacDonnell's body will soon be. 'Who was that man you were talking to?'

A shudder passes through me as I replay the scene with Mike. Did she simply overhear our conversation, or was she somehow watching us? I wonder if she thinks I'm a monster because of the work I do, the words I exchanged with Mike.

'He seemed mad. And sad, too.'

'Trecie – '

'He's not your boyfriend, right?'

That long-buried dread of being introduced to my mother's latest lover resurfaces. We are too much alike, Trecie and I. I shake my head, struggling for control.

'Good, I don't like boyfriends.'

My voice, trained by years of living with my grand-mother and then the dead, remains steady. 'What is it you want?'

Trecie continues twirling the flower, staring at it as her voice softens. 'A story.'

'I have work to do. Maybe your mother could tell you a story on your walk to the store later.'

'What about *your* mother?' She lifts her chin, her teeth small and neat behind her smile. She's still so young. 'Did you ever have any adventures when you were my age?'

She blinks, waiting for me to begin. She pulls free a petal from her flower and it drifts to the paisley carpet. I want to catch it but can't move. If I were a storyteller, one clever enough to craft something wondrous out of the mundane, a fairy tale from a nightmare, I would tell her about those first seven years with my mother. How when I was an infant, she carried me in a pack, north along the Appalachian Trail each summer into fall, stopping in Maine as winter drew near. How as I grew older, I toddled behind and later ran ahead of my mother, splashing in streams, discovering turtles and arrowheads (*that's a big one, Baby Doll!*). She was a wood nymph with her own loose hair, glossy and smooth, her young body limber and thin. At least that's how I like to remember her. There are no photographs. We owned only what fit in our back-packs, relying on the generosity of those we happened upon. Only later did I understand what provoked such acts of kindness from all of those men, though at the time I regarded their presence as an intrusion. As the weather grew brisk, we'd leave our tent rolled in its pack and find shelter at one of the campsites; the only one I recall is Poplar Ridge.

My mother managed a business of sorts, hiring herself out to the more adventurous hikers who started the trail in Maine in the weeks before winter formally made its debut. She drove their cars south, me curled beside her, meeting them in such faraway places as Pennsylvania or Maryland, once in West Virginia. She took her time, knowing the car wouldn't be needed for weeks more. We'd live in those cars during the coldest months, until it was time to begin the hike north again. But I couldn't tell Trecie any of this. Not every story has a happy ending.

'No, no adventures,' I say.

She nearly laughs, running the flower against her cheek. 'You're lying again.'

I don't allow myself to imagine how a girl so young came to be so suspicious. Instead, I think of places nearby where a child could roam, a place a girl could have an adventure. 'It's a beautiful fall day. Don't you have any friends you could meet at the park?'

She drops her chin, frowning, as she plucks another petal from the flower. 'Aren't we friends?'

Patrice – no, *Trecie*, the hair, the mouth, so familiar from my own childhood – pulls another petal free, and as it pirouettes to the floor, I sense myself floating alongside it, a dizzying descent.

'You should play with other children. Adults have adult friends.'

With one smooth gesture, Trecie flicks the head off of the daisy, gathers her hair between her hands, and grimaces as she ties it up with the stem of the flower. A ponytail, just like mine. 'But I'm your only friend.'

'That's enough.' Linus must deal with her. He's the one who invited her to stay, so he must be the one to tell her she has to go. 'Stay here, I'll be right back.'

I pivot and walk to where the wake is taking place. Linus, his swollen hands laced atop his belly, is speaking with the son of the old woman. I compose myself and then make my way over to him.

Standing behind Linus, waiting for him to disengage from conversation, I'm unnoticed by the son, his face so like his mother's with her prominent cheekbones and dimpled chin, the same sharp widow's peak along his forehead. Linus knows I'm there. He encircles my wrist, rests a thick finger against my hand, taps it there once, a slight brush of the fingertip, and then laces his hands across his stomach again.

'First Mary Katherine last January, now my mother . . .' the man says, that chin beginning to quiver.

'Have you tried talking to little Mary?' Linus asks. 'I talk to my own boy every day.'

'You lost a child?'

'Going on thirteen years now. Alma and me had him late in life, after we'd just about given up hope of having one of our own. It was God's plan. Course, once you think you know God's plan, He goes and changes His mind again.'

The man begins to weep, pulling out a wad of tissues. 'Why would He take my little girl, Mr. Bartholomew? And your son?'

'No sense in that, is there? But something I heard at a service once for an itty-bitty thing seemed about right. The preacher got up there and he said, 'I don't know why children have to die, but can you imagine Heaven without them?' It's something to hold on to, I guess. We all know the Lord giveth and the Lord taketh away. As people of faith, we've got to believe the Lord will giveth back again.'

The man presses the fistful of tissues to his eyes and then looks back to Linus. 'Does your son ever answer you, Mr. Bartholomew?'

'In time. All in good time.'

The man clasps Linus's shoulder, nods, and then rejoins his family near the old woman's casket to continue greeting mourners.

'Ah, Clara.' When he speaks, Linus's bass is a smooth rumble and the flesh between his eyes becomes deeply grooved. 'What is it, then?'

'It's that girl, Trecie. She's in the other set of mourning rooms. And she's been *here*, spying on the guests.'

'I see.'

'I think you should tell her to leave.' I keep my voice steady.

'Let's go talk to the child.'

He lumbers down the same set of hallways I just traveled. The turn in weather has inflamed his knees, slowed his gait. I follow him until finally we round the corner. There's a flash of hair, the tremor of footfalls vibrating through the carpet as she darts past us and away.

'Was that her?' Linus says, pointing down the corridor.

'Yes.'

'She was in here?' Linus asks, gesturing into the dimness. His hand seeks the light switch along the wall, catches it, and the room is illuminated. Bouquets remain on the ledge, chairs still waiting to be arranged.

I wonder how long I've been gone; more than a minute? Five? 'She might have gone back to spy on the wake.'

Linus's hands resume their place across the breadth of his stomach. 'What did she want?'

It's impossible to mislead someone like Linus, someone whose whole is true.

'She likes the flowers,' I say, careful to avoid his eyes, 'and the companionship.'

'Clara.' His tone is enough. 'I know it's not your way, to trust, but can you find it in your heart to help this child?'

I've been to the houses of families like Trecie's, with neglectful mothers and abusive boyfriends. Usually it's the woman's body I'm there for; sometimes, though, it's that of her teenage boy, killed defending his mother. Homes known to children's services, addresses the police are called to after a long night of arguing and whiskey. Not places I choose to visit. Not again. 'I suppose I can call the community center. Or Reverend Greene, see what after-school programs his church is offering this fall – '

He exhales a million frustrations, appearing to settle himself before he continues. 'A little girl like that must be in a world of pain if a funeral home is where she turns to for comfort. She's not asking for much and I know you don't have much to give, but you're obliged to do what you can.'

Not even my grandmother's belt could sting as much.

'She chose you.' That tone again. 'We can't turn our backs to a child. It ain't right.'

'I have no experience with children. You do.' I stop there, afraid the implication will pain him.

'Clara . . .' Linus starts and then interrupts himself, disappointment etched in his jowls. I can't face him, ashamed of what he'll see, or worse, what he won't. 'I remember some time ago a stray found its way to my door. She had a long brown tail and big brown eyes, and an empty gut, a real hollowness to her. She needed taking care of almost as much as *I* needed to care for her. Alma and me welcomed her into our home and loved her best we could, though it wasn't always easy, a kicked-around pup like that. But seeing as how we was orphaned parents and she was an orphaned pup, it just felt right. Do you understand what I'm saying?'

'Linus – '

'The Lord has sent you this little lost pup and you got to help her. It's the right thing to do.'

'There's a difference between caring for a dog and looking after a child.'

He shakes his head and lets loose a long rush of exasperation before returning his gaze to me. Over his shoulder is an arrangement for Mr. MacDonnell – the Woodland Greens basket with an adolescent hosta (*faithful companion*). I search my memory for an appropriate spot in Mrs. MacDonnell's yard where she could plant it – under the rose of Sharon? – imagining how over the years she would come to regard a perennial from her husband's funeral arrangements. Would she surround the tree with more hosta or feed the plant one too many aspirin, poisoning it in the process? When Linus shifts his weight from one swollen knee to the other, I'm pulled back. I suppose he's waiting me out. He's pushed before when he's wanted more from me. So far I've managed to resist. Not today.

'Perhaps *you* should help her,' I say.

'Clara, now a grown man can't be spending time alone with a girl who's no relation.'

'I don't think it's appropriate for her to spend time with me, either. Not here.' My fingers find a button that's come loose from the cuff of my jacket. I yank it free.

'A child's got to believe in someone. She chose *you*. Help her.'

He walks away and I'm left with only the flickering shadows cast by the lone candle to guide me. His voice carries down the hall, staying with me, *'that saved a wretch like me . . .* 'I rest on one of the chairs, listening to the door in the next set of hallways finally slam closed, pinching the button between my thumb and forefinger. Then I spot something out of place, several feet in front of me.

Lying on the floor where Mr. MacDonnell's casket will soon be is the stem of the daisy tied around a lock of hair.

CHAPTER FIVE

Brittle leaves skitter at my feet as I head across the parking lot. Though it's a short walk from my cottage to Linus and Alma's Victorian, I can't help but pull the collar of my wool coat snug around my neck. Our New England autumn has settled in with a frosty vengeance, leaving my solitary birch naked and the hostas that ring it bedraggled and rotting.

I enter the back staircase without knocking – Alma prefers it that way – and take the steps up to their living quarters. This is how it is each Sunday afternoon: I arrive promptly at one o'clock to help Alma with the final preparations for dinner, at which point she allows me a simple task, chopping carrots perhaps, and then sits me at the kitchen table with a cup of tea. While she stirs the gravy – there's always gravy – I'll listen to her talk of the week's events and pretend not to notice the flask of sherry she keeps hidden in her apron pocket.

As I enter the kitchen, the pungent aroma of ham and cloves assails my nostrils. I allow myself only shallow breaths. A second wave carries with it the succulence of sweet potatoes, brown sugar, nutmeg, and melting marshmallow. Alma is at the counter, grinding the pepper mill over a casserole dish, a carton of heavy cream beside it.

'Clara, I hope you brought your appetite, because I'm making all your favorites,' Alma says, turning to smile at me. Today she's wearing one of her better dresses, navy blue with white piping. I've never seen her in pants. She's full-figured but could not be described as plump. In spite of her sixty-eight years, her hair still holds much of its color and has a glossy sheen from her Saturday-morning wash and curl. Though the skin around her neck has begun to relax and her once mahogany complexion has taken on an ashen pallor, her teeth betray nothing of her age. They are large and white, mesmerizing when she speaks. I am always humbled by them.

'My grandmother's buttermilk biscuits, sweet potatoes, and some of that green bean casserole you like so much, in the cream sauce,' continues Alma. 'I have carrots, too. You can pick at them, I know how you are. And for dessert, I made my mother's apple pie.'

Long ago, I stopped bringing contributions to our Sunday dinners. The cookies from Beech Hill Bakery were always put aside in favor of Alma's rum raisin cake (*quick, while it's still warm; we'll save those cookies for tomorrow, if you don't mind*). Wine would never do, as Linus is a confirmed teetotaler. Instead, when my outdoor garden is lush, I'll bring her a bouquet for her table. She likes that.

This is Alma's show, and her Victorian kitchen is the stage on which she shines. With its original cherry cabinets and bead-board backsplash, a vintage O'Keefe and Merritt stove with two warming drawers and six burners, and a matching cobalt blue Crosley Shelvador refrigerator, it's as traditional as Alma herself. She takes a copper pot from its hook and motions me over to her grandmother's kitchen table, where a pot of tea is already steeping on its lace doily, her mother's china cup at the ready.

'It smells wonderful,' I say. I've never told her I'm rarely hungry, that food holds no real appeal for me. It would sting her to the core, and she's already suffered enough for one lifetime. 'What can I do?'

She hands me the butter dish and two trivets. 'Put these on the table?'

My eyes need to adjust from the cheerful kitchen to the dimness of the dining room. Sconces hang on either side of the sideboard, barely illuminating the walnut wainscoting and cranberry velvet drapes. The chandelier is not yet on. In another house, I would assume the poor lighting was an attempt to mask dust and cobwebs, but in Alma's home, the scent of lemon oil is a constant. If I were to touch the chair rail, I know my fingers would be slick with it. There are five place settings instead of the usual three; the cabinet that holds her good china is half-empty, the contents dotting the embroidered tablecloth.

'Who's joining us?' I ask Alma, taking the tea she offers and settling at the kitchen table.

'The Reverend Greene is coming and he's bringing his elderly mother, visiting from Elizabeth City, North Carolina. She must be near eighty-five and took the Greyhound by herself. Imagine that?'

Alma's back is to me, so she doesn't see the tea slosh my saucer. I haven't seen Reverend Greene in the two weeks since Mike visited me in the basement. I wonder what Mike has told Reverend Greene about his Precious Doe, about me. I cup the tea, chasing the chill from my hands, and listen to Alma whisk the gravy: it smells of butter, brown sugar, and cider.

I didn't do anything wrong. Silence is not a crime. The child's life had been one long hell-storm and then it was over in a moment of terror and violence. But finally over. Nothing any of them did after the fact could help the little girl; she's dead. Probably the only kindness she was ever shown came afterward: the public outcry in the newspapers; the donations that poured in for a reward to track her killer; the funeral Linus gave her attended by nearly all of Brockton's and Whitman's finest – police, firefighters, clergy, every stripe of politician. Save Linus and Alma, I wonder how many of these people, if they'd seen her being slapped in the produce aisle of Shaw's, would have stopped to help her. Mine were probably the only dry eyes at her service; only I seemed aware death was her release. Life is suffering. They think Doe is somehow still attached to this world, but her life is over.

I didn't do anything wrong by remaining silent.

'Clara, honey. Clara?' Alma has stopped her whisking and is staring at me. 'Would you get the front door? I believe that's the reverend and Mrs. Greene.'

I wind my way out of the kitchen, down the hall, and into the grand foyer, just as the doorbell sounds again.

'Why hello, Clara,' says Reverend Greene from behind a woman hunched over a wooden cane. She's a tiny person, seemingly about to topple over in her sensible shoes and heavy woolen coat. A plush brown hat, attached with hairpins positioned above each ear, matches the gloves that do nothing to hide the gnarl of her fingers. Below her proper collar, a single strand of pearls rests at her throat. Raising his voice and grasping his mother's shoulders, Reverend Greene says, 'Mama, this is Clara Marsh. She's Brother Bartholomew's child.'

'No.' Reverend Greene knows this isn't true. 'I'm Linus's assistant.'

'No matter,' says Mrs. Greene as her son takes her left elbow and offers his other arm for her to push herself up into the house. She steadies herself, in spite of the persistent tremble besieging her body. 'We're all God's children and that's what counts.'

Before I've a chance to explain, Alma rounds the bend and calls out, 'Come in, come in.' Gathering her hands into her apron and wiping quickly, she extends both to Mrs. Greene. 'Mother Greene, we're honored you're joining us for Sunday dinner. The reverend here is like family to Linus and me, so please make yourself at home.'

In one smooth gesture, Alma embraces Mrs. Greene and slips the old woman's coat from her shoulders. For a moment I wonder how the buttons were undone, but there is no time to dwell; Linus has filled the room.

'Israel, welcome,' Linus says as he clasps Reverend Greene's hand in his own. He then turns to Mrs. Greene and hovers in a slight bow, eyes downcast. 'And this must be Mother Greene.'

At first I think Mrs. Greene is overwhelmed by the convergence of all of us in the foyer, her hesitation a sign of wear from a long bus ride north, until she pulls her hand from Linus's and removes the glove, catching his hand again in both of hers.

'You are surrounded by spirits,' she breathes.

Linus scans her face but doesn't speak, a tired smile hovering at his mouth.

'They are all around you.' Her left hand arcs across Linus's shoulders as if sprinkling him with holy water. 'They like you; they feel safe in your presence. They think you'll show them the path home.'

Reverend Greene pulls at his mother, urging her toward the kitchen. 'Mama, you've had a long trip. Maybe you need a glass of water.'

We all follow, Alma looking toward Linus, and he at the floor. 'Would you like a cup of tea, Mother Greene?' Alma asks, her thumb plucking the corner of her apron pocket. I watch as a stitch, then two, are pulled free. 'I've got a pot all ready. Or a glass of lemonade instead?'

Linus trudges over to the kitchen table and slides out

the head chair, the one with the generous seat and cushioned armrests, while Reverend Greene eases his mother down. Alma hurries to the stove, churning the skin from the top of the gravy before it can harden into unsavory bits. I don't know where to go.

'Tea would be lovely, dear,' says Mrs. Greene, unpinning her hat and folding her gloves into it. 'Thank you.'

I reach for them, grateful for something to do, as Linus pulls Reverend Greene away to the sitting room. I head to the foyer closet, listening to Linus's bass and the whisper of Reverend Greene's response, but I can't make out the words. Wandering back toward the kitchen, I linger over familiar photographs lining the hallway. They are all of their son, Elton, from infancy through high school graduation, an eerie montage of the capricious nature of life. I squint at the boy in his cap and gown; his eyes, aglow from the camera's flash or perhaps accomplishment, show no prescience of the aneurysm that would burst within his brain days later.

When I step into the kitchen, the old woman's eyes are upon me. Though she moves slowly, shaking sugar crystals across the tablecloth while fixing her tea, her eyes are spry.

'Did I take your seat, dear?' She gestures toward my empty cup and saucer, which someone moved aside.

'No, not at all.' I sit across from her, though still close enough to notice the familiar odor of mothballs and lavender splash. Many of my clients use the same.

'Mother Greene,' Alma says as she sets a tray of malt

crackers and block of sharp Wisconsin in front of the old woman, 'I hope you don't mind the loose-leaf variety. I can get you a tea bag if you prefer.'

'You know, all the ladies in Elizabeth City come to me to read their tea leaves,' says Mrs. Greene, rolling one of the pearls at her throat between a thumb and forefinger. 'They're all looking to find true love, see how many babies or grandbabies are in the future. Money, too. I don't charge them, course, but they usually leave me some sort of something. A banana bread or pork chops. Some such. Most slip me a little cash to supplement my widow's pension, but they don't have to.'

'Oh, Mama,' says Reverend Greene as he and Linus enter the kitchen.

Mrs. Greene drops her necklace, and I expect to hear a thud when it strikes her collarbone. She braces herself against the table to turn slightly, glowering in her son's direction. 'Israel, you know God blessed me with the gift. I told you the night you met Dorothea she would be your wife within the year, and thirty years later I told you to get her to a doctor.' She turns back to face Alma and me. 'She died two weeks later when her heart gave out. Been almost fourteen years now, isn't that right, Israel? God rest her soul.'

In the silence that follows, Reverend Greene fishes in his pants pocket for the wedding band he keeps there while Mrs. Greene, her back returned to her son, slurps her tea. The rhythm of Alma's whisk clicking against the pan lulls me away from the tension.

'Can you commune with the deceased, Mother Greene?' Alma asks, her eyes never straying from her gravy.

'I can.'

'Do you need tea leaves—'

Linus starts, but she silences him with a look.

'Do you need the leaves to see, Mother Greene?' Alma whips the gravy, *click, click, click.*

'I do not,' says Mrs. Greene, replacing her teacup in its saucer, her eyes on Alma.

'Can you commune with my son?' With her free hand, Alma wipes at her cheek. It's almost certainly sweat from her brow, or a wayward splash from the whisk. I've never seen Alma weep.

'I cannot,' said Mrs. Greene, folding her hands into her lap. 'Your son is at rest. Only those who cannot find their way to the next world, who are trapped still in this one, appear to me. They are tortured souls. Your boy was at peace when he died, filled up with the *love* you and your husband gave him. You were wise to let him go on.'

Alma turns to Mrs. Greene. Lips quivering, teeth firmly clenched, she nods. 'Thank you, Mother Greene. Thank you.' I avert my gaze.

'But your husband here,' Mrs. Greene says, pivoting in her seat to see Linus, 'he is surrounded by spirits looking for someone to show them the path home. You know that's right, don't you?'

'Yes, Mother, I do,' says Linus, patting her shoulder.

'Everyone wants to go home.'

Mrs. Greene cackles, a joke she shares with Linus, who also smiles. I look to Reverend Greene and am reminded of the teenagers from my youth. The ones who squirmed whenever their mothers chaperoned a school field trip, as if the unconscious caresses and homemade lunches were a humiliation. I especially disliked those students.

'And you, Miss Clara,' Mrs. Greene says, turning to face me. Her head quivers atop her neck, her eyes unblinking. Though I know these are signs of Parkinson's disease, as is the dementia she appears to have succumbed to, still she appears otherworldly. 'I've peeked into your teacup. There are things you need to know.'

The odor of cloves clogs my throat. The ham is perched on the cutting board, waiting for Linus and his knife. The scent that's filled my nostrils has settled into an ache, pulsating deeper and deeper into my head. Reverend Greene fumbles his hands within his pockets, and I can just make out Alma poking the carrots, watching me.

'No, thank you.' I can't imagine how I'll eat, reminded of the clove potpourri my grandmother kept in her armoire.

'Clara, wouldn't you like to know?' Alma asks before turning her attention back to her guest. 'Do you see a man in her future, Mother Greene?'

'There are two men in your cup.' Mrs. Greene's eyes are firm, even as her body trembles. 'Mind my words, dear, both will lead you to danger. One will die trying to save you and the other trying to kill you.'

Reverend Greene reaches for his mother's shoulders, shaking her gently. 'Don't say such things, Mama.'

'She needs to hear,' Mrs. Greene hisses, watching me.

I inhale deeply the scent of cloves, of my childhood, my head throbbing in response. Many of the old women who've wound their way along the mourning rooms below this kitchen have wanted to share their prophecies with me. Near the end of their lives, they all speak to their god.

'And the little girl, Lord have mercy, that lost little girl.' Mrs. Greene places a hand to her heart, her eyes looking past me. 'She thinks she's found a home in you.'

I turn to Linus, but he's focused on Mrs. Greene. I imagine he told Reverend Greene about Trecie and that's how the old woman has come by her 'gift.'

'No one should know the pain she's felt,' said Mrs. Greene, balling her skirt in her fist. 'You're the only peace she's ever known in her little life.'

'Mother Greene,' Linus says, patting her arm. 'Clara will see the girl through. She's agreed to help. It's all been arranged.'

Tears fill the crevasses lining Mrs. Greene's face, shifting course as she grimaces. She shakes off Linus, straining across the table, grasping for my arm. The strength of her shrunken hand startles me. I'm more used to the submissive touch of my elderly clients. 'She will bring sorrow into your life.'

'Mother Greene,' says Linus. 'Clara will take care of the girl. It's all in God's hands.'

'But your girl's in danger,' says Mrs. Greene, pleading with him.

Linus reaches up and swipes away her tears with his thumb. 'Fear is the underbelly of evil; it's how the devil gets his power over us, you know that. Our faith must be stronger than our fear.'

Without intending to, I snatch my teacup from Mrs. Greene, snapping free the handle as I do.

'My goodness, Clara, you're bleeding!' Alma rushes toward me with a dish towel, wrapping my finger within it. It's just a scratch, but her cup is ruined. Her gaze falls to the broken bits of her mother's china – *oh!* – and then back to my finger. 'That's okay.'

Before I can apologize to Alma, tell Mother Greene of my intention to send Trecie to her son's church filled with other children in need of after-school activities, my cell phone rings. I pull my fingers away from Mrs. Greene and Alma both.

'Clara, it's Ryan from Brockton PD. I got a body for you.'

'Just a minute.' I step out of the kitchen as Alma helps Mrs. Greene from her seat, hiding my hand within my jacket pocket.

'Mother Greene,' I hear Alma say in her kindest tone. 'Why don't you rest on our bed before dinner? You must be exhausted after your trip.'

While I'm speaking to Ryan, Alma half carries Mrs.

Greene in a one-step down to the other end of the hall toward the staircase. Alma turns to me, frowning, her brow curdled. I don't try to interpret her expression; I've never been fluent in the language of another's body. Instead I focus on Ryan, a man who requires no translation.

'Got assigned a well-being check,' says Ryan. 'Neighbor called to say they hadn't seen Charlie Kelly in a couple a days, newspapers piling up outside. Died watching TV. Must've been something good, 'cause he's not wearing his Underoos.'

I ask for an address and am about to hang up when Ryan catches me.

'Take your time,' he says. 'I don't mind kicking back here with Charlie awhile. The Stooges are on.'

CHAPTER SIX

It can be odd picking up the body of someone I knew in life. Charlie Kelly was a local fixture in Brockton, known as the Lucky Leprechaun for his diminutive size and affinity for scratch tickets. Like most living out an existence in this grizzled manufacturing city, he was born, raised, and, now, died here. I often saw him in his DPW pickup, dragging on a cigar and sipping Dunkin' Donuts coffee, supervising as younger workers filled potholes. Years ago, he was named an Everyday Hero by the *Brockton Enterprise*. It was his idea to have DPW crews make weekly passes of elementary schools to clear the smashed beer bottles and used condoms from the playgrounds. In the spring they planted flowers, and always he had pockets filled with candy for the 'little rugrats.' In the article, he said he'd never had children of his own, that being Brockton's 'Uncle Charlie' was enough.

I check the house numbers on Aberdeen Street; Ryan has taken the space in front of Mr. Kelly's house. Searching for street parking, I notice a long berth two doors down. I imagine the neighbors will be distressed to have a hearse parked in front of their bungalow with its chain-link fence and cardboard cutouts of smiling turkeys taped to their bow window. Death isn't in keeping with the Thanksgiving spirit.

I scan the street for Mike's Crown Vic, but it's not here. In neighboring Whitman, a detective will make a pass when there's an unattended death; this happens in Brockton, too, but not always. Brockton's police force is consumed with vehicular fatalities or garden-variety domestics resolved with kitchen knives and fists. In recent years, gangs filtering south from Boston and across the ocean from Cape Verde have brought their grievances with them. Gun violence rarely makes the front page of the *Enterprise* anymore.

Approaching Mr. Kelly's ranch-style house, I'm struck by its tidiness. This street is a pocket of relief within the city. Here the dusty grit that showers everything is kept at bay by washable vinyl siding and vibrant bunches of chrysanthemums lining some of the walkways. His lawn was given an end-of-season clip, and while there's no color to break the brief expanse of green, the hedges are neatly trimmed below the windows. I suspect his DPW crew made a pass here as well.

I ring the doorbell and hear Ryan call out above the yipping of a small dog. He snaps open the door, sweeping away a Chihuahua caught underfoot.

'Hey, you didn't have to rush over,' says Ryan over the barking. He's holding a bag of potato chips. When he sees my eyes fall to the bag, he shrugs. 'Evidence.'

Save Ryan's gun belt lying on the floor, there's nothing distinctive about this house; it's a common five-room ranch. The entrance opens directly into the living room with its gray couch and matching chair, navy blue area rug over worn hardwood, and stock floor lamps, the shades cracked and yellowed. A standard nineteen-inch TV blares the Three Stooges, interrupted in spurts by the explosive crackle of the police radio from Ryan's abandoned belt. The only color in the room is from an ancient green and white afghan covering Mr. Kelly's entire torso and legs. I wonder if it was knit by his mother, if I should tuck it into his coffin.

The shades are pulled, an odd consideration for a single man. Many of the bachelors whose bodies I pick up live amid disarray, if not outright filth: overflowing ashtrays litter every room; uneaten pots of food span kitchen counters and coffee tables; laundry, pornography, and liquor bottles lie strewn throughout. But as distasteful as these houses are, none compare to those of cat ladies. All are hoarders – magazines and newspapers mostly – rot and filth spilling from between the pages. And cats too numerous to count. Years ago I considered getting a pet, but walking through one too many cat-lady homes cured me of such notions.

Ryan, with the chips in one hand and more in his mouth, bends to scoop the dog under his left arm. It immediately stops yapping and begins to lick the grease from Ryan's palm. I walk past them to the body, where an ankle pokes out from beneath the afghan. It's mottled purple and blue down through the toes. The foot that rests on the floor is wholly black where bodily fluids, pooled by gravity, have settled. All of the hairs on Mr. Kelly's exposed body are white and his eyes are nearly closed. His mouth, however, is twisted, as if his death had been particularly painful.

'He's naked as a jaybird under there,' says Ryan, crumpling the bag. He leaves it on the coffee table, next to a blank video case and Red Sox ashtray, a cigar stub wedged in its nook with a lighter in the shape of a baseball beside it. There's the requisite bottle of Jim Beam, too, paired with a half-filled tumbler. The remote is resting on the arm of the chair, where I expect Ryan left it. 'He must have been watching *the movies*.'

Though the house bears the stench of death, it's relatively mild, nearly overwhelmed by the odor of stale cigars. I take a step toward the thermostat; it's set at fifty-five degrees. I'm grateful for Mr. Kelly's frugality. Any warmer and advanced decomposition would have made this removal unpleasant.

'Watch your step. Peanut here left some land mines,' Ryan says.

'Peanut?'

'That's what his tag says.' Ryan fingers the bone-shaped pendant hanging from the dog's collar. 'I figure I'll drop him off at the SPCA on my way home. I'd love to take him home, but the wife don't like dogs much. No, she doesn't.'

Ryan's voice has taken on a singsong quality as he

nuzzles the dog's snout. Peanut begins to lick his mouth, his tongue darting in and out of Ryan's lips.

I consider Mr. Kelly instead. 'How long do you think he's been here?'

'There were two newspapers outside.' Ryan sets the dog down and starts to pick at his teeth with a nubby fingernail. I imagine the salt from the chips must sting where his cuticles are red raw. 'The guys over at the DPW said he was in on Friday, so my guess is Friday night? He probably got one of the movies, had himself a good time jerking off, and' – Ryan lifts his shoulders in the world-weary manner of cops – 'died a happy man. Poor bastard.'

There's another hiss from Ryan's radio and this time he bends to the floor and pulls it from its holster. I listen to the back-and-forth, incomprehensible mumbles, followed by the only words I can distinguish, 'ten-four.'

'Mike's on his way over,' Ryan says as he grabs his belt and clips it around his waist. 'Chief wants him to sign off on this, seeing as how it's Charlie. I better take a look around, make sure everything's copacetic. Hold off until he gets here. You know how Mike is.'

'I'll wait in the car.'

'Don't bother. He's already on Centre Street, he'll be here any minute.'

I've no choice but to stay. I concentrate on the sound of Ryan clumping around Mr. Kelly's bedroom, rolling open closet doors and slamming shut drawers. The dog is in there with him, and I can hear Ryan murmuring to him in dulcet tones. A pause and then he shouts, 'Man's got some nice cigars.'

He emerges from the room, a small wooden case in his right hand, the other dragging a cigar under his nose. 'To the victor go the spoils,' he murmurs before tucking it into his breast pocket. The dog scampers behind him, looking up at Ryan, his eyes wide and body trembling.

'Oh, poor little Peanut, all alone,' says Ryan, his voice high-pitched. He picks up the dog again, cuddling him under his chin. 'Who's my little buddy?'

Just then a car door slams. There's nowhere in this tiny space for me to hide. I shrink against the wall that divides this room from the kitchen.

Ryan puts the dog in Mr. Kelly's room and closes the door. There's an outburst of barking and the tiny dog's nails frantically scratching at the barricade.

Mike's on the steps now; I can hear him wiping his feet on the rubber mat outside and then see the knob turn. When the door pushes open into this room, it's as I've been blown back too.

I focus on his shoes, and then he says my name. 'Hello, Clara.'

My breath comes quickly, but I loosen my coat around me so he can't see the rise and fall of my chest. I glance a little higher and see his hands resting on either hip. I don't know what to make of his tone and can't look to his face.

'Hello, Mike.'

'Hey, Mikey,' says Ryan, holding out the humidor, bending slightly at the waist. 'Care for a cigar?'

I can stare at him now; his attention is directed at Ryan. Mike appears more tired than usual, and there's a slump to his shoulders I haven't seen since that first year after his wife was killed. I wonder if I'm the cause.

'Bolivars. Cuban, right?' asks Mike, eyeing the box. 'Didn't know Charlie was plugged into that crowd. Those got to have a street value of a few hundred.'

'Yeah, we liberated some of these when I was overseas,' says Ryan, before nodding toward Mr. Kelly. 'He won't be needing them anymore.'

Mike winces. 'When you're wearing *this* uniform, you leave everything as is.'

I steal a glance at Ryan and notice the hinges of his jaw bulge. Then he smiles.

'I was just kidding,' he says, but doesn't remove the cigar from his pocket. The dog has grown quiet in the other room, as if he too is awaiting the verdict of his owner's final moments. Ryan puts the box on the end table and waves his arm around the room.

'Nothing suspicious here. When I came in, the victim was on the couch. I felt for a pulse, there was none. He was cold to the touch and showed signs of rigor mortis. I phoned it in to the M.E., explained the body's state of undress, the Lipitor in the cabinet, and the M.E. called it a heart attack.'

'Have you called Charlie's doctor for his medical history?' Mike asks.

Ryan has the look of a pet caught voiding on the floor. 'Looks pretty straightforward. His license says he's sixty-two, puts him in the age bracket. My guess? He was watching TV, had himself a smoke' – Ryan purses his lips, *plbbt* – 'and expired.'

I interrupt. 'I'll call the doctor. I'll need a signature for the death certificate.'

Mike walks to the coffee table, picks up the video case, and turns it over before showing it to us. 'I don't know, looks to me like he was watching a movie. No label. And he's naked.'

'Oh.' Ryan smiles, his eyebrows flexing. 'He was having himself a good time watching *the movies*.'

He leaps across the room to Mr. Kelly's television stand, a simple particleboard and veneer cabinet, the kind popular with Wal-Mart shoppers, and begins fumbling with the VCR. I imagine Ryan is a more sophisticated consumer who outfits his compact living room with a forty-inch flat screen and cable-ready DVD player. I have neither.

'Ryan,' starts Mike, 'just look for the doctor's number.'

But Ryan ignores him and continues with the VCR. Mike lets loose a rush of air and returns his hands to his hips. Still, he turns to watch the screen. I do too.

A Gold Bond commercial exhorting the benefits of bath powder is replaced with silence as Ryan pushes a button before walking back to Mike's side. An instant later the screen goes blank and then flickers to a scene of a single bare mattress laid out on wooden boards. The wall behind it is dingy and naked, save for what appears to be a child's abstract scrawl in green and blue crayon. Mike picks up the remote control and turns up the volume.

'Uh, Mike?' Ryan starts, but Mike shushes him.

A man and a little girl are walking over to the mattress, their backs to the camera. She's wearing a sundress, pale blue and rumpled. He's wearing a gray sweatshirt, but his head is beyond the camera's frame. They turn in profile, the girl's face obscured by her long, dark hair. We see only the man's torso.

'Mike – ,' says Ryan, reaching for the clicker.

'Wait.' Mike raises his hand, and Ryan freezes.

The man on the video whispers something to the girl. It's unintelligible, but her response is clear. She shakes her head *no* and a curtain of wavy tendrils drapes against a cheek, hiding her expression. The man's tone changes; that's all I know for certain, because the only word I can distinguish is 'now.' The child raises her right hand to her shoulder and slips the dress strap down. Before she removes the other, she turns to look at the camera. Her face is expressionless, but her eyes plead with me. It lasts only a few seconds, but it's enough. I can't help myself – I cry out.

'Shit,' Ryan whispers, leaping over the coffee table and punching buttons on the VCR.

'Turn it off!' Mike says before striding across the room to me. He places a hand on my shoulder and squeezes. I've never felt his touch before; it burns. 'I'm sorry you had to see that.'

His hand still on me, he turns to Ryan. 'Secure the premises; this is now a crime scene. I'll call in a search warrant while you get his doctor on the phone and take a medical history. If he says he had a heart condition, at least Clara can get him out of here. We're stripping this house.'

Mike returns his attention to me, and I wonder if he can feel me tremble, if he can smell the acid from my stomach searing my throat. Both of my hands go to my head. Not here, not now. Instead, there's a sore from the other day, vivid and ragged. I scrape the scab free with my nails.

'Are you okay?'

'That girl—'

He interrupts. 'I know, it's sick. I didn't know Charlie was a ped.'

'No,' I say, meeting Mike's eyes for the first time, 'I know that girl.'

His grip tightens and I falter under his touch. I can't tell if it's the same flush of rage as the last time we spoke of Precious Doe, or if he feels as ill as I do. My ponytail is beginning to come apart.

Though his fingers bore into me, his voice is soft. 'Clara, you have to tell me. No games this time. Who is she? Is she from around here?'

'Yes,' I say. 'Her name is Trecie.'

CHAPTER SEVEN

I don't often have visitors. On a warm day when my garden is in full bloom, a mourner might take a break from the confines of the bereavement room and wander outside to the parking lot. He or she might spot my cottage behind the weathered fence overcome with wisteria boughs. Perhaps the clumps of colorful gerber daisies (*simple beauty*) planted at each post draw them, the flowers' sunny disposition a respite from the burden of lilies.

Occasionally, one might be bold enough to walk under my arch, to rest on my bluestone patio. What makes one person lounge in my chaise, face turned toward the sun, and another sit on the concrete bench, head gathered in her hands, I don't know. I often watch them through the French doors, though. It doesn't occur to them that they've trespassed, that this cottage of mine is not simply an extension of the Bartholomew Funeral Home. Some will even jiggle the handle of my glass door or peer through a window. They're never aware of me staring back at them.

Today I will have a guest, someone invited. Well, not

really. Mike called this morning wanting to discuss Trecie – 'strategize,' he said. Yesterday, after executing the search warrant at Mr. Kelly's house, he found many more videotapes. There were only four of Trecie, but she appeared in dozens of still images on his computer. I'm glad he told me all of this after I'd prepared Mr. Kelly's body. I'd known too much as it was. Truly, I tried to reconfigure his pained expression, tried to remove the ugly grimace that contorted his face in death. I am not a magician.

The kettle wails as a car pulls into the adjacent parking lot. Through the bramble of hibernating wisteria, I see Mike bound from his police car. It's a newer-model Crown Vic, dark green with tinted windows. Before closing the door, he reaches across the driver's seat and removes a large cardboard box. Looking around my sitting room, I'm grateful I don't own a VCR.

The kettle continues to call, so I busy myself in the kitchenette with the ritual of tea: a china pot and my two matching cups; a bowl with sugar cubes and twin creamer; a serving dish for a coffee cake I purchased this morning; dessert dishes, a knife, forks, and spoons. This is something Alma would do, not I. Never before. I remove the knife from the tray and cut two pieces of cake.

He winds his way through my garden path, but I can't wait for a knock. The box is too full, too awkward in his hands; I'll have to meet him at the door. Reaching for my hair, I feel for the spots, careful to shield them with layers of hair pulled from other parts. Then I readjust my ponytail. I wish he could come another day, or never. When I turn the handle, his presence staggers me. In the glare of the fading afternoon sun, it's difficult to believe this is the same man I saw ripping the sod from his wife's grave. His hair is fixed and his clothes starched; he smells of peppermint. There's no trace of the beaten man I saw that night. I lean into the frame and am cooled by a bitter wind.

'Hello, Clara.'

He walks the few feet over to my coffee table and places the box down. He doesn't look to me; instead, he looks around the room. I latch the door and once again my face grows warm. He's a policeman, a detective, after all. Perhaps he's seeking clues about me I can't see.

What does it mean that my couch and chair are camel colored with striped blue pillows and a matching down throw? That I spent too much for a Pakistani oriental, but that the rest of my hardwoods are bare? He must notice that my living room is a jungle of Boston fern, palm, ficus, and ivy. I've never been anywhere that inspired a photograph; there are no pictures on the walls. He walks over to a row of bookcases, sturdy oak things I bought from a consigner in town, a savvy man who haunts the houses of the dead, offering cash to families intent on cleaning out and quickly selling Grandmother's house (unlike most of the residents of this town, he didn't think it odd when I arrived in my hearse). I don't have the kind of life that produces bric-a-brac, so the shelves are cluttered only with books. Mike's head tilts sideways as he scans the titles, and I feel as though he's peering into me. What must he make of my Dickinson and Pearlman, Dang Thuy Tram and Albert Camus, Dalai Lama and Dostoyevsky, an entire shelf of Sibley's guides to birds?

'Don't you have a TV?' he asks.

So that was all. 'No.'

Mike ruffles his hair, exhaling loudly. 'I sent most of the tapes out to the FBI. They have profilers there who can break them down. They'll look for jewelry, tattoos, birthmarks – anything about the perp or victims that can help ID them. It'll take about a month. But from what I saw, it's a room of horrors, a regular setup. This guy's a pro, probably working within a ring.'

'Victims?' I say, before covering my mouth. I didn't intend to speak.

'Yeah, there's another girl.' Mike's gaze shifts away, his expression growing slack. The iridescent shadows under his eyes match my own. It's clear neither of us slept last night, knowing what we do. I wait for him to return and then he does, raising his chin, straightening his shoulders as he speaks. 'How about looking at some photos? We need to positively identify the girl.'

'I'm sure it was Trecie.' The child must be afforded some dignity.

Mike has already lifted the cover of the box and is rummaging through files.

'Please,' I say, backing away, 'don't.'

Mike's fingers stop their searching; his face softens. 'Just some head shots, nothing else. I wouldn't do that.'

He turns back to the files. He's all business, and that's why I've forgotten my manners. Even today, his day off, he's wearing a button-down shirt and tie. His badge is clipped to his belt, and the gun is in its holster. It suddenly occurs to me that I've never had a gun in my home.

'Would you like some tea? There's cake, too.'

Mike's hands leave the box to perch on his waist, and he turns to me. It seems as if minutes, hours, pass as he considers this. I've often thought there's something reptilian about Mike's eyes. No, not the coldness, it's more about the layers. There's a certain ambiguous quality to them. Like an alligator before it slips underwater, hiding its intent beneath a transparent shield that covers the cornea, allowing the animal to see as it protects itself from harm. It's the same with Mike. But right now there's no shield. Now his eyes are naked, wild, still, and deeply, deeply pained. It's impossible for me to look away.

'Tea, huh?' he says. 'Yeah, let's have some tea first.'

I walk the few steps to the kitchen and stack everything onto a tray. My back is to him, and I wonder if he's chosen to sit at the table or on the couch. The roar in my ears makes it impossible to hear. The table would be easier with its straight-backed chairs and curved oak between us, but it's small, a round pedestal that seats only two; our knees might brush. Steadying my hands, resisting the urge, I place the last dish on the tray. I turn and he's seated at the table, his blazer hanging over the back of his chair.

'You didn't have to go to any trouble,' he says.

'Alma sends me too many leftovers. I could never eat this cake alone.'

'Boy.' Mike rubs a hand along his cheek and there's an audible scratch of bristles against his weathered palm: a nod to his day off. 'I haven't had tea in years.'

A long pause is filled with the sounds of spoons against china, the clink of fork against dish, Mike clearing his throat. The heat of the Earl Grey rises in my cheeks as the time passes in silence. Finally, he speaks.

'Can I ask you something?' The cup is at my lips, so he simply continues. 'Do you like your job?'

I return the cup to its saucer. 'I suppose.'

'I mean . . .' Mike pushes his plate away and grasps his tea as if it were a coffee mug, his index finger looped all the way through the handle. 'It's got to be pretty hard sometimes, what you do.'

'Not really,' I say, surveying the box he's brought with him. 'I would think your job is harder.'

He stops and drops his chin, his free hand scratching absently at his cheek. His eyes are still bare. 'Maybe, maybe not.'

There's another long silence, but I can feel him setting up. My mind races to deflect the questions I sense coming. His leg is too close to mine under this table.

'Have you ever been down there,' he says, nodding in the direction of the funeral home, 'and thought you were being watched? Like they're waiting to see what's happening to their bodies?'

I wonder if he's thinking about his Jenny, if he thinks she materialized as I prepared her body. Does he hope she hovered nearby while I laid her out in her mahogany casket with alstroemeria (*devotion*) alongside her thigh?

'No, I don't believe in that sort of thing.'

Mike leans forward, all of him motionless. 'You don't believe in what?'

'In any of it.'

'You don't believe in God?'

I can't answer. How can there be such a thing when one little girl lies unclaimed in a grave across the street and another is forced to lie in that bed, dying a little more each time someone lies beside her? I know how it is to die in bits and pieces. But it's a terrible thing to kill hope, especially when it's all that sustains a man.

Mike slumps in his chair, setting the cup on the table, his finger gliding along the rim. He's no longer looking at me. His gaze is fixed downward, on visions only he can see. 'I guess, sometimes, I don't either.'

There are no words to console a man with nothing. Platitudes are worse than silence.

'Did you know my wife was pregnant when she died? Just a couple months. I've always wondered if you knew.'

It was in the medical examiner's notes. I was careful with the trocar that day, careful not to disturb all that was in her abdomen. It's too much to tell Mike, no one really cares to know the details of my work. I remain silent.

'She always wanted kids, you know?' As he speaks,

three fingers of his left hand hold aside his tie while the forefinger creeps between the buttonholes nearest his heart. Where it gapes, there's a splash of freckles. 'But seeing what I see, I couldn't.' His voice is thick, one finger circling the rim of his cup, his other hand restless under his shirt, until Mike clears his throat. 'So, what do you believe?'

I look again to the box Mike brought with him, then through the window to the back entrance of the funeral home, and beyond that, to Colebrook Cemetery.

'I believe it's important to breathe.'

Mike's head jerks up and his eyes drag me back. I want to turn away, but they've pulled taut the thread between us. 'Breathe?'

'Yes.' I don't know why I continue, but no one has ever asked, and it's all I can give him. 'When we concentrate on the breath, we're aware only of that moment. And that's all we ever have, really, is a moment. And when we no longer breathe, we no longer exist.'

Mike's eyes are full now. If I could look away, I wouldn't see his lip tremble, but he pulls the thread tighter. 'Do you ever find it hard to breathe?'

'Yes,' I say, 'it's always hard to breathe.'

'Me too.'

He's quiet for what seems like an endless stretch, too much. He then springs from his seat, his back to me. He gestures to the box. 'You're going to help me, right? You're going to help this Trecie?'

I think back to Mother Greene, to her warning about sending away the little girl. I don't truly think someone will try to kill me, or that someone will risk his life to save mine. And though I don't believe in Mother Greene and her ghosts, I do know that the image of Trecie in that video would haunt me the rest of my life if I were to abandon her. I won't do that. Not me of all people.

'Yes,' I say, 'I will.'

He nods, pausing before closing the few feet between himself and the box. He removes a photo from the top folder and hands it to me. 'Is this Trecie?'

It is, of course it is. Her hair, nose, even the same expression. I will have to help, though it's a terrible burden to be needed. Mike and I talk for a while, or rather he does about what it is I'm supposed to do when she shows again. He starts by asking me to relay every conversation I've had with Trecie, pressing for details about her clothing, her accent, any distinguishing marks, earrings. I don't tell him that I could barely look at the child, how I tried to turn her away again and again. He explains how the next time she comes by I should draw her out: find out where she lives, her last name, names of friends and family members, her school. That I should check for a bicycle leaning against the funeral home's wrought-iron fence, see if it's a simple rebuilt version or something with a pretty white basket and handlebars with streaming pink ribbons. Ask her if she's willing to talk to either Mike or one of the women detectives. He hands me his card with his cell phone number.

'Call me day or night, whenever you make contact,' he says. 'I live just a few miles away.'

'I will.'

'Anytime, day or night.'

He removes his sports jacket from the back of the kitchen chair and swings his arms through the sleeves. The muscles of his chest strain against the thinness of his cotton shirt. I can't help myself, I look for those speckles along his breastbone, but they're hidden away, tucked beneath the surface again.

I hold the door for him as I did when he arrived (*less than an hour ago?*), but he pauses after saying good-bye. 'Thanks for the tea, Clara. It was nice.'

I hug my sweater around me and nod. I have no more words for him. After closing the door, I step back to my kitchen window and watch as he walks back to the Crown Vic. He replaces the box on the passenger seat and lowers himself into the driver's side. Before starting the car, he bows his head and touches his forehead, heart, left and right sides. I see his lips move, and then he crosses himself again, starts the engine, and drives away. From me.

CHAPTER EIGHT

I've been kissed before.

The first time was in high school. I was a sophomore at North Smithfield Junior-Senior High, just over the state line in Rhode Island. After my mother died, I lived with her mother in the village of Slatersville. Though the town's proper name had been North Smithfield since 1871, my grandmother and other locals held firmly to Slatersville, as if one could take pride in a name.

Slatersville was, and is, a small town, not quite ten thousand residents when I lived there. Most were older: middle-aged housewives working mother's hours as receptionists or substituting in the schools, and their blue-collar husbands, thirsty for a six-pack on their way home from union jobs. Narragansett was bottled nearby. There were few children, a thousand maybe, and so, few opportunities for a fifteen-year-old girl, especially one as different as me.

Many afternoons were spent in the school library, doing my homework, biding my time until dinner and then bed, until I turned eighteen and could lose the past.

I told my grandmother I earned extra credit after school. I'd purposefully failed an English test; the resulting welts that laced the backs of my legs were worth the price of those precious hours away from her house. After that, I was sure to earn A's and suffered only a few quick strikes of her wooden spoon across my wrist when Mrs. Daher gave check minuses in gym. The library was where I met Thoreau and Austen, Heathcliff and Cathy, where I read and read again *Sonnets from the Portuguese*, where a girl could dream of her first kiss. At my grandmother's house, the only books allowed were the Bible and *Merriam-Webster's Dictionary*.

That October, Tom McGee sat two tables away, surrounded by textbooks. He was a junior and it was well known around school – even to me – that he had been benched from the football team because of poor grades. For several days we sat there while Miss Talbot restocked the shelves and scrubbed away pornographic graffiti in the easy-reader section. Miss Talbot was as close to a friend as I had. Once she told me that my mother also had been a frequent visitor to the library. A part of me wanted to know if she had known my mother's circle of friends, if she suspected who among the boys might have been my father. Perhaps my mother was the kind of girl who confided her secrets to the silent well that was Miss Talbot; my mother hadn't told anyone else. I never asked Miss Talbot, of course; it was enough to wonder, to hope my mother had had friends. Though Miss Talbot and I hardly spoke, we were comfortable together in that everyday silence, each in our too-big cardigans, enveloped within the intimate world of books. Tom's presence disrupted this world of ours.

While Tom pretended to ignore the sounds of his team practicing in the field beyond the library, I pretended to ignore him. He was broad with dark hair and Irish blue eyes. His beauty reminded me of the fashion magazines that sat on the racks of the general store. Once I looked inside those pages and saw a sumptuous coat. It was red with black fur trim, long and sleek. The woman who modeled it was unlike any of the women around town. Only Mrs. Hansen with her flaxen hair and Nordic cheekbones was close. When I read the caption beneath the photograph, $8,175, I replaced the magazine on the rack and was never tempted to look again.

One day while Miss Talbot took a call at her desk, Tom approached me. 'You got a pencil?'

A stack of books formed a barrier between us: novels, memoirs, poetry, some biographies. I kept my eyes trained on the page before me while my fingers sought the beveled edges of a number two from my book bag. I raised my hand but not my eyes, and extended the pencil to him. When he took it, his fingers brushed mine. I could feel the chafe of his dead skin against my own smoothness.

He didn't leave. Instead, he lowered my wall by lifting my science text. 'Hey, aren't you in my chemistry class?'

I didn't bother to respond. It would have taken too

many words to explain why I was in an advanced class. No need to carry on when the conversation would end within seconds anyway. It was delusional to think otherwise.

'Did you already do the homework? I'm stuck on number three.'

Still, I pretended to read. I wasn't coy enough to play hard to get. The first couple of weeks after I'd arrived in Slatersville, following my mother's funeral, a few of the children tried to befriend me. In the end, none had the patience.

But Tom persisted. 'You a mute? My cousin's retarded. You dumb or something?'

I looked up then. 'No.'

'Did you do number three?'

I handed him my chemistry notebook and he brought it to his desk. He kept it there, turning the pages as he copied my work. After Miss Talbot returned the phone to its cradle and rounded the corner with her spray bottle and sponge, Tom came back. He slapped my notebook down, but by then I'd spent too many years living with my grandmother to be caught off guard by the startle of a bare smack.

'You ever read this book?' He was clutching a worn school copy of *Hamlet* in his right hand. I noticed a page was dog-eared, something Mrs. Johnson forbade. Seeing Tom's folded page thrilled me in a way I'd never known possible.

'It's my favorite,' I said.

'You're not into that *Romeo and Juliet* stuff?'

I tried not to cringe, knowing most of the other girls swooned over the lovelorn pair. 'We're reading it now in Mrs. Johnson's class. *Hamlet*'s better.'

Tom leaned his thigh into the corner of my table. I noticed his flesh didn't give against the hardness of the wood. When he bent over me, I could smell the sourness emanating from his mouth, feel the heat radiating from his body. 'You get this?'

I nodded, sensing as he looked to his right and left, and then out to the football field, where the coach's whistle trilled across the schoolyard. Tom finally settled on me, or so I hoped. It was too much to look up. It was as if I'd taken my first breath when he said, 'Maybe you and I could read it together.'

We met like that every day. I'd hand over my chemistry notebook and answer his English lit handouts, and in return, he'd talk to me. I'd listen to his stories of our class-mates, stories I'd never been privy to before. Stereotypes are born of truth, and so it was with high school, where football players made it with cheerleaders, chugged from kegs, and sought their neighbors' high-and-inside mail-boxes with their Louisville Sluggers.

As he spoke, I'd let my eyes drift over the broadness of his chest, glance at his hand spread-eagled across his thigh. I'd inhale his sweat and the musk of his cologne, which had faded by the late afternoon. After many days, I could almost meet his eyes. I remember that first time, when he asked me to show him where the biographies of his sports idols were kept, I stood on unsteady legs, hugging my too-long sweater against me as I walked ahead, conscious of his bulk behind me.

When I turned to him, pointing to the shelf, he caught me in his arms. He bent low to reach my mouth, tilting my chin upward before he kissed me. I felt everything in that instant: his tongue prying open my chaste lips; the press of hard muscles against my own bones; an awakening of something long ago put to rest. I felt tiny and alive. Every sense was keenly attuned, but none more so than my hearing, listening as Miss Talbot pushed her squeaky cart, paused to return books to their shelves, and then the pop of her knees as she stood again.

That first kiss was as unexpected as a crocus baring itself during a February balm. I've seen some bloom from time to time in my own garden, straining through a crack in winter's soil. They are so hopeful, so lavender lovely, so blithely unprepared for the brutality of an approaching nor'easter.

After that first time, Tom and I would return to the stacks once I finished his homework. Each day his hands grew bolder, more insistent. After a couple of weeks, I took to wearing skirts with high cotton socks, providing easy access and a ready cover should Miss Talbot round the corner. Though he'd thrust himself inside of me again and again and again, it was his kisses that filled me whole.

During school, if we passed each other in the halls, neither of us would acknowledge the other. I might stare for the briefest flash as Tom surrounded himself with teammates and the cheerleaders who wore their letter jackets. I wasn't jealous of the cotton candy girls and their easy banter. I knew our afternoons in the library were beyond the scope of their simple experiences.

That day, that Friday, he arrived at the library as usual, though this time he brought a friend, someone I recognized from the halls. He had the same thick neck and muscled shoulders as Tom, the same football insignia on his letter jacket.

'Clara,' said Tom, 'this is my buddy Art.'

I was thrilled. Tom was ready to introduce me to his circle of friends. He wanted them to know me, to finally know of me. The junior prom was in a few months and I'd already made preparations should Tom ask me. For weeks I'd hoarded scraps of material in home-ec class. The girls there preferred the pastel fabrics, leaving me long swaths of gray and black. I could make do. My grandmother was the greatest obstacle. I knew better than to introduce the subject of dating in her house. She liked to remind me that my mother's harlot ways were what had driven her to an early grave, and if I wasn't careful, I would follow the same wayward path.

'God punished the whore for her sins,' my grandmother would say, gesturing to the mantel where she haphazardly taped torn magazine pages with Hollywood divorcées, newspaper clippings of serial killers, and my mother's black-and-white senior portrait with me concealed beneath a girdle. Above us all, reaching for the ceiling, hung a crucifix. Her hand was clammy when it grabbed mine, cold and desperate, her eyes beseeching. 'Stay true, Clara. Suffer for Him. He'll provide you everlasting life if you reject sin!'

I'd remain quiet – it was usually safer that way – and she would pull me down to my knees. 'Let's pray for forgiveness.'

But I didn't want forgiveness, I wanted Tom. I was prepared to be like my mother, the whore-child, and climb out of my bedroom window to be with him for one perfect night. Welts and bruises would heal, I reasoned, and death was inevitable.

So when Tom stood before me with his friend Art, the flush of adventure seized me. 'Nice to meet you.'

'I've heard a lot about you,' Art said, deep acne scars twisting as he smiled.

My heart skipped.

'Hey, Clara,' said Tom, 'I got some good news. I got a B on my English quarterly, so I'm back on the team.'

Forgetting myself, I threw my arms around him, right in the middle of the library. 'That's great!'

'Yeah, so I won't need to come here anymore. But see, my buddy' – Tom took a step back from me and put his arm around Art – 'he could use some extra help. Coach said he won't be able to play unless he gets a C average. I was thinking maybe you could help him, the way you been helping me.'

Tom and Art exchanged a look. There was a malevolence to Tom's expression, and in that moment, I realized I'd been overlooking it for weeks. It was too late now. When I looked to Art, his eyes were dim and his mouth hung slack.

'I told him how good you are with science and English,' Tom said. Had I really not noticed that smirk before? 'And other stuff.'

My breath came then in short, quick bursts, leaving my lungs just as swiftly.

'I don't think so.'

'Come on, Clara,' said Tom. 'Give a guy a break. Do it for the team.'

I took a step back, and then another. Tom's nostrils flared and I wondered if he could smell me, smell my regret. I don't know how I found myself back at my table, but I sat there, taking a book from the pile, as if seeking out the shoulder of a constant friend. But Tom wouldn't leave. He swaggered over, placed both hands down on my desk, and then pulled the book away.

'I wonder what your grandma would think if she knew her grandbaby was a whore. What would happen then?'

I looked at him. I could find no trace of the boy I'd spent weeks and months longing for, the one into whose ear I'd whispered my secrets. Instead, I saw the same face his opponents on the field must have seen, an adversary who thought nothing of crippling anyone who got in his way.

The tears nearly choked me. 'I can't.'

'You don't have a choice,' Tom said. 'It would kill your grandma.'

He grabbed my chemistry notebook and threw it to Art. 'Here you go. Just give her your English homework, she'll do it. When she's done' – Tom looked at me then, smiling as tears scorched my face – 'take her over to the biography section. She likes it there.'

Tom left, and in that moment I almost prayed. I almost prayed Art would feel some sense of compassion, a sense of dignity, but he simply took his English folder from his backpack and handed the worksheet to me. I stalled, giving superficial answers to the questions the way I had with Tom's homework. *Let the clock run out*, I begged my grandmother's silent god. But Art wasn't patient the way Tom had been in the beginning. After only ten minutes he stood before me, an erection visible through his cotton chinos.

'Hey,' he said, grabbing my hand. I tried and failed to pull free as he glowered over me. 'Don't make me tell Tom.'

And so I followed him, dragged by the wrist. He watched Miss Talbot stroll down the contemporary-fiction aisle and then he yanked me into European history. Within seconds he slammed me against the rear shelf. I could feel the corners of the books digging into the small of my back. A quick turn of his wrist and his pants were down. He fumbled with my skirt, gathering the wool and pushing it aside, pushing himself into me. I stopped him when he bent to kiss me.

'No,' I said, pressing against his shoulders, my face covered with tears and snot.

He stopped moving a second, two, his face clouded and dull. Then he shrugged. 'Fine by me.'

Art was only the first of Tom's friends who would seek me out in the library. Tom was right: I didn't have a choice. As Art burst inside of me, I heard a sound, a squeak. I looked past him and saw Miss Talbot. She stood at the end of the aisle, her book cart brimming. Her mouth hung open, her gaze fluttering up and down my and Art's joined bodies, and then her eyes met mine. Art was unaware, his back to her, consumed only with his pleasure. We stood like that, my friend Miss Talbot and I, our eyes locked. And then she pushed her cart to the next aisle and I heard her knees pop once again as she bent to return a book to its shelf.

I've thought of that moment a lot lately. I imagine the shock Miss Talbot must have felt. I imagine she must have seen a little girl, her face expressionless but her eyes pleading.

I imagine she saw a girl much like Trecie.

CHAPTER NINE

I wish Linus were here. He and Alma are attending the opening performance of *Black Nativity*, as they do the first week of every December. Lifts their holiday spirits, they say. He bought the tickets weeks ago, to the matinee performance rather than an evening show, an acknowledgment of their age and aversion to driving late at night. Though the play didn't start until three thirty, they set out early to sightsee along Boston Common.

'Christmas in Boston is a withered man's shadow of his former self,' Alma says once the holiday lights start to appear. This time of year she likes to tell me how, when she was a child, she and her three sisters would set out early from their South End apartment to spend hours in the Jordan Marsh department store touring the Enchanted Village.

'Reminded me of *It's a Small World*, only for Christmas,' Alma says. Now she's forced to accept whatever paltry Christmas substitute is available in the city. One of the disadvantages of living above the funeral home is she can't string colorful lights or hang festive evergreen boughs this time of year.

Here in the mourning room, there is no recognition of the holiday. There is only Mrs. Molina whispering as she kneels over the body of her twelve-year-old daughter. Her shadow, cast by low-lit sconces and the five-pronged candelabras on either end of the casket, undulates against the far wall. Whether it wavers from an unsteady flame or the woman's mute sobs, I can't tell.

If Linus were here, he would know where to stand, know the words to soothe her. He would probably kneel with her, though lately his knees have made it difficult for him to regain his footing easily. Still, he'd swallow the pain.

I don't know why he asked me here instead of canceling his plans. Always the families of the bereaved are invited to come the night before the wake to say a private farewell. It's been his role to host them, to guide them through the strain. Perhaps this too is an acknowledgment of his age. Maybe he thinks he's grooming me to take over the business. Though I dread the conversation, I need to tell him I prefer my standing, here in the shadows. I could never fill his shoes.

I try not to look at Mrs. Molina, her body a waterfall tumbling over her daughter's. Instead I scan the flower arrangements, identifying as many blossoms as I can.

Like many children stricken with cancer, Angel Molina was known to the community. Over the years, I've seen the flyers down at Tedeschi's corner store advertising a bone-marrow drive. Or the story last year in the *Brockton Enterprise* when a local car dealership donated a van with a wheelchair lift. She was beloved. Now that she's dead, her status is reflected in the numerous bouquets and funeral wreaths that overflow the room. There are the mandatory calla lilies in faux brass vases; a red, white, and blue carnation wreath mounted on a stand from her grandfather's VFW; and pink amaryllis (*proud*) sent by Mrs. Brown's class, where Angel was a student. I like the pots and pots of wholly white arrangements: roses, aster, and, as at every child's funeral, white daisies. There is an especially healthy one near the head of the casket with blossoms the size of my fist. I wonder if Mrs. Molina would mind if I took a stem to seed my own garden. I look at her, and as if sensing my attention, she turns.

'Clara, did you do this?' She straightens herself as she speaks, pushing up on the kneeler to stand, and then stops to caress her daughter's cheek. I returned Angel's complexion to its original olive tone and styled the glossy black wig, a girlish bob, so that it curled in to highlight the graceful lines of her neck.

'Yes, ma'am.'

She glances back at her daughter, her voice trembling. 'Everyone's been so generous, I don't know how to repay them. And now this.' She gestures to the casket, her arm casting an enormous shadow against the far wall.

'Linus never charges for the children. Not anyone.'

Mrs. Molina nods, both hands clutching the strap of a worn tan purse that dangles before her. She's petite with dark stockings and comfortable shoes. She wears her dress like an afterthought. Her only adornment are the intricate plaits spun in dizzying loops atop her head, streaked black and gray. I notice for the first time that though her face is plain and her body settled into the thickness of middle age, she is beautiful. It's the kind of beauty exuded through pores, through lustrous eyes, through inner peace. 'She looks lovely, Clara. Thank you.'

I don't know what would be a proper response, so instead I say nothing.

'I always wondered what Angel would have looked like if it hadn't been for the chemo and steroids,' Mrs. Molina says, turning to her daughter again. 'Of course, she was always beautiful to me.'

I listen for Linus's step, the sound of his car pulling into the parking lot, but I'm alone. 'I'm sorry for your loss, Mrs. Molina.'

'No, not a loss.' She hurries toward me, shaking her head and grabbing my hand in hers. I can feel the skin along my wrist begin to itch. If I look, I'll see hives blossoming there.

'Angel was a gift.' Mrs. Molina's eyes are glossy, her words strong and assured. 'She brought such joy to my life, a purpose after her daddy died. Her favorite thing in the world was to go for walks at World's End. You know the park, in Hingham? We'd bring a picnic lunch and our binoculars, and watch as red-tailed hawks flushed the sparrows. But that was before.' She pauses and looks back at Angel, her face softening. 'I like to think she's flying with them now, above them even. Her daddy by her side.

'You know, some people go their whole lives without love, but my little girl gave me enough in twelve years to fill me up for a lifetime.' She reaches for my hand and squeezes. Her fingers graze my inner wrist, an exquisite tease along the hives. I want nothing more than to rake her nails along my arm. 'No, I have not suffered a loss. I choose to believe my time with Angel was a gift.'

She smiles at me, nudging and sweet. It would be too cruel of me to share my own thoughts; silence is the better choice. Rubbing the tender part of my wrist against the woolen sleeve of my suit jacket, I let my gaze fall to her belly. I can't help but imagine Angel lying there within Mrs. Molina's womb. Before life, they were tethered by an umbilical cord; after, by hope.

'Do you have children, Clara?'

'Me?' I shake my head and pull my hand from hers.

'None at all?' Mrs. Molina asks, sadness overcoming her features.

'No.'

'Well, I'll pray for you,' says Mrs. Molina, gathering her coat from a nearby folding chair and shrugging it on. 'I've got my Angel. Something as insignificant as death won't ever separate us. I pray you get the same.'

She moves swiftly to the exit, the door pounding

closed behind her. For a moment I stand in place, wondering what's expected of me, if there exists an appropriate reply to Mrs. Molina's pity, but she's already gone.

There's no use in considering it further. Tomorrow will be a long day with a steady stream of mourners. It's time to extinguish the candles. I first blow out the ones at the foot of the coffin and then walk over to the candelabra at the head. Before I do, I look at Angel. Her mother's features overwhelm her face. I wonder if she appears to be smiling because Mrs. Molina's words still ring in my head or if her expression was always so. Somehow I can't remember. I feel alongside her thigh for the pink camellias (*perfect loveliness*). I imagine the flowers there over the next few days, staying vital through the wake and funeral, and then buried with the girl, their remains eventually blending together, back to the earth.

Looking at Angel's face, touching her hand, I wonder what my mother would have said had she lived and I died that rainy night. If she would have claimed her love for me was eternal, that I was her heart and soul and breath.

'Clara?'

I nearly shriek and stumble backward, attempting to regain my composure. I look at Angel, her expression fixed, but then I see Trecie emerge from behind an arrangement of asphodels (*eternal sorrow*) located on a console behind the casket.

'What are you doing here?' I take several more steps back.

'Are you sad?' Her hair appears windblown and knotted, and her delicate legs are bare beneath her skirt in spite of this New England night. Her eyes are so deep and dark, I feel as though I could plunge into them and never touch bottom. All I can do is shake my head.

'How did she die?' Trecie moves around the casket to stand before Angel. Looking down, she reaches out a hand, her fingertips perilously close to skimming the dead girl's arm.

Mike's words come back to me, counseling me to remain calm, to gather as much information from Trecie as possible without frightening her away.

'She had leukemia. She was sick for a long time.'

'Oh,' says Trecie, her hand now resting on the girl's. 'I saw her momma crying.'

'Losing a loved one can be difficult,' I say, wondering how I can draw her out of this room. But Trecie is mesmerized by Angel.

'Her momma loves her a lot.' Trecie turns to sit on the kneeler, facing me. She slumps over, resting her chin in her hands. 'My mom would cry if she came to my funeral. She'd feel real bad. And my sister would cry too.'

My heart lurches in my chest. I feel in my pocket for Mike's card – I've carried it with me since that day at my cottage; I should call him now. 'What's your sister's name?'

'Adalia.'

'And your mother's? What's her name?' I take a step toward her. Trecie doesn't answer, just looks at me with those bottomless eyes, and I can't help but see her on that video. 'You said your mother has a boyfriend, right?'

She nods.

'What's his name? You told me before, but I forget.' My head hurts as I flip through the possibilities: Vincent? Vito? Rick? I sense she's pulling away and don't want to waste time going over questions she's already answered. This must end tonight. I can't let her go home. Not to that. I'll call Mike and he will come take care of all of this.

Trecie stands and looks at Angel before asking me, 'What's *your* mother's name?'

Mike said she might try this; deflection, he called it. Try to engage her in conversation, he said. He must have felt so hopeless giving me these instructions.

'Mary.'

'What is she like?' Trecie is stroking Angel's hands, fingering the rosary beads wrapped in them.

'I don't remember really. She died when I was seven.'

'Do you think she would have been sad if you died?'

I can't help but wonder if she eavesdropped on my thoughts. My imagination gets the better of me and I feel a scraping sensation the length of my body as if she's raking my insides. I reach for my hair. 'I expect most mothers would.'

Trecie walks away from the casket and heads for the sitting room. As she turns, the back of her head is before me. Patches of scalp glow like orbs caught in this light. If only there were a salve for this sort of thing. I quickly extinguish the candles and follow her. She's standing in the middle of the room, waiting for me.

'I saw that man again,' she says.

'What man?' I don't really want to know anything about the man on the videotape. I rub Mike's card, wondering if I could excuse myself. He's the expert, he would know what to ask, how to ask. He could bear her answers. I need to believe she would talk to him.

'I saw that man go into your house. Are you sure he's not your boyfriend?'

That man, Mike. 'No, just a friend.'

Trecie eyes me. 'Do you have a boyfriend?'

'No.'

'No one at all?' she asks. I can't answer, her pity is too much to bear. 'I don't either.'

We fall silent, though I know I should direct the conversation back to her, somehow back to the trauma of her life, away from mine. I begin to pick at the hives on my wrist, then rub them against my hip, awaiting inspiration.

'She got a lot of flowers,' Trecie says, peeking back into the mourning room. 'More than that big man.'

'Mr. MacDonnell? Yes.' I remember back to the flowers she plucked from the arrangement the last time she was here – or rather, the last time I was aware she was here – how she tied a stem around a fistful of hair. Mike said to do anything to gain her trust and keep her around until he could get here. 'So you like flowers?'

Trecie nods her head. I wonder if it's a mistake, if I'm crossing some sort of boundary – my own – but I'm not clever enough to think of another way.

'Would you like to see my flowers?'

She smiles. Her cheeks seem almost full and there's the implication of a dimple along her chin. In this cold room, on this cold night, I begin to feel an ember of hope glow within me.

CHAPTER TEN

Her presence, inches away as I fumble with the lock to my patio door, is oddly comforting. It's near six, night falls early this time of year, close to four o'clock, yet she seems in no hurry to be anywhere but with me. I wonder if she's hungry, how long it's been since her last meal. There's fruit in my refrigerator, a splash of milk, and some cheese. There are crackers in the pantry, along with a box of cereal, and a can of soup in the cabinet. That's all. A roast? Sliced carrots in dill sauce? Twice-baked potatoes? I should have brought her to Alma's kitchen instead. If only they were home.

'It's so pretty,' Trecie says, stepping into my living room, her face aglow.

I look at the simplicity of my space and wonder what about it could be attractive to a child. There's nothing bold about the colors or style of furniture. No whimsical mementos to enchant the eye. But there is a general softness to the textures, a bland palette that's restful. And the greenery always warms me.

She pushes past me and walks over to the bookcases.

Her fingers glide along the spines of the hardcovers as she walks the length of the shelves. 'You have a lot of books.'

'Do you like to read?' I scan my memory for something appropriate I could share with her. I wonder if she's too young for the collection of Nancy Drew I keep tucked away on my bedroom shelves. Nancy, Bess, and George were my only friends in the early years. I bought the complete collection with my first paycheck from Linus.

Trecie lingers over a *Sibley Guide to Birds*. 'I don't know how.'

'You can take that if you like,' I say, motioning to the book. 'It has lovely pictures.'

It's too much to contemplate the entirety of this girl's life. When I first went to live with my grandmother, she enrolled me in the local elementary school. My vagabond life with my mother hadn't included classrooms and children my own age. With their colorful lunch boxes and sensible department store clothes, my classmates appeared to be characters from the picture books Mrs. Morrison read aloud to us, books the other kids could already read on their own. Trecie's prison is even worse than I first realized; it seems her only escape is this underworld of mine.

I feel like a tomcat stalking a flightless chick, every muscle flexed, every movement stilled. 'Aren't they teaching you to read at school? Where is it you go?'

She stops fingering the book and walks toward the kitchen. 'I don't go to school.'

I remain motionless. 'Does your mom home-school you?'

Trecie stops and turns to me, smiling. Her face is wan, reminding me of Mrs. Molina offering her prayers to me. Between us my ficus wilts in its corner, and I reach for a leaf. How did it grow yellowed at its edges without my noticing? Its roots must be straining along the sides of the ceramic pot, a mass of guts rolled into themselves at the bottom. I've neglected it; without attention, a larger container and fresh soil, a chance to stretch beyond it limitations, it will smother and die.

'Do you have any pictures of when you were a child?' she asks.

'Sorry.' There are no baby books, no detailed records of my first steps or first words, no school pictures marking my life through the years with adoring captions underneath. I pluck the leaf from the tree and put it in my pocket. Tomorrow I'll go to the nursery.

'What did you look like?' Trecie's standing so close now, this wisp of a girl, and I feel in every hair and fiber just how much she yearns for me to reach out and lay my hands upon her head, cup her chin, give her a careless hug. Something playful and affectionate. I finger the leaf instead.

'I don't really know. My hair was long, like it is now, just as dark, but thinner. I was always small for my age, I guess, skinny. In the summer, I'd turn brown as a nut.'

'Like me.'

'Yes, I suppose I looked a lot like you.'

She tilts her face and she is beautiful. Without intending to, my arms begin to lift, reach of their own volition for her, but then she takes a step backward and hurries toward the other side of the living room, swiveling her head as she moves. I wrap my arms around myself instead.

'Can I see the flowers now?'

Yes, of course, the flowers.

No one has seen my secret garden. Well, that's not true. I asked Linus and Alma's permission before starting construction, and when the greenhouse room was finished, they brought me the ficus to celebrate. But I intended the room for flowers. Once they left, I moved the ficus to my living room, where it could thrive against my bookcase, exposed only to filtered light, where it could weep its teardrop leaves in private.

Linus insisted on sharing the expense, since it increased the value of his property, but I refused. An undertaker makes a healthy living, and I've nothing else to do with my savings. Initially, Alma would stop by with lemon bars and her desire to help with my flowers. Sometimes I'm stricken when I think of how I discouraged her, never even inviting her in for a cup of tea. Still, I don't try.

My garden is tucked away off the lone bedroom, in the back of the cottage, where a wall once obscured the southern light. It's not something a guest passing my room would notice; no, one must be present to see it. And if for some reason a repairman needs access, I have the option of obscuring it with drapes. My bed is positioned with a view of the glass doors across the room leading to the greenhouse. On clear days, both rooms are bathed in sunshine. No one can see my garden from the parking lot, hidden as it is by the fence and privet that encircle my side yard. I doubt even Trecie has noticed it in spite of her prying ways.

I stumble over the edge of my bedroom area rug, steady myself against my chest of drawers. Trecie's eyebrows lift and she reaches for me without actually touching. Having her walk through this room with its odd assortment of tag sale furniture and plain white bedding, with books lying askew across my pillows, a robe cast off onto an upholstered chair, more bookcases . . . It's too intimate a step. I usher her over to the French doors and move aside the drapes as my hand searches in the dark for a light switch. I leave behind my anxiety when the bulbs catch and we step into my haven. I can't help but look at her face when, after several seconds, her eyes adjust.

'It's beautiful,' she gasps.

Though it's a simple structure of sheer glass and a fieldstone base, it houses wonders. Like the prep room in the funeral home's basement, there are drains in the tile floor. Here they're for water to nourish my flowers. Here, bright lights nurture growth and warm the living. In this room, the scents are only kind: rolling waves of citrus and butter, wet sugar and subtle musk, the promise of contentment. Instead of the thermostat being set at an intemperate fifty-five to prevent further decomposition, in my greenhouse it's an ardent eighty-three for seeds to compose themselves into roots and stems; leaves and buds; and then blossoms of petals or spathes, and the comely pistils. This room favors life.

In the far corner is a galaxy of dazzling sunflowers (*you are splendid*). In another, with a filter covering the glass panel above, is a party of elegantly dressed orchids (*flattery*), frozen midwaltz, curtsying and bowing. On benches and along the floor azaleas, primroses, dahlias, aster, lupines, morning glories, pansies, asphodels, marigolds, narcissis, a color wheel of roses, daisies (a complete palette of gerber and the virgin white Shasta), cosmos, lilacs, and on and on, with only narrow pathways for me to navigate a hose. The one bit of true furniture is a potting table with my supplies. There are no chairs. I've found that when I'm here, I want only to wander, to touch and to marvel.

'Let's close the door before the heat escapes,' I say.

Trecie begins to make her way into the room. Soon she turns the corner and is hidden by a cluster of lavender zinnias and Indian jasmine.

'Why did you do this?' I can hear her voice though no longer see her. She's lost in the dense thicket.

'I don't know,' I say. 'Everyone has a hobby.'

'Which flower is your favorite?' Her head is now visible through towering hollyhocks (*ambition*), their cowbells pink, droplets of water still hovering in the flowers' cuffs.

'I don't think I could pick.' Overcome by my garden, I've forgotten why we're here. I reach into my pocket for Mike's card and instead find the leaf, a stark reminder of my carelessness for the lives in my charge. I wonder if he would be home on a weekend night or out somewhere, with someone.

'Just tell me.'

'I don't know. Hydrangea, I suppose. Shasta daisies. Poppies are nice, but they wither so quickly.'

'Mine are the daisies. I like roses, too. Yellow ones.'

My guess is she chose the daisy and rose because they're the only flowers she knows by name. She's been given no education in life. She must recall the one of Mr. MacDonnell's I let her keep. The one she left behind.

'Would you like a drink? Something to eat?' The chrysanthemums, all the way toward the back of the room, shudder; she must be kneeling there.

'No.'

'I'm going to get a glass of water. I'll be right back.' I close the French door behind me, hoping she doesn't mind, expecting she'll be lulled by the serenity. The kitchen is just a bit away and I pull the card from my pocket as I hurry there. Reaching for the phone, I dial the number. He answers on the second ring.

'Mike Sullivan.' I can't tell if I've disturbed his dinner out or roused him from a sandwich in front of the television.

I try to make my voice firm as I speak. 'It's Clara, Clara Marsh from the Bartholomew Funeral Home.'

'Yes, I know who you are, Clara.'

Is he smiling? The phone cord twists in my fingers, weaving itself into an intricate knot. 'Trecie's here. She's at my house. Can you come get her?'

'Don't let her leave. I'll be there in ten minutes.' His voice becomes sharp, but still it reassures me.

When I hang up the phone, the cord snakes back into place. Looking to my fingers, I realize it's not the cord at all, but my hair that's knotted. I want to let go, gently uncoil the mass of kinks. I want to. But as I think of Mike driving here, imagining his hands on the wheel, what his profile would be like in the cabin of his car, I pull hard and moan. I brace myself against the counter until the panting quiets. Shoving it all into my sweater pocket – too much this time – I briefly finger the coarser strands. Later – right now I must hurry. I fill a glass from the tap, sloshing it onto the floor as I rush back toward my bedroom and the greenhouse beyond. I pause before opening the door to face her. Steadying my hand, I step into the greenhouse.

'Are you sure I can't get you something?' There's no response. 'Trecie?'

I follow the paths around the room, looking under stands and pushing back flowers as I go. 'Trecie?'

I'm at my potting table and place the glass there while I walk on. It feels as though the barometer has dropped; there's that odd sense of stillness after a storm's raged. I reach into my pocket for a reassuring touch, but the hair is no longer there. I'm at the French doors; I've come full circle. Though I call her name again, I know she won't scamper out from beneath the gladioli. For now, all I can be certain of is that she's gone.

CHAPTER ELEVEN

He's a bull, pacing with nostrils flared, neck muscles bulging. My living room is too small to contain him. I lean against the wall, hoping to fade, but his anger – or his disappointment – commands me to stay.

'I'm sorry.' My wool cardigan is my terrapin shell. I pull myself into it, drawing the collar up along my neck, just over my chin, my hands receding into the sleeves.

'I know.' Mike's feet pound back and forth along the floorboards, wrenching a moan from the same swollen plank with each pass. One hand is curled around the back of his neck; the other gestures as he speaks. He stops, looks at me, into me, and so I tuck my mouth under the wool collar.

His hands move to lie astride his hips. His voice is tight, each word carefully spoken, controlled. His complexion turns from its usual alabaster to a molten flush. 'Where was the last place you saw her?'

I don't want to share my secret garden with Mike. It's enough that Trecie saw it. I don't know what I expected, showing it to her. No, that's not true.

I expected my special place to be a wonderland for Trecie, too, that it would somehow ease her pain. I hoped that transplanted in that world, warmed by the lights and quenched by a fine mist, she would unfold, extend herself like a blossoming crocus.

But she didn't, and now there isn't a way to say no to Mike.

'Here,' I say, and feather-step my way to the bedroom.

I can feel him behind me, the heat radiating from his body. I slip deeper into my sweater as I reach for the light in my room. I walk across to the far side, keeping my eyes fixed on the French doors before me and not on the bed that blurs in my peripheral vision. I will him to do the same. The handle is suddenly in my hand and I pull it open, switching on the greenhouse lights.

'I left her in here.'

'Jesus,' Mike says. He pushes past me, a hand at the small of my back, before taking the two slate steps down into the greenhouse.

My teeth settle around my thumbnail, my gaze focusing on the corner of the floor nearest the slider. A garden spider with graceful legs rests among a scattering of fruit flies caught in its web. I wonder if the tiny flies are still alive and have simply tired of struggling, if they're simply waiting for the spider to sink its trocarlike fangs into their rigid thoraxes and suck their lives away. After a certain point, they must welcome death, a preferable alternative to the angst of waiting for the spider to decide their fate.

'What is this?' Mike says, wending his way around the greenhouse, his gaze springing from my face to the flowers and then back again. He crouches to look under the gardening table, pauses to touch a dark red geranium (*melancholy*), and then continues on, watching me. 'Are all these flowers for the funeral home?'

'No.'

'You just do this? For no reason?' He's at the back of the room, finally turned away, jiggling the knob of the door that leads outside.

'She must have gone out that way,' I say, thankful for the distraction. It's a simple door with a deadbolt and outer storm door. In the summer, I replace the Plexiglas with a screen, locking the main door when I'm away. At night, I like to lie in bed with the French doors open, listening to the peepers' hopeful calls to lovers while a warm breeze flows through my greenhouse, carrying with it the cacophonous perfume of my garden.

Mike turns the doorknob and pulls, but the lock is set. 'Was this open before?'

'I don't think so. Maybe.'

'Where are your other exits?' He strides toward me, brushing aside a dense thicket of cosmos (*longing*), and walks headlong into my bedroom. I follow, closing the greenhouse door behind us. He seems larger here in this room. His reflection passes in the mirror that hangs over my chest of drawers, and it staggers me to have two of him so near.

'There're only two exits,' I say, smoothing a wisp

that's come free of my ponytail. 'That's all the fire code requires.'

'Tell me again where you were.'

'I went to the kitchen to get a glass of water, to call you, but wouldn't I have seen her pass me?' I lead him through the living room and point to the French doors just off the kitchen. 'How could I have missed her?' There were those moments of distraction; I don't tell him. I can't.

'She must have followed and heard you talking to me, slipped out while your back was turned. Unless . . . ,' Mike says, looking around the sparsity of my living area, 'she's still here. There's no place for her to hide in this room. Have you checked all the closets, under your bed?'

I shake my head and he walks back toward the bedroom. 'Wait,' I say. 'I'll do it.'

He nods as we make our way. I head for my closet and he moves back to the greenhouse. Pulling open the closet's louvered doors, I know there isn't a little girl hidden among my black suits and white oxfords. There are the usual three pairs of black loafers, but no soiled white sneakers with faded cartoon characters. I check under the bed, but only because Mike might be watching.

'Clara!' Mike left open the greenhouse door, and I can feel the warm air wafting out, carrying with it the fragrance of my garden. I hurry to him.

He's standing at the back of the room, next to my rainbow of daisies. When he bends, only the crown of his head is visible behind the rows of flowers. I take the two steps down and stop when I reach the ruins he's crouched over.

'Did you do this?' Mike picks up a Shasta daisy and holds it to me. There are more on the floor, an enormous bunch, all snapped from their planters with only shredded stems remaining in the soil.

'Trecie,' is all I can manage. It will take months to grow more.

'What the hell?' He sifts through the carnage and lifts a length of curls tied up with a stem. 'Is this yours?'

No, though it could be. It's long like mine, just as dark, and there are the familiar white tips where hair meets scalp. But this is finer, lovely. It can't be mine. He must see the difference.

I can't explain any of this to Mike, so I shake my head. He springs to my potting table, snaps free a plastic sandwich bag, something normally used for storing seeds, now meant for evidence. Mike tucks the sample into his breast pocket and strides back to me.

'There's no place else to look. She's gone.' His face is hard, the way it was when I told him about Precious Doe's birthmark. He won't look at me. Instead, he picks up a daisy and with a jerk of his thumb decapitates it, then flings the stem away.

He reaches for his cell phone and hits a button. 'This is Sullivan. I need the dogs and the infrared light at Bartholomew's Funeral Home in Whitman. Now. Call the Whitman PD and get them here too. We've lost contact with the girl.'

I kneel beside him, scraping for the remaining flowers, trying to gather them all in my arms, grabbing as if plucking them from the floor and pressing them against me will save them, impart what little life I have into them.

How could she have escaped? Did I watch her creep past me and subconsciously turn away because to help her would have stirred too much? Am I that way? Am I Miss Talbot? (No, no. Mrs. Molina's words, her loss, she was a good mother to a good daughter. Perhaps I wanted too much to save someone, anyone, the girl I used to be. I didn't sleep well last night, I haven't in years, and now all this talk, chasing the ghost of Precious Doe and trying to help – or not? – yet another little girl in need. There are too many of us.) I bury my face in the bouquet, inhaling its tangy musk (*one-two-three, breathe*).

'Clara.' Mike is extending a daisy, one I missed. He takes me by the elbow and raises me to my feet. He's still holding my arm and his voice is soft now, a smooth hush of silk. 'It's okay. Everything's going to be okay.'

I hear a murmur, a strangled puff, and then someone crying. It swells, bursting into heaving, gasping sobs. He wraps his arm around my shoulder as he leads me into the kitchen. The sound grows as he shepherds me. She must still be here. I search in the corners, behind the ficus, but I can't see her. Mike doesn't appear to notice. He lets go when we reach the counter separating the kitchen from my table and chairs. He walks on, opening the cabinets above my sink, pulling out an enormous ceramic pitcher I found at a yard sale last summer. I tighten my grip on the flowers and listen to the sobs catch and then resume. I turn, expecting to see Trecie, and when I don't, I look to Mike for direction.

'Mike?'

He doesn't hear, his back to me as he fills the jug at the sink, the sound of rushing water smothering her cries and my lone one. He appears so strong, his shoulders so sturdy. I imagine the weight they bear, his life the way it is, and wonder why they don't bend and warp. I wonder if he ever carried his wife there and if he has room for one more.

He turns and places the pitcher on the counter and then extends his arms to me.

'She's still here, Mike, I know it. Can't you hear her?'

He meets my eyes with his free of pity. 'Here, let me take those.'

Gently, with a tenderness I haven't seen from him in a long while, he takes the flowers from my embrace and places them in the water, careful that each stem is in the pot and not marooned, thirsting while the others drink their fill.

Even now I hear the crying. 'We have to find her.'

He stops. He places both of his palms on my shoulders, his fingers pressing into me. 'Clara, it's okay.'

Suddenly I feel myself gasping for a whole breath. I raise my hands to my face and feel how sodden it is, catch the mucus flowing from my nose and my swollen eyes. I hear the sound from my lips, a great heaving of air. Smell the metallic odor of my sorrow. It's me, my tears all along.

Mike removes his hands from my shoulders, leaving those spots mournfully cold. He reaches into his pants pocket and removes a handkerchief. His eyes never leave mine and I force myself to meet his gaze. Finally, there is quiet. Gently, gently, dabbing at each eye, he traces the path of my tears down one cheek and down farther, pressing the cloth against my throat with such delicacy, stroking, a whisper of touch. Then he arcs up to the other side and begins again. My eyelids flutter against the cotton, a warm salve against my grief. It smells of peppermint and detergent, and I can't help but lean my cheek into his covered fingers.

'I'm sorry I let her go. I let you both down.'

'Shhh.' His other hand moves from my shoulder and finds a place to rest along my side. His thumb presses there, against my hipbone, his fingers curving around my back. My body bends toward him, seeking his warmth the way a flower seeks its sun.

His fingertips, unsheathed from the handkerchief, glance along my hairline, brush down, and then curve into my lips. I can smell him now. He is ginger and rain, salt and blood, he is pungent with humidity and life. He strokes the fullness of my bottom lip and I feel it slip open, his finger inside, touching the wetness there.

His thighs, hard and stringy, press against mine. His breath is ragged, warm as he exhales against my cheek. The thread I've felt before, waxing and waning between us, is being reeled at either end, twanging as it's drawn. Closer. With stunning clarity, I see the burn spots on his neck where his razor cut and his blood hardened; the ropy thickness of veins pushing against his throat; his pulse throbbing along his carotid artery. The urge to lay my lips there overwhelms me. I need to feel his life flow through him, against me.

Headlights pour in through my kitchen window, blazing a path along my living room wall, snapping the thread. The catch and roll of the Buick's engine are as familiar to me as Linus's own voice. In the distance, not too far, is the less familiar wail of sirens.

Mike releases me, pressing the handkerchief into my own palm as he clears his throat and steps back, his attention now focused out the window. 'I've got to take a look outside and then talk to Linus. Maybe he saw Trecie hanging around here earlier.'

I nod and lead the way to the patio doors, my step tentative, my head mottled. We walk into the bank of cold air, and the wind stings the damp spots Mike missed along my face.

CHAPTER TWELVE

'Is that so?' Linus says, his eyes turned down toward his cup. He blows into his tea and a steam cloud billows forth.

Linus remains quiet, save the occasional 'uh-huh,' while Mike recaps the investigation. I trace the familiar grain of Alma's kitchen table as my other hand fingers the handkerchief tucked in my jacket pocket. At the center of us all is Mike's police radio issuing a constant whir, interrupted only by sporadic updates as police canvass a two-mile radius of the funeral home.

The air is warmed by the scent of orange pekoe and pine swags. Alma fusses above us, refilling the teapot, laying a banquet with minicakes, glazed brownies, sliced pepperoni, malt crackers, and chèvre garlic cheese. She's still wearing the festive red dress from her trip into Boston. A jingle-bell brooch with metal holly leaves, pinned above her left breast, tinkles with each step. She hums as she hovers about our heads. I stop listening to Mike and try to place the melody. After a moment I recognize it: 'Joy to the World.'

'Our investigation didn't turn up any type of video equipment at Charlie Kelly's house where we found the tape,' says Mike. 'He was just a customer is my guess, but he probably knew the guy who filmed it. We can't positively identify the adult male on the tapes, because he knew enough to keep his head out of the shot. It was the same setting, same guy, same girls in all the tapes.'

'And the children,' asks Linus, methodically balancing a slice of sausage on a square of cheese and cracker, 'how many children?'

Mike's plate is pushed off to the side with only a polite mouthful missing from the cake Alma plopped before him. His hand cups his tea, the same hand that minutes ago encircled my waist. His gaze remains on Linus; he hasn't looked my way since before we came here.

'Two from that room,' Mike says. 'We know one, Trecie, but the other hasn't been identified. She's about the same age, same coloring. That girl was in only a few films.'

'Clara,' interrupts Alma, 'would you like to join me in the parlor? I bought a CD from the *Black Nativity* show today and we could listen to it if you'd like.'

Alma smiles at me as her hand grips the back of Linus's chair. Her dark knuckles turn a warm pink from the strain and her gorgeous teeth are clamped one neat row atop the other.

I start to speak; there's so little I can contribute to this conversation, but I understand my duty is to remain here. Through the window, flashlights direct their beams around my cottage, and I can't help but try to decipher the static coming through Mike's radio. I turn back to Alma, but before I can answer, Mike does for me.

'I'm afraid I'm going to need Clara to stay.'

Alma folds her arms and lays them across her chest, her eyes boring into Mike's. 'I don't see why she can't take a break from this unpleasantness and listen to some holiday music.'

It isn't often Alma reveals her emotions and never has she betrayed her dignity. In the twelve years I've known her, twice she's been stricken with the flu. Both times, though feverish and obviously pained, she denied the illness any hold. Still her dinners were cooked, laundry was washed, floors were swept clean.

'I'm sorry, Mrs. Bartholomew, but I need Clara here while I speak to Linus. It might jog something free.'

Alma's lips purse thin. '*I* believe Clara has heard enough for one night. I don't think she has anything more to contribute to your investigation, *Detective* Sullivan.'

She leans across the table and snaps up his cake plate. Her chin aloft, her back scolding, she turns and drops it into the sink, where it clatters against the soapstone. Mike looks to Linus, raising his brow as if to implore his assistance. Linus nods and then pushes himself up from the table, placing an arm around her waist.

'He's only trying to help the child.'

'He's not trying to help *my* child,' Alma says, her back erect. It's a moment before I realize she's talking about me.

Linus leans in closer to Alma; his lips graze her ear as he whispers, though it's loud enough for us all to hear. It's as intimate an encounter I've seen between them. We should excuse ourselves, but I feel inexplicably drawn into their world. 'Now, Alma, the man's got a job to do and Clara has got to help. Nothing's going to hurt her. She will be protected.'

Alma wrenches Linus's hand away from her. 'Is that so? Well, I for one remember what Mother Greene had to say, and mark my words, Linus, if anything happens to her, I'm holding you' – then she turns to point at Mike – 'and you responsible.'

She stares straight ahead as she strides from the room, her jingle-bell brooch gaily tinkling as she goes. I can still hear it as her feet pound the stairs to the residence's second floor, growing fainter as she reaches the landing. There's a pause and then the sound of a door slamming.

Linus braces himself against the counter, shaking his head as his gaze settles along the floor. Mike slides back in his chair, intent on the spoon he rolls between his fingers. I wait for someone to speak. Linus finally turns to us, a tired smile pushing his great cheeks upward. 'You're not scared, are you now, Clara?'

After all of these years, it's reflexive. 'I'm fine.'

' 'Cause you know I'm going to take care of you, don't you? You know I won't let no one hurt you.' His eyes are steady, his smile a mask. I've never realized before tonight how well I've come to know these people, Linus and Alma. And how I can now look past his expression and see his fear, see how he's trying to shield me from it.

I want to believe him. 'I know.'

His face relaxes. 'Well then, excuse me while I go and talk to my bride.'

He leaves the room and takes with him any sense of comfort. At first I think his footfalls on the staircase lead down to the funeral parlor, but I must be mistaken. Humming seems to be coming from there, *Grace, my fears relieved* ... But no. As he said, he's on his way upstairs to soothe Alma's nerves. I settle on the rows of cakes before me, trying to distinguish trapezoids and rhombuses among the sprinkles that clutter the frosting. Mike continues twirling the spoon.

Moments pass one into the next, neither of us speaking. I've moved on to the more plentiful triangles on the platter when Mike clears his throat.

'You know I won't let anyone hurt you either,' he says.

My eyes flick to his face, but he continues to fix on the spoon. 'I'll be fine.'

'I'll take care of you,' he says.

My vision blurs then, and, without my realizing, the hand that's been tucked in my pocket, fingering the handkerchief, slowly rises from beneath the table and begins moving toward Mike's. I can't feel my hand, there exists only numbness beyond my wrist, but still it moves closer. I want to pull back, imagining the sting when it touches his, but it continues on. He remains focused on the spoon. My hand closes in. I want only the warmth of his skin, the texture of his calluses, the brush of his hairs. Almost there, almost there.

I startle when the trill of his cell phone blasts the quiet. He fumbles the spoon and it clatters to the table. I reach instead for the sugar bowl. He sits up, grasping in his back pocket for the phone.

'Sullivan.'

I stare at the spot where his hand was, only half listening to the one-sided conversation.

'Are you sure?'

Mike pulls a pad of paper and a pen from his breast pocket, begins scribbling. He stops and shifts his body toward me. My eyes move upward along his torso, linger over his neck, and finally meet his. He's staring at me full-on.

'Reverend Greene, will you agree to a trace on your phone?' There's a pause and then, 'Reverend Greene, a girl's life is at stake. I'll get a court order if I have to.'

The muscles of his face bulge as his teeth clench; his breath is audible now. Mike flips off his phone, folding it into his palm. He stares at me before speaking.

'Reverend Greene had another tip from the anonymous caller about the Precious Doe case.'

I reach for my cup of tea, hoping there's enough left to warm my hands. 'Mike, I told you everything I know. There's nothing more.'

'Clara, Alma might be right. We're dealing with some real sick people who're probably making a lot of money off these videos. That's enough of a motive to do just about anything to end this investigation.'

I think of Trecie tracing the spines of my books, wandering the paths of my secret garden. I can see her face on that video and know I cannot be another person who lets her down.

'I'm not afraid.'

Mike places his phone on the table and takes both of my hands in his. They're as cold as my own yet somehow warm me. 'Remember I said there was another girl in one of the videos? The caller told Reverend Greene the other girl was Precious Doe.'

I feel the blood seep away from my face just as Mike's radio crackles to life and he reaches for it. 'Sullivan.'

'Yeah, Mikey,' says a man's voice. It sounds like Ryan. 'Trail's gone cold, we got nothing.'

'What about the dogs?'

Ryan's words are clipped. 'Never picked up a trail, nothing to go on. You want us to do an Amber Alert?'

Mike rests his head against the radio and waits a moment, and another, until he finally raises his chin. 'No, I want everyone back to the point of origin in five.'

'Affirmative,' says Ryan.

Mike replaces the radio on the table. Now I understand how he felt back in my greenhouse when I let her go. I don't know if it's shame or fear that fuels my words, but they're spewed from my mouth. 'Why not call an Amber Alert? One girl is already dead. We have to save Trecie.'

He's burning with the same fire that's engulfed me. He stands, knocking his chair onto the floor, causing Alma's decorative copper plates to rattle against the wall. They hum as they find their way back to silence. 'You think I don't know that? What do you think I'm doing here? If I alert television and radio, what's going to happen to Trecie?' He snaps his fingers, his face enflamed with rage. 'That pervert will make her disappear just like he did to Precious Doe.'

He clips his radio to his belt and then drags both hands down the length of his face. 'I can't lose another child. I can't.'

I go to him then. I take the few steps, stumbling as I cross the chasm. Finally, standing before him, I raise my arms, feeling the sinew and muscle grow within my limbs: connecting, thickening, aching. I ring his waist, finding the courage to look at his face, but he's looking past me.

I rest my cheek against his chest, satisfied with the whoosh of his heartbeat. And when his body begins to shake, I say, 'It's okay, Mike. Everything will be okay.'

CHAPTER THIRTEEN

The Brockton Police Department foyer is a narrow passageway with dingy floors and overlapping notices taped to cinder-block walls. There's a large collage of men's faces staring out, their two-dimensional eyes leaping beyond the black-and-white photos: !WARNING! They're just a few of the city's level-three sex offenders, some of the most violent among criminals. The papers rustle as I pass. Though I try to keep from meeting their eyes, I glance up, half expecting one to wink.

I walk past an older woman and a teenager I assume to be her daughter, both seated, wearing tired expressions and snug parkas with fur-trimmed hoods. I approach the police officer sitting at the desk, a tempered-glass window and locked door between us.

'Can I help you?' His words are mumbled and his face is expressionless, though his neck wattle quivers as he talks. He's older, heavyset, with thinning black hair gelled into place. He has the ashen pallor of some of my clients.

'I'm here to see Detective Sullivan.' I glance behind me to see both women staring back.

The cop picks up a phone and suddenly his face comes to life. 'Yeah, Mikey, she's here.' When he speaks, his chin disappears into the pool of flesh beneath it.

The utilitarian clock above his head, grimy from years of wear, reads eight thirty. In the next instant Mike opens the door, ushering me through to the other side.

'Thanks for coming.' His voice is even and his eyes cling to the sign-in sheet he's filling out. His face is clean shaven and set. It bears no sign of last night after he left the funeral home just past midnight, appearing battered and worn. Before that he had come back to my cottage once more to check for any sign of Trecie, any clue, but found none. I walked him to his car from there. Our fingers may even have brushed before he turned to lift the door handle. But now, though he's only inches away, I can feel the gulf between us. I wonder if I imagined holding him, imagined his hand at my waist. It's probably best if I believe that.

'Sorry to make you come in so early.' Mike pulls open a door leading to a stairwell, taking us up one flight. He walks first, so I can't see his expression, but I can hear it. 'You probably didn't sleep much, huh?'

I pause just a moment, less, my hand clinging to the railing. 'I'm fine.'

He reaches the landing and again holds the door, allowing me to pass. This time he looks at me, but his eyes are sheathed now by that familiar reptilian shield. 'You didn't have trouble sleeping?'

'No.' I wait for him to direct me, but still he stands in the doorway, watching me. 'I went straight to bed after you left,' I say.

He lets the door slam behind us and walks ahead. I follow, plucking at a loose button on my coat, noticing his stiff back, and I can see the bulge along his right hip whenever his suit coat brushes against his gun. I know what he wants me to say, but it's too much to part with. Yes, I had to bring the daisies Trecie pulled free to Precious Doe; I can't have dead things in my house – not there, no. I didn't see him at first, overcome by what I found propped against Doe's marker: a Mass card Linus had printed for Precious Doe's service, the prayer of Saint Anthony, the saint of lost things, on one side, and on the other, an image of a child's hands pressed together in prayer. The card's edges were frayed, the upper right corner bent as if it had been kept someplace where it was thumbed regularly. Last night, it was Mike's turn to hide among the shadows. It's better to pretend I didn't hear him call out as I hurried away. Grief is not meant to be shared.

I've never been to Mike's office, though I've had reason to be at the station from time to time. Occasionally a Brockton cop will ticket the hearse when I'm picking up a body. Narrow side streets and winter parking bans cannot justify a body languishing in a loved one's home. The police chief assured Linus years ago that he could simply ignore the tickets; 'Just bring them in,' he said. Neither Linus nor I has ever abused that courtesy.

Mike opens another door and we turn a corner into a large room with several rows of desks facing three enclosed offices. Nearly all of the desks are filled. Men with suit jackets draped over the backs of their chairs focus their attention on the computer screens before them or into a phone. I recognize a few from pickups of unattended deaths. There's only one woman whom I've never met. She's petite with natural blond hair and a stylish beige pantsuit. She appears to be in her early thirties but could easily pass for younger. As we walk past, she smiles as she speaks on the phone, a large framed photograph of two young girls with the same blond waves and toothy smile before her. I suppose this woman was both homecoming queen and class president in high school.

This room has the same air of dinginess as the foyer, only more so. The ceiling is yellowed drop panels, soiled from years of cigarette smoke and water damage. There are several missing altogether, exposing free wires and once-white pipes encased within brown film. It's easy to imagine the colony of mice that must make the walls and rafters their home. Bulletin boards encircle the room, all overflowing with notices and mug shots. I scan the one nearest me, an Interpol warning of a gun disguised as a cell phone.

Mike walks over to one of the desks and lifts the phone's handset. He presses a button and says something unintelligible to the person on the other end. He nearly looks at me, one hand worrying along his waistband,

and then turns his back. I assume this is his desk, though there are no obvious mementos laying claim to it. I position myself to see if I missed photos of his wife but discover only crumpled napkins and a chipped blue coffee mug, half filled, with a swirl of cream thickening in the center. Then I spot it behind a dead ivy. It's in a wooden frame, a color photo of the two of them taken at a beach, their faces tanned and pressed close together. They look like a couple.

Since he hasn't offered me a seat, I continue scanning the room. Behind me is an interrogation suite. Through one door is a narrow room with a window and adjacent to it is a larger room with a mirror and a long table. On one side of the table, the side opposite the two-way mirror, is a single straight-backed chair, and across from it are two more. I'm surprised to see the room looks just the way they do in movies. I suppose I expected more subtlety.

'Can I get you a cup of coffee before we start?' Mike asks, flipping through a stack of papers on his desk while gesturing to a near-empty pot.

'No, thank you.'

'Here they come.' Mike lifts his head and looks past me, straightening.

Two men walk into the room, both wearing suits. They have the familiar grittiness and confident gait of cops. When they approach, Mike greets each with a handshake, and together they form a circle with their backs to me, leaving me to stand mere inches and yet miles away. After several minutes of familiar chitchat, Mike turns.

'Clara, this is Will Peña – he's with the Plymouth County district attorney's office – and this is Detective Frank Ball with the Whitman police. They're assigned to Trecie's case.'

I nod. I learned long ago people weren't eager to shake my hand. It's no different today; the two men remain motionless. Will Peña is shorter than Mike, thick and hard with a clipped, no-nonsense haircut. Frank Ball is tall and wiry, the kind of thin that displays a bobbing Adam's apple. Both have the same cagey eyes.

I expect to sit in one of the interrogation rooms, but instead Mike pulls chairs from adjacent empty desks and sets them around his own. He removes the lid from a cardboard box; I assume it's the same one he brought to my cottage that day. He takes out the still from the video and the copy of the head shot. There's another box beside this one, the words *Precious Doe* scribbled in black marker on the sides and top. I wonder if it's Mike's handwriting.

'Clara,' says Peña from the DA's office, 'Mike has relayed all of your conversations, but why don't you tell us everything you know in your own words.'

'Where should I start?'

'From the first day you met the girl,' says the Whitman detective, Ball. As I start to speak, the woman detective hangs up the phone and crosses the room to us. She sits on Mike's desk, her legs dangling over the side.

It seems a familiar pose to her, a comfortable slouch. I wonder if this is something she does whenever she and Mike work a case or simply talk over a cup of coffee. I notice she's wearing elegant suede heels, and it strikes me she doesn't leave this room often. They're not the type of shoes I'd expect a police officer to wear while giving chase. She has an ease about her, a sense of effortless authority among these men. I glance at Mike, but he seems not to have noticed the woman lounging on his desk.

At different points I'm interrupted by one of the men asking me to elaborate on a particular point, though each time I'm unable to. While I try to recall the exact version I told Mike, I'm careful not to focus too much on the way their hands race to copy my words across their yellow legal pads. I notice that neither Mike nor the woman is taking notes. I can't decide which is more unnerving. When I finish, the men turn to the woman, who finally speaks.

'Clara, I'm Lieutenant Kate McCarthy. I'm head of the sex crimes unit here.' She leans toward me and I find myself pushing back against my chair. 'Did Trecie ever mention school, where she goes, what grade she's in?'

'As I said, she told me she didn't go to school. She appears to be about eight, but I can't be sure. I don't know a lot of children – '

Detective Peña interrupts: 'Should we still take Clara around the area schools to look for the kid at recess?'

Kate shakes her head and turns her attention back to

me. Smiling, she says, 'Can you describe what she looks like?'

'She's in the video. Mike showed me one of them.'

Kate looks from Mike to me. 'I know' – that smile again – 'but in your own words.'

I don't understand where Kate is going, but I'm overcome by that familiar sense of otherness: them and me. 'She has long dark hair, wavy. She's quite thin, small for her age. She acts older than she looks. Her eyes are brown, I think. It's hard to say. I don't know. Her skin's a bit sallow.'

'Sounds a lot like you,' says Kate, peering into me, and it's as if all sound is sucked free of this room. And then, 'That hair sample Mike found at your house, it looked like it was yanked out. Ever notice any bald spots on Trecie's head?'

They know enough about her life, they have the videos. I can't betray her, reveal any more of her shame. Her secret's safe with me. 'No.'

'What about her eyelashes?'

Before I can answer, Detective Peña interrupts. 'What are you getting at?'

Kate continues to watch me as she answers. 'The psych said there's some kind of anxiety disorder where girls who've been abused pull out their hair or eyelashes.'

'Trichotillomania.' I hadn't meant to speak.

Kate's next words come slowly. I dare not look toward Mike. 'Yeah, that's right. Twirling their hair hypnotizes them or something, and then they just yank. They don't even know they're doing it. Some eventually go bald, others try to hide it under a hat.' She cocks her head, looks me over. 'Or a ponytail. How is it you heard of it, Clara?'

'I've seen it from time to time. I see a lot in my line of work.' I sense them all regarding me.

Kate finally breaks the silence. 'When she came around, was it always the same time of day?'

'Once in the afternoon and twice at nightfall,' I say, mindful that I must hold fast to the seat of my chair.

'When she was there, do you recall hearing any car doors slam, seeing any strange cars in the parking lot? A bike maybe?'

'No.' I look to Mike, but he's weaving a pen between his fingers, his focus steady on his mug of congealed coffee. 'Last night, the only cars in the lot were the hearses. Linus and Alma were out with the Buick. I didn't notice a bike, but we didn't go around to the front at all.'

'Hey, Frank,' Kate says, turning to the Whitman detective, 'how many apartment buildings are within walking distance of the funeral home?'

'Depends on what you mean by walking distance,' says Frank. 'Maybe six within a mile up and down Washington Street, more like eight if she cuts through the cemetery. But what little kid is gonna walk alone through a cemetery, especially at night?'

Kate raises an eyebrow and uncrosses her legs. 'The kind of kid who hangs out in a funeral home.'

'I think we should do stakeouts where Precious Doe's body was found and at her grave,' says Mike, his eyes boring into mine. I will my face not to burn. 'See if anyone is acting suspicious around there.'

Mike remains silent while they discuss the danger to Trecie if they were to canvass local apartment buildings and convenience stores with her picture. I only half listen as Kate makes the case against it, citing the same reasons Mike gave last night. Instead, I turn away so Mike is no longer in my line of vision. When I do, I spot Ryan across the way dropping a file onto one of the empty desks.

He sees me staring and waves. Before I can pretend not to have noticed, he's walking toward us, smiling broadly.

'Hey, what's going on?' Ryan's voice is too loud for this room, for this conversation.

Mike only nods, but Kate turns to greet him. 'Hey, Ryan.'

He walks over to the coffee machine, just feet a way from us, and grabs a foam cup. 'Did you haul Clara in here because of all her parking tickets?' He shakes powdered cream into his cup, his savaged cuticles a raw contrast to the neat blue canister. Then his tone becomes serious, almost kind. 'Is this about that little girl?'

'Looks like that case Mike called you to last night is related to Precious Doe,' says Kate, getting to her feet.

Ryan rips open four packets of sugar at once, making low *tsking* sounds as he taps them into his cup. He takes a used plastic spoon from the coffee cart to stir, the sockets of his jaw bulging. 'No shit. How'd you figure that out?'

'Our anonymous caller,' Mike says, breaking his silence. 'Reverend Greene called me last night while I was at Linus's place.'

'Can we put a tap on his phone?' asks Peña. 'I'm sure the DA himself would put it before a judge.'

Mike shakes his head. 'I asked Reverend Greene and he said no. I don't want to wait a year for a court order, so I already put in a request to subpoena all of his incoming and outgoing calls since Precious Doe's death. We should have that in a couple of weeks. Maybe sooner.'

Peña cocks his head. 'How do we know our Reverend Greene didn't make up this anonymous caller? Could be he's trying to cover up the crime himself. Has anyone done a background check?'

'Sure, Reverend Greene's a stand-up guy,' says Ball, holding on to his lapels as he shakes his head. 'He's worked with my guys at the Whitman PD for years on community outreach, especially at-risk kids, so we're required to do a CORI background check every year. Hell, I been in this business long enough to never be shocked, but if he has anything nefarious to do with this case, I'd be surprised.'

'But the details our anonymous caller is providing are details only the killer would know,' says Mike. 'So why won't Reverend Greene let us put a bug on his phone?'

'It's always the ones you least expect,' says Ryan, nodding his head knowingly. He's rolling back and forth on his heels, his left hand snapping and then unsnapping the belt that loops through his holstered gun. I'd forgotten he was standing there. He seems somehow out of place, a uniform among the suits.

'Trecie had a sister, right?' Kate's looking to me, and I'm reminded that I'm a part of this conversation too.

'Yes.'

'She said her name was Adalia? Did she say if she was younger, older?'

'Younger, I think,' I say.

Kate turns back to the men. 'All right, I'll call the state, child protection, see if they have any cases in the area with two sisters, names Trecie and Adalia.

'Peña, can you check the state police crime-lab files? Tell them we'll be dropping off that hair sample just in case. See what physical similarities, if any, there are between Precious Doe and Trecie. If our perp has a certain type he goes after, see if there are any matches with our local level-three offenders. Now might be a good time to touch base again with the FBI agent assigned to Doe's case. He might be able to hook us up with a profiler.

'Frank, you know Reverend Greene, but my gut tells me he's hiding something. It's time to take a closer look at him. You know how to do that without letting on.'

Kate pauses to take a breath. She squares her shoulders

and looks at Mike. 'And Mike, you stick to Clara like glue – she's our only contact with Trecie. Sleep at the funeral home if you have to, or her house. I don't care. We can't let what happened to Doe happen to Trecie.'

I can feel my cheeks burn even as ice flows through me. Mike's face flushes as well and still there's more: an overwhelming air of dread about him.

'Look, people,' Kate says, placing her hands on her hips, her jacket pulled back. Though I shouldn't be surprised, I start when I see a gun there. 'I don't care what laws we have to bend, break, or flip upside down, I want to find this little girl and the man responsible for these tapes.' She places a hand on the box as she speaks. 'Whatever it takes.'

As everyone starts to stand, I will strength into my legs. I wobble, clutching the back of my chair for encouragement, but no one appears to notice. Steady now, I reach in my pocket for my keys, eager to leave this room, but Ryan pulls us back.

'Lieutenant? I want in.'

Kate pauses and then smiles at Ryan the way I imagine she would to indulge her young children. 'Why don't you distribute Trecie's photo to all the patrols in Brockton and Whitman?'

'No,' says Ryan. He crumples his cup, sloshing coffee down his thigh as he does, then whips it into the nearest trash can. 'Some rat bastard is hurting little girls and I want to help catch the son of a bitch.' He turns to Mike, his tone changing as he speaks; it's high and pleading. I can't help but look away. 'Come on, Mikey, I been gone a long time. I want to get back in the swing of things. Let me in.'

Mike runs a hand through his hair. He looks as worn as he did last night, after he left me. Worse. 'Yeah, sure. Another set of eyes and ears won't hurt. You can help stake out the funeral home.'

Ryan nods, settling back into himself. The nearness of these people begins to press against me. I find myself fading into the wall, hiding there. I could melt into the paint and filth and nicotine that have accumulated over the years. Together we could be a mishmash of gray, of nothingness. At night, when shadows fill this room, I could watch the mice scurry at will, scrambling for crumbs and other bits of waste along the floor. I would be privy to the secrets that pass across these desks, among these people. I could observe Mike, his every sigh, each blink, the way he gestures while talking on the phone. And when he passed my spot, here inside the wall, I could reach out an invisible hand, allow my fingertips to brush his sleeve, and he wouldn't notice, safe, knowing he would never again have to suffer the indignity of my touch.

Instead, Ryan sees me, looks at me, and rests a tattered, gnawed hand on my shoulder. 'Looks like you and me are going to be spending a lot of time together.'

I don't respond. My words would only extend an

already awkward moment. I want only for Ryan's hand to be gone from my body. And for Mike to realize not all lies are born of deceit.

CHAPTER FOURTEEN

It's been two weeks since I sat at Mike's desk. Four days since he decided Trecie wasn't coming back and that his time at the funeral home was done. The first five, he wandered around the mourning rooms, avoiding eye contact and conversation. He never ventured downstairs where I laid out the dead. The next four days and well into each night, he stayed in his car. Every hour or so, I'd hear him turn the ignition. I'd listen while the engine ran, precisely fifteen minutes each time, and then the silence would return. I expect the cold was getting to him.

I couldn't help but imagine Trecie hiding outside too, waiting for Mike and Ryan to leave so she could return. Wherever I was in the house, I'd check the windows to search for her. I may even have left a child's coat and mittens behind the holly bush that obscures one of the basement windows. A Christmas present two weeks early. Pliable fabric to hug her body. No doubt it was my imagination, but on Mike's fourth day here, I saw her watching me from that window. I caught only a glimpse, a movement, a flash of hair swinging just out of sight. I wasn't certain, so said nothing. The coat and mittens are still there.

On his last day, day ten, Mike wandered around the property, then walked back and forth along Washington Street. I wondered what he thought about during those long hours, his wife in the cemetery across the street. I tried not to consider what he thought of me, one floor below.

I was walking up the stairs from my workroom when I saw him. He must have been waiting for me, sitting in one of the leather wingbacks in the reception area, avoiding Mrs. Shannon's body in the adjacent mourning room, the Adonis (*sad memories*) tucked against the dead woman's thigh. I could hear Mike's fingers drumming against the armrest, the whisper of his radio turned down low concealed beneath his suit coat. He stood when I reached the top step.

'Clara.' Though his face was smooth, save for the constant furrow of his forehead, and his suit crisp, he himself appeared threadbare, as if he had been rubbed raw against something coarse and unforgiving.

'We're closing down the stakeout for now. I appreciate your cooperation, but we have to direct our resources to other investigations. If Trecie comes back, you should call Kate, let her know.' His words were slowed, his gaze steady on a spot above my head. I looked away when he placed a business card on the table next to Mrs. Shannon's guest book. 'Here's her number.'

I didn't move, I didn't speak. We stood like that for what seemed several minutes, but I was more patient, more used to awkward silences.

Eventually, his gaze steady on the floor, he said, 'I'll see you around.' Then he was gone.

A part of me was relieved. With him gone, Trecie might return. I wouldn't call Mike if she did. I would give Linus Kate's business card and he would call.

Ryan had been here too, but he was sent back to patrol after a week. He spent each day of his stakeout pacing the mourning rooms, unwrapping peppermints from the candy dishes, then crinkling the cellophane between his fingers. I refilled the dishes each night after he left.

His last day here, Ryan walked in as I was finishing with Mrs. Shannon. Her elderly mother dropped off a simple black dress from her daughter's closet and a strand of paste pearls. After preparing Mrs. Shannon's hair, framing her face with soft curls to distract the eye from her eternal frown, I began layering the foundation across the flabby part of her nose, where an explosion of blood vessels laid waste to what might once have been flirty and coy. With my back to the door, it wasn't until I heard the clack of the peppermint against his teeth that I turned.

'Sorry, I didn't mean to scare you.' He raised his hands as if to surrender.

He closed the door and took his time crossing the room, stopping when he reached the floor drain at the end of my worktable, at Mrs. Shannon's feet. Other than

Linus and my classmates at mortuary school, no one has ever seen me prepare a body.

'How'd she die?' he asked, nodding to the table while his right foot toed in and out between the bars of the floor drain.

'Cirrhosis.' My forefinger glanced the edge of the curling iron, singeing the cuticle. I tried not to wince.

'She's young, huh?'

'Forty-two.'

'She have kids?'

'No, just her parents and brothers. Divorced.'

Ryan went silent, fixing on the woman's face, though his foot never stopped digging into the drain. Without warning, he let loose a queer belch of air. I put the iron on my worktable and reached for the comb.

'She kind of reminds me of my mother, you know?'

'Oh, I'm sorry.' I turned in his direction, but his focus remained on Mrs. Shannon. He waved me off.

I lifted a curl near the front of the scalp and teased some body into it.

'My little sister looked just like her, you know, a real live Mini-Me. My mom said I took after my dad, but no one really knew him, so I don't know. She said I was just like 'im.'

Once I smoothed the hairs back into place, I partitioned off a section toward the back, curling it while Ryan spoke, his voice losing its volume, its vigor, though his foot still spasmed within the grate. Another length of hair around the iron as his foot went in and out. Straight, glossy hair. I counted four screws fastening the drain to the floor; chemicals used to sterilize the bodies wash over the surface of that grate. He wiggled the tip of his shoe under a bar and lifted, creasing the leather. The screws held. Steam rose from the curl as I released it.

'God, she really looks like my mom.' His voice became a whisper and his foot finally stopped. I followed his gaze to Mrs. Shannon's face, her left eyelid shiny from a trickle of glue that seeped from the area of the tear duct, clumping the lashes gathered at the corner. A cotton swab and nail-polish remover were all it needed. Later.

'Must have been some life if she was hitting the bottle that hard.' He rolled the peppermint against those yellowed teeth. 'I guess we all have our ways of dealing, huh?'

I reached for the can of hairspray, super hold – Mrs. Shannon's wake was a few days away – and depressed the knob with a hiss. The scent of artificial grapes nearly masked the odor of embalming fluid. Ryan pulled his foot free and loped toward Linus's painting.

'So, no sign of this girl Trecie, huh?'

'No.'

'You sure it was the same girl from that video?'

I nodded and looked at the basement window where the child's coat remained, the nylon probably stiff from the cold.

Ryan shifted his weight between his feet, crunching the peppermint as he moved. ''Cause Mikey and me was talking and, I got to tell you, they're starting to wonder.'

'Wonder?'

'I probably shouldn't say nothing, but Kate thinks maybe you're confused or, you know, spending too much time down here with no one to talk to' – he swept his arm out, gesturing to the shelves – 'all these chemicals and stuff.'

He wouldn't stop. 'Mikey's got a lot riding on this, you know. The chief's been pushing him for disability. He can't screw up again. And Mike listens to Kate.'

'Excuse me,' I said. 'I need to finish with Mrs. Shannon.'

He shook his head and then made for the doorway before turning. 'Look, I believe you, I really do. We get a lot of women who spend too much time peeking out from behind their curtains, looking for a little attention. They start calling us with hot tips, happens all the time. I know you're not like that.'

'I'm not lying.' I started backing toward the door then, my hand feeling behind me for the handle.

'No, course not. It's Kate, she thinks you might be sweet on Mike or something. 'Lonely,' I think she said. What does she know? Like I say, I believe you.'

'Please.' I needed him to leave, but I didn't want to touch him, I didn't think I could. Instead, I hid myself behind the door, pressing against it with my body, against him. He wouldn't move. My fingers ached to release the humiliation, to seek those places that were raw and pure. To create a new one. I rounded the edge of the door and repeated, 'Please. Excuse me.'

Though I tried to focus on the floor, I could feel the weight of his eyes on me. Before turning to leave, he said, 'I'm not the one who thinks you're crazy.'

In the days that followed, the few times I caught Mike's eye, I heard his words, an endless loop in my head. But I can't dwell on such things. There's much to be done: Brockton PD just called for a pickup. This is what requires my attention now. The cop on the scene, Andrew Browne, said the body had been in the Vanity Faire apartment at least four days. There's some relief knowing he'll be the officer on site.

I park the hearse just outside the entrance and regard the metal staircase through the glass doors. Like many low-income apartment buildings in the city, there's no elevator. It's only three flights. As I reach the landing I snap open the stretcher, and a mouse, brown and fat, races across the vinyl tiles. It dives into a hole in the crumbling plaster, a wall connecting the stairwell to a third-floor apartment. I've already paged one of the removers to help me. He should be here soon.

When I open the door to the hallway, keeping it propped with my foot to slide the gurney through, the stench assaults me. Decomposition has become a familiar odor, but for the residents up and down this hall, as well as those directly above and below, the past two days must have been unbearable. Someone finally called this morning. I can feel their eyes, pressed against their peepholes, watching my arrival. A couple of them are bold enough to stand in their open doorways, arms crossed. One woman has a small boy wrapped around her leg, her belly filled with another. She calls to me as I approach, a finger and thumb pinching closed her nose.

'That smell is nasty. I always knew she was trouble.'

I nod, watching the child clad in an expensive-looking sweat suit suck on a lollipop, his enormous eyes staring up at me.

'We never had cockroaches till she moved in. How long you gonna take, getting her out of here?' Her eyes narrow as she speaks. Still holding her nose, she raises her other hand to purse her mouth around a cigarette.

I glance at the police officer standing at the opposite end of the hall and shrug. Listening to the wheels of the gurney churn as I make my way toward him, I'm careful to avoid a mound of knotted plastic grocery bags resting against the peeling door frame of one apartment. The upbeat theme song to a popular game show blares from within as I take shallow breaths. The odor of cat urine emanating from that apartment challenges the stench of death.

The pregnant woman exhales smoke as she persists. 'You've got to open some windows in there or something, 'cause that's a big case of nasty.'

I finally pass her, finally reach the police officer and notice his breathing is labored. I realize it's because he's both inhaling and exhaling through his mouth.

'Hey, Clara,' says Andrew, his arms crossed, his complexion pale. 'Looks like she OD'd.'

I don't open the door. As horrific as the smell is, it will be worse once this hollow barrier is removed.

I reach into my satchel and pull out the jar of Vicks VapoRub, extending it to Andrew first. 'Did you talk to her doctor?'

'Nah,' says Andrew, smearing a glob of gel under his nostrils. I notice he's still breathing through his mouth. 'People like her don't have doctors. M.E. didn't even come out. You'll see when you get in there.'

I nod, reaching for a pair of gloves and a mask. As I turn the knob to enter, Andrew stops me.

'Sorry, but I can't help with this one. It's too disgusting.'

Inside the efficiency apartment, it's the expected scene: scraps of paper and unopened bills littering every surface; half-eaten plates and cartons of food forming an unsavory banquet across the one counter; tattered furniture and a filthy white sheet tacked over a pair of windows. The only object in the room that has any luster is a newer television preening on a scavenged wood crate. Everything is covered in a film of grit.

And there is the body. The woman's eyes are nearly closed and her brown hair wound through an elastic. She's wearing a soiled tank top and underpants, half sitting on the couch. Though her face and legs are dangerously bloated, her arms are skeletal, mapped with bruises, all connected by meandering track lines. I avoid looking at those places where her blood and other bodily fluids have pooled. But I'm drawn to her upper arm, cinched with a rubber band, a needle sticking out of the crook of her elbow; two more lie on the couch beside her. A small Baggie is on the floor, floating in a puddle of her own making. It was an intentional death. I marvel at her courage.

There is no dignity in this room. Death doesn't allow for it. She must have felt relief with that last breath, when she was delivered from the excruciating pain of a labored life. Looking at her there, her face melting into itself, I'm reminded of a similar scene, one of blood and ache and loss. I stand there for a moment, lost in the constant parallel between birth and death.

I hear a brief rap on the door before Andrew steps into the room. He stares at me as I stand over the body.

'I told you it was bad,' he says, his eyes darting over the woman. 'Your guy is here, the remover. Carlos? Okay if I send him in?'

'Yes, thank you.' Before he turns to go, I stop him. 'What's her name?'

Andrew's hand covers his face, so his words are muffled. 'Craig. Eileen Craig.'

Carlos nods when he enters. Of all the removers Linus has contracted, he is my favorite. I wonder about his past in Cape Verde, why he's never once grimaced while handling a body. He's young and strong, quiet in the homes and around the families, his presence somehow reassuring as they watch their loved one now safe within his sturdy arms. But this woman has no family living with her. Carlos makes the sign of the cross while standing over her, whispering in Portuguese. He then pulls on a pair of gloves, shaking his head when offered the mask. His hand moves to her arm and, with his usual deftness, swipes the needle from her vein, dropping it alongside the others. He pauses and then brushes a clump of matted hair from her face. After several minutes, we manage to place her in the body bag and lift her onto the stretcher. As we roll through the door, I hear Andrew start, but he's facing the wall. I look away when he begins to retch.

I glance past Carlos to see if the pregnant woman is still there, waiting to offer her opinion on what remains of her neighbor. There's only a girl standing in another doorway toward the middle of the hallway, a tiny whimpering dog in her arms. He sniffs the air and cries louder.

As we near, I notice something familiar about her. The way her long dark hair hangs to her waist, wavy and slightly unkempt; the frail bones under her olive skin; the dark, haunting eyes that plead with me. Though I'm masked and wheeling a body heavy with the odor of rot, she faces me unafraid. My heart hurls itself against my chest: Trecie is here. The wheels of the gurney catch under the weight of the body and begin to grind. Seeing her makes me dizzy. The hall looms, becomes telescopic, the little girl fading in and out of focus at the end. I can hear, feel, my mask collapsing and inflating with each breath (*one-two-three*). My whole begins to tremble. It's Trecie. I'm ready to let go of Miss Craig, to gather Trecie and the dog in my arms, when I realize my mistake.

She isn't the little girl I've been searching for. She isn't Trecie. And yet – she could be. The resemblance is startling: the same nose, narrow eyes, though she's older; nine, ten? I can't help but stare, and she doesn't look away.

As we pass, she tucks the dog, a Chihuahua, under her chin and speaks to him, rubbing her nose, that familiar lovely nose, along the top of his head. 'É aprovado, Amendoim. Não scared. Oh, Amendoim, é aprovado.'

Carlos opens the door to the stairwell, careful not to let the door hit the stretcher and jostle the dead woman. Soon we're outside, where the odor can begin to dissipate in the crush of December air. We load Miss Craig into the hearse and I slam the door behind her. With a wave, Carlos turns to leave. I stop, realizing he can help.

'Carlos.'

He turns. We've never spoken much beyond the briefest of instructions. He appears curious but still doesn't speak.

'What did that girl say?'

'What girl?' His words are heavily accented, his voice low and careful.

'The one in the hall, the one holding the dog? She was speaking Portuguese, right?'

He blinks.

'What did she say?'

Carlos waves his hand and shakes his head. He begins to walk away again.

Though mindful of my soiled gloves, I don't hesitate

to lay my hand on his shoulder, smearing his jacket. 'I have to know.'

Carlos looks from his shoulder to me. 'She said, "It's okay, Peanut. Don't be scared."'

He gets into his car and I'm still standing, watching as he drives away. I finally strip the gloves and pull off the mask. As I do, I remember what it's like to be held captive in the cold grip of fear.

CHAPTER FIFTEEN

It was Tom's baby. Not really. It was mine.

Spring of my sophomore year, I was sixteen. The signs had been there for months, though at first I didn't know. I was so slight, so thin, my cycle was irregular at best and mostly nonexistent. It wasn't a matter of missing it. Fatigue overwhelmed me, but I was never nauseated. Odors became more intense. After several months, there was a thickening to my waist, nothing more. I ignored it all until I felt the flutter, the awakening of something, someone, inside of me.

I managed the courage to stop going to the library after school, though I'm not sure it was courage: more survival, desperation, a desire to protect my child from their intrusions. There were no repercussions. I was a distant memory to Tom. And once the pretty, popular girls, hot with spring fever, blossomed under the football team's attention, they didn't miss me at the library. If only I'd realized that sooner.

I began working at Witherspoon Florist. My job was to count stock, freshen the buckets of water, sweep the discarded stems and leaves littering the back room after Daphne finished creating her vast arrangements. Mulrey's Funeral Home was her best customer.

After she closed shop at five, I would stay on an extra hour to clean and ready the store for the next day. Often I stayed later, learning the names of the flowers, their textures and scents. Once my chores were done, it would soothe me to wander the stockroom, where buckets were filled with all manner of flowers. It was my haven to be surrounded by buttery roses, sharp lilies, demure orchids.

And I was earning money, saving it from week to week. In the town library, I scanned the *Boston Globe* classifieds, seeking an apartment and a job that could earn enough to support the two of us. I found everything I needed: a summer rental, cheap until the fall, when college students returned and rents were raised; plentiful jobs, the kind I could do, anyway; and advertisements offering cash for diamonds, no questions asked. At night, my grandmother kept the ring in a box on her chest of drawers. It had been her mother's.

I knew the bus schedule and planned to leave within weeks, when concealing my condition, by then nearing my eighth month, would be difficult, especially when spring cardigans were exchanged for summer shifts.

But it's the curse of the young to be hopeful.

The cramps started sometime in the night. I woke in my bed, under the crucifix my grandmother had nailed above my headboard, waiting for them to pass. The pain twisted in my belly, gripping my insides, wringing them around and then round again.

When it stopped, I slipped from between the sheets, pressing myself against the wall to avoid the swollen floorboards that ran along the middle of the hall. Though my grandmother was well into her sixties, her hearing was still sharp. It took several minutes of careful toeing before I reached the staircase. As I started down, another spasm caught me. I pushed the meaty part of my palm into my mouth, biting down hard enough to leave teeth marks for days to come. But I didn't scream.

I recall this being the first time I was relieved that the lone bathroom was on the first floor. After all those years of dreading the middle-of-the-night trek in the creaky old farmhouse, now I was grateful. More than that. I closed the bathroom door just as I was caught in another grinding contraction. When it passed, I climbed into the ancient claw-foot bathtub and lay there, a towel bunched under me, another stuffed in my mouth. It all happened so quickly.

My legs were spread wide, feet pressed against the bead-board wall, my back against the unforgiving porcelain. She was born minutes later in a spasm of fluid and blood and desperation. When I looked between my thighs, my breath came in quick, heaving bursts, but hers did not.

She was the length of my forearm and just as thin. Exquisitely tiny veins were visible through her transparent skin, and her eyes were closed. Her hair was thick and brown, plastered to her head, blood smearing the crown. She was beautiful.

Carefully, I lifted her to me; she was weightless in my arms. I took the towel from my mouth and swaddled her with it, instinctively pressing her to me for warmth. I wiped at her face with the corner of the fabric, and then with my own cheek. It never occurred to me that she should have been crying.

I peeked at her beneath her makeshift blanket. Her chest rose and then collapsed in quick, raspy succession – once, twice, three times – and then stopped. I waited for her to move again. Of course she didn't.

'Breathe!' I begged. The single word shattered the night.

I don't remember walking outside, the mile along Preston Road leading to the main square, carrying my daughter in the chilly night air. When I came to the florist shop, I must have reached into the mailbox to retrieve the key, unlock the door. I must have, but I don't remember.

Her casket was an elegant ivory box reserved for long-stemmed roses and baby's breath, for happier times in a person's life. I washed her in the back room with soap and a soft cloth, stroking the length of her little body, feeling her skin beneath my fingertips. When I was done, I kissed her mouth and laid her naked on a bed of daisies, purely white.

It was a simple ceremony in the village graveyard, free of words and promises. She's buried along the tree line near my mother, between two grand evergreens. Her only marker is a shower of pine needles. I know she's there.

I do remember returning to my grandmother's house and making my way back to the first-floor bathroom. The sound of the pipes rattling when I ran a bath must have woken her at that early hour. She didn't knock, just walked in; locks were forbidden. The sight of her thin housecoat and worn slippers, the front of her legs a fireworks display of exploding spider veins, made the moment somehow sadder. Her face was soft with sleep, though her mouth retained its hard edge. She carried her boar's-hair brush in one hand, expecting the worst of me.

'I had cramps,' I said. My grandmother's eyes lingered over the bloody water and then back to my face. 'It's that time.'

She stood there watching me, both of us dangerously still. Then, without speaking, she closed the door and returned to bed, leaving me alone with the blood and ache and loss.

CHAPTER SIXTEEN

Mounds of cigarette butts grow in the abandoned flower beds, their expanse broken only by perennial clusters of trash. Standing at the entrance of the Vanity Faire apartment building, caught in a wind tunnel, my core is overwhelmed by the bitter cold. A middle-aged man exits the foyer, a watch cap pulled snug around his head, the fingers of his gloves cut away. He holds open the door for me, a cigarette dangling from his lips, but I pretend not to notice him. He appears annoyed and whips the cigarette atop the others, shaking his head as he walks away. The odor of Eileen Craig still lingers.

I can't stay much longer. I need to make final preparations for Miss Craig's service. It will be the briefest of ceremonies, led by Linus, without benefit of clergy. She's bound in a simple cotton sheet with scarlet geraniums (*consolation in despair*) by her side. She was discovered too late for clothing. It will be a closed casket. Only her mother and sister are expected, and then she'll be cremated. It seems money is an issue. I expect Linus will absorb his fee. Though it's well known he doesn't charge for children, I've learned he extends this consideration to some adults as well. He's never told me he does this, but family members have often returned in the days following their loved one's service, arms bursting with rich fruit pies, a father's pocket watch, and once, a pair of lobsters struggling to free themselves from the confines of a paper bag, struggling to live. All told me of his largesse. They spoke Linus's name as if he were their savior, and I suppose in some way he was. With Miss Craig, he even went so far as to order a funeral bouquet, an arrangement I'm supposed to be picking up now for this afternoon's service. But I'm here instead.

It's time to walk into the apartment building, but I know once I do, I'll be walking away from my careful life and entering Mike's world again. The doors open easily.

Nothing has changed since the day before last, other than the odor, which is less intense. I take the stairs up to the third floor and pause on the landing. I scan the mouse hole and wait for it to scurry out, but it doesn't. I don't know what I'll do once I'm outside the apartment door. Knock? Ask for the little girl who so resembles Trecie? Ask for Trecie herself?

Hurrying down the hall, I turn my face away as I pass the pregnant woman's apartment. There's the little girl's door. Careful to avoid the peephole, I press my ear beneath it and hear the murmur of a television. My heart lurches at the sound of children arguing, their many voices low. Without thinking, I knock.

There's an explosion of yapping and silence beyond that. Then the door cracks open. The girl is standing there, the little dog cuddled in her arms. He's shivering, his eyes frenzied, ears cocked. The child appears unafraid, though her expression is nearly worn through.

'Hello,' I say.

She simply stares back. The dog wriggles in her arms, a familiar bone-pendant hanging from his collar. She's wearing faded blue sweatpants and a T-shirt that looks to belong to an adult, *Cape Cod* in once green letters scripted across the front. A sour odor wafts from inside.

'I saw you the other day, with the dog' – I nod in his direction – 'and was wondering where you got him. He looks just like the one I lost.'

She continues her silence. Then I remember she had been speaking Portuguese. Shame overwhelms me. How absurd to think I could do this on my own. I should have called Kate, allowed her to handle it. Better yet, I could send her an anonymous message. There's still time.

I bow my head and turn to leave when the girl calls out, 'What's your dog's name?'

My breath catches. I think back to when I was at Mr. Kelly's house. How long ago was it? 'Peanut.'

'Oh.' She looks down at the dog now whimpering against her chest. She rubs her cheek along the top of his head. 'That's his name too.'

I try to see around her, into the apartment, but she's standing in the narrow space of the cracked door.

'Maybe I should talk to your parents.'

'Mama's not home.'

'What about your father?'

She shakes her head as she squats, laying the dog across her lap. He rolls onto his back, exposing a round belly, his eyes seeking her face. But she is watching me. I hear a whisper from inside and a younger girl tries to squirm through the narrow opening of the door. I catch a flash of her and nothing more before her older sister whips her head to warn her, 'Shh!' Turning back, she continues stroking the dog in short, reflexive sweeps.

'You must have a lot of brothers and sisters in there.' She says nothing. The only sound between us is the dog's panting.

I don't know where to go from here. My mind flips through questions, but I'm afraid of scaring her off the way I did Trecie. There's an urgency pressing into me, constricting my lungs and my legs, forcing me to make my last, best effort. She speaks first.

'Are you going to take Peanut?' Her head is bowed now, her body curled around the dog. She appears utterly defeated. It feels hopelessly cruel, but I must press on.

'Where did you get him?'

'From Victor.'

Victor. Yes, Victor. Not Vincent or Vito or Rick. Victor. I bend and reach to pet the dog. I notice how badly my hand shakes and move faster so the girl won't see too, though she's focused on him, her mouth pressed close to his ear, perhaps whispering her farewell. Within inches now, he turns and bites my finger. Peanut leaps from her lap and races around her legs, back into the apartment.

We both stand, and before I can say a word, the girl (yes, she's definitely older than Trecie, by a year, two?) whirls to face me. 'I don't think he likes you.'

She slams the door and I hear a bolt slip into place. My finger begins to throb and there's blood seeping from just above the middle knuckle. Standing there, blood coursing down my finger, I wait to see if she'll come out again. She won't, I know she won't. I walk back down the hallway. My finger's burning and my head aches. *Victor*.

I'm nearing the stairwell when the pregnant woman flings wide her door. It crashes against the wall and I find myself in a familiar stance, cowering and paralyzed.

'Don't you come to my building to buy your drugs, bitch!'

She's holding a bag of cheese curls, her mouth and fingertips an unnatural orange. In spite of the comeliness of her full womb, her expression is menacing. My eyes flash past her; the apartment is bigger than Eileen Craig's and far cleaner, though there is the faint odor of tobacco. A scented candle – apples and cinnamon – flickers atop the kitchen counter. Her little boy is watching a large-screen television, sitting cross-legged on a plush rug, his face so close to the dancing puppets it's as if he were a part of the program too. He doesn't start at the commotion.

'I was looking for my dog.'

Something inside of her clicks and she relaxes against the doorjamb, thrusting her belly forward as she does. Her fingers find their way back to the bag and she pops several cheese curls into her mouth as she speaks. 'You were here the other day. You took that nasty dead woman. How long is it going to smell? I got kids to worry about.'

It's hard to focus on her words, between the pain in my finger and the terrible uncertainty of not knowing if I'm moving toward Trecie. With my good hand, I reach into my pocket and pull out a stack of business cards. There are some for local florists, livery services, and two toxic cleaning companies who specialize in sanitizing after the dead. I give her the latter. 'Your landlord should call this company.'

'Look at you,' the woman says, gesturing to my finger with her own orange tips. She doesn't move to take the card. 'Did that yappy little dog bite you?'

I nod. It's time to move on, pick up Miss Craig's flower arrangement. And I need a quiet space to think.

'You got AIDS?' she asks, eyeing my hand. Before I can answer, she sucks on her teeth and then shakes her head. 'Come on, you gotta stick a Band-Aid on that or something before you drip it all up and down the hall.'

Though I shake my head, she persists. 'Come on in. Knowing them' – she nods in the direction of the girl's apartment – 'the dog probably has rabies. You'd think they'd have themselves a Rottweiler or pit bull. Some kind of guard dog. That's what most drug dealers around here have.'

'Drug dealers?' The little boy glances at us as his mother closes the door; we're already in her kitchenette. In the far window sits a small potted Christmas tree strung with lights now turned off. It's sprinkled with red and green balls, a plastic angel prays on top, and the base is wrapped in gold foil. The woman gestures for me to put my hand under the kitchen faucet, and then she wipes her face and hands with a wet paper towel.

'Yeah,' she says, reaching for my wrist as she floods my hand with hot water. She's surprisingly strong. Her hair smells of straightener, and her dark skin, free of makeup, glows under the fluorescent light. 'That woman is strung out. Crack, heroin, meth, take your pick. Men used to come by her place at all hours. I called the police once, about four years back, but they didn't do a damn thing. One cop stopped by, didn't even call child services. Ran out that boyfriend, though, threw him right down the stairs.'

I try to keep my voice steady. 'How many kids are there?'

'Am I hurting you?' She's pouring hydrogen peroxide over the cut now. I'm barely aware of the sting. 'Lord knows how many she's got in there. Five, six? I never see them go to school, that's for sure.'

She's winding the cotton dressing tight around my finger. Within seconds, the tip is chalky and numb.

'Have you seen a little girl? She's about seven, maybe eight, with long dark hair? Her name is Trecie.'

She puts away the tape and gauze, shaking her head, her mouth a curt frown. 'Look, living around here, you learn to keep to your own business. Only reason I called the police that time was because the mother had an evil boyfriend. But whoever came next is worse. When this new one started visiting, I could hear a lot of crying and carrying on, mostly from the children. My own boy was a baby, and I don't know if you have kids, but once he was asleep, I wanted him to stay that way.' She crosses her arms on top of her belly and glances at her boy. 'My advice is go get yourself another dog.'

I stand there, not more than a second, two at the most, but it feels a lifetime. The bright exuberance of children's television flooding my ears (it must be the same show down the hall), the constancy of living with fear and danger, the lingering odor of death. This is Trecie's life.

'So was that your dog?' The woman extends a can of Diet Coke. I shake my head and she opens it for herself.

'Pardon?' I need to pay attention.

'The dog. Was it yours?'

'No,' I say. 'No, it wasn't.'

'Good.' She reaches for the bag of cheese curls. ''Cause you don't want to take on that boyfriend. He will mess you up, and he's untouchable.'

'Victor? Why?' I can feel it again, that push forward, momentum and speed, a lurching toward something.

The woman's movements slow and the cellophane bag she's holding begins to shake. 'You got to go now. Right now. Get.'

I walk to the door and turn back to apologize, but she remains in the kitchen. As I leave, I catch sight of the little boy. He frowns at me as I pull the door closed.

When I reach the hearse, I turn the ignition and then feel in my pocket for Mike's card. I try not to think what it says about me that I carry it still.

'Mike Sullivan.'

I pause and he repeats himself before I can will myself to respond. 'It's Clara. Clara Marsh.'

'Oh.'

I tuck the cell phone against my shoulder. 'I think I have some news. About Trecie.' My nails brush a sore spot at the back of my head and a jolt of pain streaks as far down as my neck.

There's a long pause and then Mike exhales. 'You should call Kate, she's the lead investigator on this case.'

I scrape away the scab, seeking out baby hairs. They're too soft yet. 'I think I know where she lives.'

Mike's voice grows sharp. 'What do you mean?'

I allow my hands to drop to my lap. I can feel blood begin to ooze. 'I was picking up a body at the Vanity Faire and a girl came out of one of the apartments. She looks just like Trecie, they could be sisters. She has a dog, too, his name is – '

'Clara, stop.'

'But – '

'I know you want to help, really, I do. Jesus Christ.' He sighs. 'Look, Clara, we don't even know if your Trecie is the same girl in the video.'

'She is, I know,' I whisper. My free hand returns to my head, with intention this time. There's a patch of wiry curls near the crown.

'*I* don't know,' says Mike, his voice rising. 'What are you doing, anyways? First you say you don't know anything about Precious Doe's birthmark and then you say some girl is hanging out in your funeral home?'

A jerk and several strands come free, the roots a pleasing white. The sting transports me if only for a moment. 'It's true.'

'Really? So how come no one else has seen her?'

'Linus has.' I don't know if Mike hears me; my voice is nothing now.

'I wasted two weeks at the same funeral home where I had to say good-bye to my wife, chasing down some figment of your imagination, when I could have been helping real victims.' He stops and I feel the vast expanse of this hearse begin to press against me, the way it echoes with Mike's voice. 'Look, I'm sorry, it's got to be tough working there, living right there, it must get lonely, but . . .'

I don't hear the rest. The phone drops to the floor of the hearse. I shift the car into drive and peel away. My fist is full now. I press it to my face, swipe at my tears, then hide it all away in my pocket.

MINIVANS AND SUVS crowd the lot of Kennedy's Country Gardens. Men can be spotted here and there tying Christmas trees atop their cars as mothers fuss with infants' hats. Speakers affixed to poles throughout the grounds play 'Jingle Bell Rock' while swarms of children in brightly colored parkas roam free among the blue spruce. I pull the hearse into the farthest corner away from the holiday cheer, trying to forget Mike's words, straining to remember both the arrangements Linus ordered and a pot for my ficus. A comb I keep in the glove box helps restore my composure.

Without slowing to admire the row upon row of wreaths with tasteful bows – some dotted with starfish, others with holly berry (*foresight*) – I enter through a side door, careful to ignore the mistletoe (*need to be kissed*) above me. If I were to wander through the front rooms, I would have to bear witness to the crowds picking over the trendy amaryllis and common poinsettias (*very beautiful*), knowing each of those perennials will be tossed out with a dead balsam fir in a few weeks' time. It's better to take the long way to the florist shop and avoid the carnage. When I cross the threshold, I remove my hands from my pockets and notice the dog bite has bled through the dressings. It will need stitches.

This time of year, the rear greenhouses are a forgotten warren where fertilizer, soil and seeds, all manner of pots – glazed ceramic, foam, cedar, terra-cotta, concrete – are stored until gardeners emerge from their winter respite, ready to splurge on the riches of spring. Here provisions are stacked everywhere, caked in dust, one on top of another, against the walls, covering every table. The scent of peat moss and cedar chips spilling from their bags onto the floor welcomes me. I pause at a haphazard display of birdhouses. They are intricately crafted, with lovingly designed shingles and white clapboard; several have roofs made of copper. I reach out to one; it's cold beneath my touch, and when I start to pull away, a sparrow darts past me. If my grandmother were alive, she wouldn't rest until she chased the bird from this place, mindful of the old wives' tale that a bird caught indoors is a harbinger of death. In her own way, she tried to capture me, too. She tried. I take my time, stopping to admire a squared-off planter – cobalt blue – and then I remember my ficus.

Lifting it from its place on the shelf, I struggle to carry the pot through the narrow passageway. A rough edge on the bottom, untouched by the glaze, scrapes my injured finger. I feel it with each step. I don't notice him at first, intent on that spot, but as I make my way to the florist's desk at the rear of the shop I hear a voice call out, 'Hey, Mikey!'

When I turn, there's a man I nearly recognize just a few feet away, beckoning to someone I can't see. Even as I need to flee, my feet won't carry me from this place, and I stand exposed in the middle of the aisle. A salesclerk, Jeff, his arms overflowing with balsam greens, hurries past me, knocking my arm on his way.

He stumbles, I do too, and then rights himself, never appearing to notice me.

'Mikey!' The man motions to someone just beyond my sight. I can't bear the thought of facing him, not now. It's as if a tide has risen within me and is about to burst forth. I feel the pot slipping. Then a toddler appears from around the corner carrying with him a gaudy ornament.

'C'mere, buddy,' the man calls to the boy.

My grip strengthens and calm descends; I can't allow the panic to swell again. I quicken my step, retreating to the florist's shop in the adjacent room. It's vacant save for the giant blue macaw dozing on her perch amid the display of silk poppies (*extravagance*). Many years ago she escaped and smashed the windshield of a delivery truck pulling into the lot. Now she's capable of little more than brief bursts of flight, mainly hopping from roost to post, careful to drop her waste in a corner of the room. Mirabelle's been here as long as I've been a customer, longer still, a fixture among the dried flowers and vine wreaths. There are photos of her everywhere. Bea is the manager of this department, the owner's daughter, and the bird's 'mother.' She often uses the bird's discarded plumage in some of the arrangements, though never ours. Usually I have a treat for Mirabelle in spite of the *Do Not Feed the Bird* signs Bea posted in her Palmer's cursive.

The pot has grown burdensome, and as I head across the room toward the counter to set it down, Mirabelle begins to coo. I check my watch; Miss Craig's service is soon. If I hurry, there will be time for a cup of tea to help put away this day.

'Hello?' I say, hoping Bea is just in the back room and not among the holiday throng. I don't have the energy to search for her. This place, this home away from home, is beginning to feel claustrophobic.

'Hello.'

It comes from behind me. When I turn, no one's there. 'Hello?'

'Hello.' It's Mirabelle.

I've never heard her speak. I laugh in spite of myself, an unfamiliar sound that jangles my nerves still more. It's a day for odd circumstance. The macaw is peering out at me through her white irises, her face drawn in alternating stripes of black and white, though the rest of her is a painter's wheel of yellows, blues, and greens.

'Bea?'

'Hello, Clara,' the bird says again, though her mouth hardly moves. I can't help but smile when she cocks her head to the side, leaning toward me. I take a step and then another closer to the bird. If only I'd brought her a biscuit. She stretches her wings, flapping them ever so slightly, and I notice for the first time that while the underside of her tail is sunburst yellow, the top is sapphire. She extends her neck its full length so that her hooked beak is mere inches from me. I lean in and she nuzzles my cheek, her feathers a cushion of velvet. Closing my eyes, I lose myself.

'I thought I was her favorite.' Bea's at the register,

Miss Craig's modest arrangements on the counter waiting to be rung. She rips the ticket from the pot. 'This too?'

I pull myself away from the macaw and she flits to another perch. 'Yes, separate check.'

Bea's a no-nonsense woman with gray streaking her once-blond hair, blue eyes gone watery, her figure resigned to the pudge of middle age, hidden beneath a red T-shirt bearing the nursery's logo. There's always dirt under her clipped nails, caked into the palms of her hands; today's no different. When the time comes I'll bury her with white violets (*unabashed candor*): She does not suffer fools gladly.

'That must have been some treat you fed her,' says Bea, reaching for my check, each of us avoiding eye contact. She flinches when my fingertips graze hers but says nothing about my wound. 'How'd that compost work out for you?'

'I'll know this spring.' I slide Linus's credit card across the counter, mindful of my hand this time.

'Let's hope winter brings us some snow. I'd hate to start the spring off with a drought. I lost all my cosmos last year.' She puts both receipts into a small bag and then places it and an arrangement into the pot. She stands expectantly. 'Did you get your tree already? We have some real corkers out front.'

I shake my head.

Bea's voice grows quiet, her mouth turning down at the corners, twisted as if she's bitten into something sour.

'I don't suppose you'd celebrate Christmas, would you?'

I take the pot in my arms and turn to leave. Mirabelle swoops to her roost nearest me, leaning toward me. The down that collects along her throat is iridescent, a thousand colors blending to one. I can feel Bea's eyes on me.

'She said my name,' I say.

Bea comes out from behind the counter, collecting Mirabelle in a protective embrace. Though her voice is light, teasing, Bea's expression has taken on the guarded facade I've come to know so well from so many. 'I think you've been spending too much time at the funeral home, Clara. Since the accident, Mirabelle can't talk.'

CHAPTER SEVENTEEN

Miss Craig's mother stands in the open doorway leading out to the funeral home's rear parking lot. Gusts of frozen air whistle around her, flooding the vestibule as she takes a long last drag of her cigarette. Her nylon coat is too thin for this weather and there's nothing to protect her hands or head; stringy hair whips her face. A navy blue handbag hangs from her shoulder, its contents bulging through a broken zipper. She wears polyester slacks, as if from a uniform, and I imagine Miss Craig's face looked very much like her mother's toward the end: a battlefield of hopelessness and yearning.

'Hi, I'm early,' she says, stepping inside. Her voice scratches her throat; the blackened phlegm that lines her esophagus and lungs vibrates with each word. 'My daughter's on her way. She'll be here in a minute.'

I listen for Linus's footfalls creaking down the hallway. He's never forgotten to greet a family member before.

'Hello, Mrs. Craig,' I say. Linus would shake her hand with both of his. He would hold her there, offer his condolences, and while she spoke of her daughter's life and death, he would extend a hand to her shoulder and she would fall against him, comforted by his sheer mass and ability to absorb her pain, soothed if only while in his presence. I offer what I can. 'May I take your coat?'

'No, I'm still freezing.' She shoves her fists into the pockets of her windbreaker and lifts her shoulders around her ears. 'Is it okay if I wait for my daughter here? I don't want to go in . . . *there* . . . by myself. You know.'

'Of course not. Let me show you to the sitting room. You'll be more comfortable there.' It's just off of the waking room where Miss Craig's casket rests, set with leather wingbacks and comfortable sofas. I sit her in one of the chairs, knowing from this angle she won't be able to see the simple box that houses all that's left of her child. 'May I get you a glass of water? Coffee or tea?'

'Yeah, a coffee, regular. That would be great.' I turn to go and then, 'Miss?'

'Yes?'

'The cops say she been in her apartment a few days before she was found.'

'Yes.' The fresh bandage is snug around my finger. I gave myself the six stitches; it barely hurt. A brief nap and cup of chamomile tea helped me regain perspective. I'm fine now.

'Who brought her here?' Mrs. Craig's words are strangled. Her eyes fill, magnified and wavering until the tears are loosed.

'I did.'

'She must have looked real bad, huh?' She begins to rummage through her pocketbook, piling the detritus of her life – a plastic comb, mints, cheap lipstick, store-brand cough drops – onto the end table.

I take a tissue from its box on a nearby table and hand it to her. She stops her searching and presses it to her nose, her breath coming in jagged bursts now.

'She looked beautiful, Mrs. Craig.' I pat her shoulder, lingering there. I almost give it a squeeze. 'I'll get you that coffee.'

Where is Linus? With this terrible cold, his arthritis has been bothering him. He could have fallen. I can't imagine it would be anything worse than that, but when I turn the corner and see his office door is closed, the gnawing within me builds. He's here, but ignoring his duties. Something must be dreadfully wrong. I reach for the handle, ready to burst through, when I hear him.

'Lord, forgive me, I am not *perfect and upright*, no I am not that.' His voice carries through the oak door, his baritone vibrating through me. 'Sometimes, Lord, I am overcome by the evil that lurks among us, within us, *walking to and fro in the earth and back and forth among it.*'

The anxiety within me settles. Looking at my watch, I realize Linus isn't late at all, he's simply preparing for Miss Craig's rites. He does this first, cleanses himself, he says, before conducting a prayer service. Those families who've never before affiliated themselves with a religious institution still crave some semblance of ceremony.

They believe Linus holds sway and can help direct their loved one into the next world. It's their fervent hope that it's never too late.

'Lord,' Linus says, 'I am a sinner. There's a boil down deep, growing, worrying at me, making me question if what I'm doing is pure of heart.' I start to leave, give him a few more minutes to compose himself. 'Don't make much difference if it's a lie of omission or flat-out denial of the truth, and to lie like this to Clara . . .'

I stop when I hear my name and press my ear against the wood. Down the hall, the back door opens and the cold air snakes its way here. The door crashes shut and a woman's voice calls out, 'Hello?'

I will her to silence and continue listening to Linus. 'Makes me feel like I should be reading Genesis instead of Job, Lord. All these years I never could understand how Abraham could pet the downy head of his boy, even as he laid his own child out on the altar, a knife behind his back.'

The women's voices rise and I press a hand against my free ear, blocking them out.

'Can't say I'm much different from Abraham, Lord, willing as I am to sacrifice my own child.' He's taken by a hiccup, stumbles over his words. It's not a sob. No. 'What scares me, what has me looking round corners and *back and forth*, is wondering if I really am doing Your will. I've got to believe the lies, the deceit, have a purpose. That I really am doing right by Clara and Trecie. 'Cause in the dark days, faith is all a man's got.'

It's as if a bind has been placed around my ribs, pulled fast and tight, the pressure intense. Pins and needles begin to work their way through the spaces in between the bone. He doesn't mean it, he's not lying, I can't believe that. Linus is a man of honor, not of deceit. Mike could forsake me, yes, it was nothing, I was nothing to him. But not Linus. And Trecie? I simply misunderstood. He was praying, prayers can be interpreted a thousand different ways.

'Excuse me!' A woman stands at the end of the hall, her stance angry and tensed. 'My mother and me are waiting in the other room here.'

'Yes,' I say. 'I was just getting Mr. Bartholomew.'

I turn the handle, but before I can push the door open, Linus has pulled it free. He catches me when I stumble.

'I got you, don't you worry,' he says, steadying me. His hands feel sure on me, the way I imagine a father's would. I straighten myself quickly. Yes, I simply misunderstood him.

'The Craigs are here.'

'So I see,' he says, stepping past me.

'Linus?' I call after him. He's already started down the hallway to greet Miss Craig's family. My insides quake, but if I don't ask now, I never will. 'How long have you known Trecie?'

'Hmmm?' He pauses, turns slowly, his expression impossible to interpret. So unlike him.

'How long has she been coming here. To play?'

'Been a while now.'

He starts walking again and I take the few steps and touch his arm, stopping him. 'How long?'

Linus removes my hand, takes it in both of his. 'Now what exactly are you asking me, Clara?'

I can't say it. I can't. He releases me and reaches the end of the hall, where Miss Craig's sister is waiting, his hands swallowing hers the way they always do. 'Miss Craig, I imagine you're in a world of pain right now. I know what it is to lose a sibling, lost my own brother when I was twenty-six. It's like losing half your memory and an arm, too. You have my sympathies.'

Her anger crumbles and she drops her head. 'It was just me and her growing up, you know? She had problems, the drugs, but she was a good person. She really was.'

'Yes, she is, and don't you worry that the Lord doesn't know that.' He enfolds her in his arms and holds her there a minute until her tears subside. 'You go to your mother now. I need to get my prayer book and I'll be right along.'

She leaves and Linus walks back down the hallway toward me. He points to my finger as he passes. 'What happened there?'

'A cut. It's nothing.' It's beginning to throb again, so I hold it within my other hand.

'Make sure you put some cream on that, wrap it up good. You don't want no fluids coming into contact with it. You could get a terrible infection that way, you know that.'

He steps into his office and reaches for his book, lying open on his desk. Before he leaves, he cups my chin in his massive palm and gazes at me just a moment too long. 'I wouldn't want anything to happen to you.'

As he retreats down the hall, he hums a hymn, loud, without any sense of uneasiness. Something dark and haunting, its melody familiar, the words on the tip of my tongue – there! – and then gone again. It's something I should know, tantalizingly close, a hint of something . . . *toils and snares I have already come* . . . I can't be sure. When he disappears around the bend, I want to call to him, to ask, but don't. I can't say why.

CHAPTER EIGHTEEN

I'm dreaming. I know I'm dreaming, but still.

An Asian woman's just ahead of me, turning back every so often to smile, urging me forward with a wave. She's tiny and barefoot, wearing a white ao dai that billows around her calves, caught in a breeze of her own making. Her hair is black, hanging in long uneven layers. She appears younger than I am, but so much older. I know her. We're on a garden path, thick with a menagerie of flowers that hang from dense, snaking vines, suspended from nothingness. I want to stop and clip a stalk of hibiscus, hydrangea, rose, all conjoined on a single trailing stem, but there's the woman. Just ahead.

She turns a corner on the path and I can no longer see her. I walk faster, but as I do the vines begin to shift and sway, extending themselves toward me, plucking at my skin, pinching and snapping. I catch sight of her ankle as she turns into darkness.

I hesitate, check over my shoulder. The path behind me has become overgrown. Leaves unfold, rustling as they shake themselves out; mature buds blossom before my eyes, their colors so vibrant it burns; their fragrance begins to smother me. I follow into the darkness.

I'm falling, hurtling, my legs kicking wildly, desperate to feel something solid. I reach and reach, but my hands find nothing to hold before I land into more of nothing. It's a dream, I know this.

Then I spot her, Trecie, sitting cross-legged across the way. The Asian woman is gone. Trecie's pressing a bundle to her and I hear it yelp. I'm reminded of the dog, Peanut, and watch as Trecie pulls it closer, pressing her cheek against its head, nuzzling it as she giggles.

Relief flows within me, rippling outward in concentric circles, growing larger as it laps against my insides. I walk toward her and my arms extend, ready to engulf her. Trecie is safe, she's safe.

She watches me approach and sits erect. There's a shift in her that fills me with dread. Each step closer to Trecie pains me, a stab arcing toward my chest. But I need to bring her home.

And then I'm standing over her. She looks at me as if she were protecting me and folds back the blanket that covers her bundle. It's a baby. The infant's cheeks, fat and round, beg to be kissed. Her mouth is glossy with drool, a string hanging from the corner. I want to catch it with my finger. Her eyes are brown and clear, innocent and fine. Daisies are scattered over her full belly, a stem caught in a fold of her thigh. She kicks it free, smiling and gurgling. She is my daughter.

Trecie raises her to me. 'Clara.'

Tears burn my cheeks as I hold out my arms, but I can't reach her.

'Clara,' says Trecie.

My arms are leaden things, as if I'm underwater. I swim toward them, struggling to breathe.

'Clara!'

I snap awake, my body heaving itself upward, lungs gasping, the book I fell asleep reading, a war memoir, askew on the floor. My eyes are burning, hot with tears. I want to go back. I need to find my way back to them.

'Clara, wake up. It's Mike.' There's a banging at my door.

I stumble out of bed, reaching for my robe, forgetting my slippers. He continues to pound the door, calling my name. Through the fog, I wonder if I'm really awake, if I'm not still caught in the nightmare.

I can see him through the patio doors now; he looks thinner than I remember, though it's been only a few days. The kitchen clock reads 7:06; I've overslept. My head is too clouded to speak when I open the door.

This is not a casual visit. Mike has not come here for more tea, to hold my hand, to reassure me that Trecie is fine, that it's not my fault, that he doesn't truly believe I've imagined it all. He's wearing a jacket and tie, his hands are red raw, and stubble coarsens the usual smoothness of his face. I'm careful to place a hand over the back of my head. It doesn't matter. He doesn't move from the mat. He won't look at me.

'Clara, I need to take you down to the station, ask you a few questions.'

In the parking lot behind him, there are more cars; three sedans and a Whitman cruiser.

'Why?' I feel the way I used to when my grandmother would question me about some misunderstanding. Then those awful moments waiting in my mother's childhood bedroom while my grandmother fetched her brush from the downstairs bathroom. I can almost hear her now, climbing the stairs.

'I'll stay here while you get dressed.' He shifts his weight from one foot to the other.

'What do you want to ask?' Is he curious about my visit to the Vanity Faire apartment?

'Just get dressed.' It's as if he's pleading now, as if we both are.

'Mike, please.'

He rubs his face with a hand until it curls around to the back of his neck, rubbing back and forth. 'We got the phone records from Reverend Greene's line. The dates and times of all the anonymous tips match up with calls placed from the Bartholomew Funeral Home. I need to take you down to the station.'

'I don't understand.'

Mike stands there, his body half turned away. 'I can't say any more.'

I nod – it's all I can do – and then head back to my bedroom. I reach for my white shirt, my fingers clumsy, shaking, missing the buttonholes again and again. As I dress, I look out to my greenhouse and wonder if there's time to water my flowers. How long will I be gone? Will they survive two days, a week? I open the door and inhale, filling myself with them, taking their comfort with me. It's only a few more minutes to make my bed, brush my teeth, put up my hair. When I return to the kitchen, Mike is in the same spot, still looking away.

As we walk to the parking lot, I see Linus and Alma. Kate is walking Alma toward one of the sedans, and Mike's partner, Jorge, escorts Linus. None of us speak. We stand too far away to reach out a hand, too close not to feel each other's dread. Alma is composed yet nervous. She clutches her purse in front of her, red lipstick carefully drawn. She looks at me and nods her comfort. The cold must be bothering Linus's knees. His gait is slow, careful. When he looks up, he stares, pouring himself into me. Then he smiles, warm and kind, as if to capture me within a protective embrace. If I could, I would go to him. I would take his hand and hold it within my own; I would press it to my cheek. I can hear his voice, *I'll take care of you.*

I swallow the catch in my throat and walk toward him until Mike reaches for my arm, guiding me to a separate car. I stop to look down at his hand, my gaze moving to meet his face.

He looks at me then and I can see him. Finally, I can see him again.

'I'm sorry, Clara.'

CHAPTER NINETEEN

My tea has grown tepid. With only powdered milk and flimsy sugar packets to accompany it, there seems little point.

We're in one of the interrogation rooms at the Brockton Police Department. I sit facing Mike and Frank Ball, and whoever may be standing behind the two-way mirror. I try not to glance at my reflection, and the person beyond, focusing instead on the Whitman detective's bobbing Adam's apple as he reads a file from the sturdy cardboard evidence box: the familiar *Precious Doe* scrawled on all four sides in haphazard print. An ancient metal table sits between us, its gray surface marked by linked coffee rings and scratched with curses and games of tic-tac-toe, the grooves black with filth and the city's ever-present grit. Mike already told me our conversation will be recorded; he didn't mention if we were being videotaped as well.

I try to imagine Linus and Alma in similar rooms, being apprised of their right to have an attorney present for questioning, being reassured that they are not under arrest. I imagine Alma's stoic facade squared off against Kate's blond cheerfulness. How her fingers must ache to scrub the table before her.

Linus will be different. Friendly – warm even – he may go too far. He's incapable of deception. He'll give them everything they seek. Or in an effort to protect me, will he try to mislead them? I must remind myself to breathe (*one-two-three*).

I keep my hands folded on my lap where they can shake at will. Mike's coffee sits in front of him untouched. He rubs his hand along his cheek, the scratch of stubble audible in this small room, but he appears not to notice. We are close enough so that I can smell his soap. It seems impossible that just weeks ago I stood with him, holding him while he shook. Now we're here. I look up and he's watching me. I wonder if he's thinking the same.

Mike starts. 'Can you tell us about the phone system at the Bartholomew Funeral Home?'

I call to mind Linus and Alma, and in their faces find the courage to begin. 'It's a two-way line, meaning two phone numbers are hooked into the same line. One number is for the funeral home and the other is for Linus and Alma's residence. Each number has a different ring tone, so we can tell if the call is business or personal.'

'What's the purpose of having a two-way line?' asks Ball. 'Why not have two separate lines?'

'Death comes at all hours, Detective Ball. Mr.

Bartholomew makes himself available when he's at the supper table, while he's sleeping — he even had a phone installed in his shower. No one likes to get an answering machine when they need an undertaker.'

'I see.' Detective Ball makes a notation on his yellow legal pad and then gestures to Mike.

'Who has access to the phone?' Mike says. He's twirling a pen along his fingers, his notepad free of any marks.

'Linus, Alma, and me.' A bright spot on his otherwise dulled wedding band catches the overhead light. He must see it too and moves his hand under the table while the other continues to flip the pen.

'How well do you know Reverend Greene?' he asks.

It occurs to me that the reverend must also be somewhere inside this building, being pushed and prodded by another interrogator. The room begins to waver a bit. The air is dense, and suddenly my throat's parched and the tea becomes irresistible. But I don't dare reach out my unsteady hand.

'I've known him for twelve years.'

Mike's pen stops its fumbling. His gaze settles on me, pulling me into his sphere. I can no longer see Detective Ball. I can no longer see or hear or feel anything but Mike. My arms twitch and a hand begins creeping away from my lap, reaching toward my head.

'That's not what I asked,' Mike says. 'I asked how well do you know him. Do you talk regularly, see each other socially? He is a widower, correct?'

I pause, studying the growth along his face. I understand the implication and want to reach out and slap him. Mike is strong, but I feel an equal strength grow within me. I refold my hands. 'How well do we really know anyone?'

His eyes flash when he asks, 'Why didn't you tell the police investigating the death of Precious Doe about the birthmark you found on her neck three years ago?'

'Why didn't you find it?'

He nearly winces. Though it's not as satisfying as a smack, it has the same effect. Yet he persists. 'You and the anonymous caller knew about it.'

'So it seems.'

'Did Linus?'

'No.'

Mike leans forward. I can smell his sweat through the soap and feel myself begin to grow warm. 'Are you sure?'

Breathe. 'If Linus knew anything that could have helped that child, he would have called you.'

'What makes you think he didn't?' Mike speaks the next part too quickly for me to respond. 'Now, what about Trecie?'

'I thought you weren't interested in hearing about Trecie.'

'You said Linus let her play at the funeral home?'

'Mike, stop.'

'Have there been other children over the years? Anyone fitting the description of Precious Doe?'

'No!' My fingernails scrape my palm. 'Mike, you know Linus. He's a good man.'

But he won't stop. 'You said yourself we never really know someone.' He waits just long enough for his words to register and then, 'Why were you visiting Precious Doe's grave the night Trecie fled your home?'

'Because no one else does.'

Mike purses his lips and looks off. 'Would you say you go there often?'

'I usually go at night,' I say, anger swelling my courage. 'After midnight, when no one's there. Well, almost no one.'

He whips his eyes back to mine, and in them I see his nakedness. I want to turn away, to reel back my words, but they've been cast out, hitting the mark I sought. It's too late.

Mike squares his shoulders and regroups. 'Do you have access to all of the rooms at the Bartholomew Funeral Home?'

'Yes.'

'Even the residence?'

'Yes.'

Mike leans forward on the table, staring at me full-on, his eyes unblinking. He's stringing my noose. 'The bedrooms?'

'Pardon?'

Mike raises his voice. 'The bedrooms. Have you been upstairs to the Bartholomews' bedrooms?'

I should tell him now, force him to listen to my story

about the little dog, about the girl who looks so much like Trecie, about the boyfriend named Victor, but I don't. He's on the other side. Not mine, not Linus's. 'Yes.'

'How recently?'

'I can't remember.'

'How many rooms are on the second story of the residence?'

I pause, trying to imagine the trap he's laying. 'There are four bedrooms, a master bath, and a guest bathroom.'

'I assume there's a phone upstairs?' Mike won't look away, and I don't know where to direct my gaze.

'I've already told you Linus had one installed in his shower. He also has one on his bedroom nightstand.'

'The night we were searching for Trecie, while we sat in Linus's kitchen, he claims he went upstairs to talk to Alma. Minutes later, a call was placed from that phone line to Reverend Greene. Then Reverend Greene called me with the news that the other girl in the video was Precious Doe. Do you recall that?'

I can't answer him. It hurts to breathe.

But he won't stop. 'What's in the other rooms?'

I reach for the tea, letting the bitterness slip along my throat. 'Alma uses one as a sewing room, and the other two are bedrooms.'

Mike removes a photograph from the Precious Doe file and holds it up for me to see. It's a picture of Trecie, a still taken from the video I saw at Charlie Kelly's house. She's staring at the camera; there's the dingy wall behind her with the crayon scrawl and the bare mattress that haunts me.

'Does this look familiar?' Mike asks.

I bob my head, turning away. I've tried hard to forget that video.

'Is this one of the bedrooms in the Bartholomew residence?' Mike's voice is a whisper, and the picture begins to tremble between his forefinger and thumb.

I place both hands on the table and push myself up, then reach for my coat from the back of my chair. Detective Ball stands and moves to the door. 'We're not done questioning you.'

He is no one. I turn to Mike and he also stands, facing me, the picture of Trecie lying on the table between us.

'There are four bedrooms upstairs.' I'm calm now; for Linus I can be anything. 'There's the master bedroom, Alma's sewing room, and a guest room decorated with a quilt Alma made with her sisters. The fourth bedroom belongs to their dead son Elton. It contains his baseball trophies and posters of his favorite band. Nothing has been touched since that day.'

My voice cracks and I need to stop, clear my throat before continuing. 'You will not find that room' – I gesture to the photo – 'at the Bartholomew home.'

Feeling the rage build, my voice drops. 'I assume you have officers searching the house as we speak. I would appreciate it if you would tell them not to disturb Elton's room. It would devastate Alma. You of all people should understand.'

Mike nods, his face slack and impossibly tired. I turn to leave.

'Clara, wait.' He reaches for my arm and I shake him free.

'Don't touch me.' I want nothing more than to leave this place. I feel in my pocket for my wallet, hoping I have enough cash for a taxi home. I won't ask for a ride. Had I really believed I could expect more of him, anything other than betrayal? My fingers knit themselves under the elastic holding back my hair and begin twisting. Not here, not now. Later. 'If you have any more questions, please contact my lawyer.'

Before I can open the door, Ryan is there. He steps into the room, blocking my escape. He nods in my direction but looks at Mike. 'We got our caller. Bartholomew just asked for a lawyer.'

CHAPTER TWENTY

My grandmother came to me at night.

I felt her there before I opened my eyes, the odor of lye soap and cloves hanging between us. She didn't say anything at first, just waited while my pupils adjusted to the light streaming in from the hallway. Though physically small, she towered over my bed, my mother's bed; her rosary beads wound tight around the knuckles of her left hand, the tips of her fingers glowing white. I began to tremble when I realized she was dressed, her clothes covered by the striped apron, the one with pockets. The head of the boar's-hair brush peeked over the lip of one pouch; the other was weighted down with something I couldn't see. I didn't look to my grandmother's face.

'Get up.'

My bed was warm and the farmhouse frigid that winter night. Still I followed her along the hallway and down the stairs, gripping my cotton nightgown on either side as it fluttered against my knees. I should have known better than to drag my bare feet along the planks of knotty pine, I should have stepped firmly toward the inevitable. It wasn't long before a splinter embedded itself in the ball of my right foot. It stayed there for days until an angry weal formed. When I touched a hot needle to it more than a week later, the bit of wood exploded through the skin, carried by a wave of pus.

As my grandmother led me through the living room, I saw it and knew. There, on the mantel below the crucifix and alongside my mother's senior-year picture, was my own portrait taken the month before. Each was defaced with red marker in her neat, purposeful cursive: *Whore*. When I had arrived at school on picture day, I freed my hair from its elastic, allowing it to hang loose to my waist. I'd hidden the photograph in the bottom of my closet along with the money saved from my job at Witherspoon Florist, a one-way bus ticket to Boston for the day after my graduation, and the calling card from my long-ago doll, Patrice, the same card I'd snatched back from my mother's casket. It was safe to assume everything was gone now.

We continued into the dining room that contained her mother's set, the crown jewel a Victorian sideboard with contrasting mahogany inlay. It was too heavy for this space, too reminiscent of guests we'd never have. Through the doorway, the kitchen was ablaze with lights. When we walked in, I understood what was to happen. It wasn't the first time, though it was the last. Or, perhaps, the beginning.

A stool waited in the middle of the linoleum floor, a

side table from the guest bedroom beside it. My grandmother's Bible lay on top of it, its worn plastic cover obscured by a hand mirror lying facedown. Torn bits of paper marked favored passages. Whatever warmth I had left me then. It was as if all my blood flowed out, leaving my body weak and malleable. I'd like to say I protested, at least backed a step or two out of the room, but I didn't.

'Sit,' she said, pointing to the lone stool.

I did. In a way it was a relief. My grandmother took her place behind me, her fury radiating from her in palpable swells. I heard the boar's bristles scrape against the apron as she removed the brush from her pocket. She then took the mirror from atop her Bible, thrusting it at me. I held it with both hands, keeping my gaze soft on a point just beyond its frame. If I focused, if I stayed within myself, the tears might come. She started at the crown, pressing the bristles hard against my scalp, and began pulling through, section by section.

'Your mother must have liked the darkies, just look at this hair. Are you looking?'

'Yes, ma'am.' She tugged with such force I was yanked from the stool. I knew enough to get back on the seat again. It would be over sooner this way. I tried not to notice the burn, the clump of hair drifting to the floor.

'All these kinks. Can't imagine why you'd take pride in such a thing.'

With her right hand she continued to drag the bristles through, and with her left she opened the Bible to her selected passage. I managed to keep my chin aloft as she ripped through another tangle of curls. A prickle came to my eyes; I dared not blink. My grandmother spread the book facedown. There was a certain satisfaction when its spine cracked. She paused to clear the brush. The strands she freed came to rest along my knee, trapped on the hem of my nightgown. For the rest of my time in that chair, they tickled my skin whenever caught in one of the many drafts.

My grandmother finally set the brush on the table. Though I knew what was waiting for me in her other pocket, I tried to believe the worst was over. But she was standing too still behind me, her breathing agitated. The mirror reflected the rise and fall of her chest, and just above it, her chin and lower lip. Spittle collected in the corners as she spoke. 'Apple doesn't fall far from the tree, does it? We know how much Eve liked her apples. Ran into Dot McGee at the market. She wanted to express her *concern* for you. Seems she overheard her boy Tom and his friends talking, how you was the football team's best cheerleader.'

I watched my grandmother's hand in the mirror, the way it slid along her navy and white striped apron into that front pocket. How I wanted to look away. 'She was just being a good neighbor, she said, didn't want you to end up like your mother. 'Apple doesn't fall far from the tree,' she said.'

With her other hand, my grandmother flipped over the Bible. I didn't see it, just heard the thump when she righted it on the table. Her voice boomed. 'A reading from First Corinthians: For if a woman be not covered, let her also be shorn.'

The scissors, her good sewing pair, caught the light as she held them to my head. The mirror shook as the shears cut. My grandmother's huffing and the scrape of the scissor's hinge raked my ears. She started with small fistfuls, but as her rage grew, so did the layers in her hand. All the while I held firmly to that mirror, righting myself onto the stool each time.

She was only partway done when a cramp dug into her left arm. A lather formed about her mouth as her chest heaved. Before she took her seat at the kitchen table, she handed the scissors to me. 'Finish.'

My grandmother died a few months later; a heart attack killed her the day before my graduation. Her mother's diamond ring bought me another bus ticket and a few months' rent before I enrolled in mortuary school. I did the rest. Later, following an apprenticeship at a funeral home, I found my way to Linus. He's tried to shelter me, find a way around my past, but my grandmother's legacy is too powerful even for him.

It was ten years before my hair grew back to its previous length. It will be many more before I forget that night, the odor of cloves, the way my hands shook. What I remember best of all, however, is the calm that descended when I finally put down the shears. How my breathing settled, the tears stopped, how everything *stopped* when I took hold of the clumps that remained. I stared first at my grandmother cradling her shoulder, turned back to my reflection, and then I began to pull.

CHAPTER TWENTY-ONE

Walking through the parking lot, I check between cars, hesitate before taking the outside corner of the bend of the ramp. A light drizzle wets the grime, freshening the odor of waste. My thighs clench as I climb the steep hill up to the Brockton Police Department; it's located high on a concrete hill, a sentinel overlooking this weary city. Sporadic halogen lamps give off a fuzzy, otherworldly light, the ever-present dust and rain whirling in their glow. There's a subway stop just a hand's throw from the main entrance; it's never seemed queer before tonight. But tonight the familiar has become alien.

It's fitting that the sky is obscured, without the moon or stars to light my way. Anything is possible now. A train screams alongside the subway platform across from the police station's entrance, belching diesel fumes from its gut. In an instant, it devours a stream of people between its snapping doors, as if stealing them away to their final exit. An off-duty cop exits the station and walks toward me, a cell phone tight against his ear, a hat pulled low against the weather. His laughter echoes through the bitter night; he doesn't know.

I open the door to the same dingy foyer from this morning, though it seems that was years ago. There are the *!WARNING!* posters alerting me to real monsters lying in wait. I wonder how long before they hang Linus's photo alongside these others.

Alma asked me to pick up Linus. She reminded me of her difficulty driving at night and of her roast in the oven. Both are true; I don't want to think there's any other reason.

The police haven't charged him, but she said they've hired a lawyer nonetheless, someone from Reverend Greene's congregation. The reverend was able to reach her in North Carolina, where she's celebrating Christmas with her family. The lawyer said she'd fly home first thing in the morning. It will be pro bono; Linus buried the woman's fiancé not quite a year ago. He was driving to their rehearsal dinner when an elderly gentleman mistook the gas pedal for the brake. It was whispered throughout the wake that Linus refused payment, that it was his gift to the bride. It would have been the couple's wedding day.

There's no one in the waiting area tonight. The officer now behind the Plexiglas is young and lean, with a boyish smile and a boxer's nose; I imagine his weekends are filled with frothy women and pickup games of touch football. He's placing a coffee order with someone beyond my line of vision, '. . . three sugars and milk, and can you get me a chocolate cream-filled?' They make the expected joke about cops and doughnuts, and then he swivels in his chair, his smile disappearing when he sees me.

'Can I help you?' He looks down at a jumble of papers, his countenance a mask of indifference.

There's that stab, a familiar sense of otherness. 'I'm here for Linus Bartholomew.'

He doesn't look at me, just lifts the receiver and mumbles into the phone. I stand there after he hangs up, waiting for his instructions, but he simply shuffles the papers before him.

I turn and sit on the edge of a metal chair, alone, invisible again. It's hard to admit, but I don't want to be here, to see Linus vulnerable and broken. Thoughts of the days and weeks to come begin to buzz in my head, a prelude to a thickening ache. Though Linus will walk through these doors tonight, I doubt he'll ever be free again. To be linked to such a crime tars a person forever. I'll need to find an unknown reserve within myself that will sustain us both.

I feel in my pockets for a wayward aspirin, anything to quiet the deafening rush of thoughts. There's a sound on the other side of the wall behind the officer, a familiar voice and Linus's own low rumble. Then the stairwell door opens and he's ushered through, Jorge holding it ajar while Linus continues speaking.

'No, no, I appreciate it.' Linus gestures to me. 'Clara's going to be taking me home now. Thanks anyways.'

Jorge nods to me as Linus shuffles across the room. He places a hand on my back, an unconscious act of affection on his part. This time I allow it to remain.

'So I'll see you back here at one o'clock tomorrow with your lawyer?' Jorge asks, holding a folder, his expression a mixture of regret and disappointment.

'Oh, I'll be here, don't you worry.' Linus raises a hand over his shoulder; he's already headed for the exit.

The drizzle has cleared, though other clouds roll across the skies. Snow? We don't speak as we walk to the car. He leans on me the entire way; there's a thin layer of ice in the pockets of blacktop. I imagine both the cold and the sharp incline are difficult on his legs, and, of course, the long, horrible day that's taxed his whole. I help him into the passenger side of the hearse, then find my keys and turn the ignition. The vents blow full-on, cold at first, the stagnant air tinged with the odors of must and rot, odors familiar to my business. I stop at the light at the bottom of the concrete hill. Once it turns green, I make the left to return to Whitman.

'Clara,' Linus says, his voice strong, his face obscured by shadows. 'Go on ahead and ask. It's all right, it won't bother me none.'

I don't know if he can see in this dim light, but I shake my head. I think he's agreed to the silence until he shifts his weight and stares out the window. Shop signs whiz by in a dizzying flash of reds and blues, magnified and blurred by droplets the rain left behind on the windows. Then, 'Do you remember the day you came to our door?'

224

I continue driving, allowing the darkness to swallow the awkwardness. As he speaks, the timbre of his voice, the smoothness of its tone, lull me.

'Those were some dark days after Elton died. I prayed, I prayed hard for God to unveil his plan to me, for my purpose to be revealed. Course once you think you know God's plan, He goes and changes His mind again.'

Driving under a bridge, its sides crumbling, I see a homeless man propped against an abutment, a shopping carriage stationed next to him overflowing with his life. Ahead is a mattress warehouse, a check-cashing store-front, and the turn toward Whitman.

'We'll be home soon,' I say.

Linus ignores me, his voice humming now, trance-like, and in spite of myself, I'm hypnotized. 'I figured since you was an orphan and we was orphan parents, it made sense. Alma and me, we love you like you was our own.'

I place my hand over his. In spite of the heat that's blowing strong now, his skin is still frigid. I keep my gaze fixed on the road as I squeeze the meat of his palm. He bends his head to meet my hand and kisses it. I feel it there, something tangible and pure, something I can carry forward with me. I need to believe him, believe *in* him. I have to try.

'Alma said she's making her roast pork.' There's a catch in his voice before he clears his throat. 'Will you come to supper?'

'I'll be there,' I say, and then pull my hand free.

It doesn't take long to get home. I turn into the back entrance, to the parking lot that stretches between Linus's house and my cottage. Alma must have heard the car approaching, because all of the lot's floodlights are on. She's standing inside their doorway, her hands clasped in front of her. It isn't possible, it's probably the fluorescent light that hangs above her, accentuating every furrow and spot, but she appears to have aged a decade since this morning. She hurries outside to help Linus from the car.

'Look at you, you've gone and made my supper late. Now you're going to have to chew the tenderloin twice.' Her admonishment is belied by an arm she wraps around his waist, the other used to bolster him as he limps away from the car.

Linus smiles. 'Sorry, I got held up.' He stops to look at Alma and she meets his gaze. 'I really am sorry, Alma.'

'You have nothing to be sorry about, Linus Alvin Bartholomew. Do you hear me? Nothing!' She shakes him a little as she speaks. They pause when they reach their doorway, Alma straightening her back while Linus leans into her.

'Clara, give us fifteen minutes, would you, dear?' Alma says without turning. 'I should have dinner ready by then.'

'Can I bring anything?' But they don't hear me and so I make my own way home. It's a relief to be in my kitchen, walking through my living room and into my bedroom. It's none of these spaces I seek; they are only the route there. I yank open both doors to my greenhouse and step into its midst. I can feel my skin warm, my brain calm, the flow of my blood pulsating throughout my body slow. I sit in the doorway caught between these two worlds, between the pull of others' needs and those of my own. I breathe the incense of my garden, several deep breaths are all I remember, and then I'm jarred awake.

Before my eyes even open, I'm looking to my watch. I must have dozed off and now I'm late for dinner. It's been nearly half an hour, what must they think? I jerk myself up and find my shoes by the patio door. In my haste I forgo my coat, and outside I'm immediately besieged by a wind that pierces my thin shirt like shrapnel.

It's darker than when I was out last. The waxing gibbous moon is still visible, though the skies are heavy with clouds, their indistinct shape and foreboding gray threatening snow all week. The flakes will start any day.

My head is still dense with sleep, numb and slow. And then I realize what's different. The floodlights in the parking lot are out. Alma always leaves them on for me. She's like that. As I make my way to their house, another wind kicks up and blows through me, churning the clouds so that the moon's light is dimmed. I hear something: footfalls scraping against the bits of sand and rock covering the blacktop. They're quick and light, gone before I'm even certain that there were footsteps at all.

I slow, wary of my imagination and of the very real black ice and wayward rocks. I stumble anyway, landing on something hard and full. Another surge of wind pricks me, whipping dirt into my eyes, freeing the moon from its cover, and for an instant I can't see, blinking away the grit that scratches the delicate surface of my corneas.

When everything clears, I wish I could return to blindness.

There's a mound of clothes, a bundle of some sort, and I think of my dream. I reach out, knowing already that life has changed.

'Linus?' He's sprawled on the ground, his knees pulled in close, lying on his right side. I kneel and reach for his throat, needing to feel the pulse of his carotid artery under my fingertips. His eyes are open and I hear him then; his breaths come in quick, raspy succession.

'Clara?' It's a gurgle, but it's life.

'What happened?' There's a quaver to my voice and I squash it. My peripheral vision narrows to his face; everything else fades to gray. In the split second between his words and mine, a thousand thoughts cross my mind: Can I lift him? If I'd brought my coat, I could lay it across him. What if I have to press my lips to his, to breathe life into him?

'I was coming to get you for supper. . .' He's overcome by a wheezy cough.

'Do you have chest pains, Linus? Is it your heart?'

I run through the steps from the CPR course I took at Brockton Hospital. I may need to lay him flat on his back, check for a heartbeat, ensure he's breathing. Three puffs, fifteen chest compressions. Is that right?

'Clara,' he says. His words are a struggle.

'Linus, don't talk. I'm going to shift you, and then run inside and call 911.'

My hands move to his shoulders, but he grabs my wrist.

'Wait.' His chest explodes into another bout of coughing and blood erupts from his mouth.

Without thinking I grab my shirttails, catching the end of my ponytail, and begin to swipe at his face and neck. I roll him onto his back, reaching under both arms to prop him up so he won't choke, but it's slick there.

My fingers are at his neck again, but my hands are too slippery. I rub them on my shirt and feel them smear. Pulling them from the shadows, I hold them to the light that glows from the kitchen window where Alma is standing, stirring at a pot, unaware. My hands are streaked with blood. Too much.

'Alma!' I don't want to leave him, but she doesn't hear me. I scream again, high and jagged. 'Alma!'

The air embeds itself into my hair, crystallizing the sweat there. The mucus within and beyond my nostrils hardens as it freezes. The only warmth I have is from Linus's blood.

I tear open his wool cardigan and a button catches and skips free across the pavement. His white shirt glows in the refracted light, but there are shadows, too, spreading before my eyes. I press my hand to the ground and feel his life pooling beneath him.

'Linus, what happened?' I try to remember how many pints a person has, calculate the amount already gone.

'A man' – he sputters again – 'run, Clara.'

He pushes me away and then collapses. I hesitate, not knowing what to do, but I know I can't save him alone.

Before I can get to my feet, I hear him gasp, then dissolve into another wrenching spasm. I race to Alma, to help. As I rip open the storm door and find my footing on the stairs, another fierce wind is roused, whipping my matted hair against my cheek and neck. Though the winter air bellows and keens, still I can hear Linus's voice carried within it, 'Lord, take care of my Clara.'

CHAPTER TWENTY-TWO

The walls of Ellison Four are beige and blue, designed to soothe the anxieties of loved ones. The lighting strives for subtlety, though the floor is a dizzying scramble of marbled vinyl squares, dribs and drabs of color intended to blend with all manner of bodily fluids. The other oversight is the steady stream of announcements calling for a particular doctor to come decide the fate of a code green or blue.

I sit with Alma, both of us waiting for the nurses to settle Linus. Though we saw him briefly in the surgical intensive care's recovery room, he was still on a ventilator and bound to anesthesia's netherworld.

He was med-flighted here to Massachusetts General. Alma and I followed in the hearse, driving mostly in silence, Alma humming along to a hymn only she could hear. When we arrived at the emergency room, Dr. Belcher assured Alma that MGH had the best thoracic surgical unit in the nation, and therefore the world. His kind eyes and gentle face didn't shy from the fear reflected in hers.

'Your husband is very ill, Mrs. Bartholomew,' he said. 'His left lung was punctured and collapsed, and it appears he has several broken ribs. He's lost a lot of blood – he's still receiving transfusions. With his extra weight, it's putting quite a strain on his organs.'

When Dr. Belcher noticed me beside her, he looked to Alma for guidance. Alma was still wearing her apron, the aroma of garlic and fried potatoes woven into its fibers; it was all the comfort I had until she laid a hand on my shoulder, nudging me forward. I could feel it tremble there, pressing hard between the bones. 'This is our daughter, Clara.'

I didn't correct her. Dr. Belcher turned his attention to me, and if it were possible, his face softened still more. 'Why don't you come with me? I have an extra sweatshirt in my locker. You can clean up there.'

I'd forgotten Linus's blood. Only then did I wonder how Alma could have stood to be near me. When I returned to her side, two Whitman detectives were waiting to speak with me. Neither was recognizable from the interrogations the day before, but I assumed both had been briefed. I nearly hated them for that. Alma had already given her account. She had little to contribute; it was my statement they wanted.

'Can this wait?' I still felt dizzy after lathering my forearms and hands, watching the soap turn a deep salmon, seeing it splatter in the sink and then flow down the drain. When I looked in the mirror there was a long ragged streak of red down my cheek, curling around my neck. That's when I vomited.

'We're here to help,' said one, who introduced himself as Detective Marcolini. He was lean and strong, the type of man I imagine people wanted beside them in a crisis. 'The sooner you talk to us, the sooner we can catch the person who tried to kill Mr. Bartholomew.'

I suppose I should have known; there was no other explanation for the kind of wound he suffered. Perhaps it was the boldness of the words, stark and spoken, that finally penetrated.

'Kill Linus?'

'I'm sorry, Miss Marsh,' said the other detective. His name was Pingree. He was older with a long mustache that curled up at the ends; it made him appear to have a constant smile just above his lip. 'The doctor said he was knifed. What we're hearing from the crime scene is that the lines to the outside lights were cut. Did you see anyone when you found Mr. Bartholomew? Hear anything unusual?'

'No, nothing.'

With their prompting, I told them about finding Linus. About stumbling over him, the weight of his blood, and then I remembered his words.

'He said there was a man. He told me to run.' That's when Alma came to me, tried her best to take me in her arms. 'My God, he told me to run.' It was the first time a woman wanted to hold me since my mother died.

Looking back, I realize I didn't know enough to put my arms around her too.

I don't know what else I said beyond that, what more I could have offered, but we continued to talk for several minutes before Dr. Belcher reappeared. 'They're going to take your husband down to the O.R. now,' he said.

'Can I go with him?' Alma asked, already gathering her purse, looking over Dr. Belcher's shoulder to the doors that separated her from Linus.

'I'm sorry,' Dr. Belcher said. 'They're already on their way.'

'Can I at least say good-bye?' The grooves and shadows I'd seen on her face earlier – a play of light, I'd thought – had settled in, as if the previous features I'd come to know were a thin veneer easily splintered and swept away.

Dr. Belcher took her hand in both of his. 'I'll say a prayer for you.' And then he left.

Alma's face was resolute. 'I think I'll go find the chapel now. Will you walk with me?'

Detective Marcolini interrupted, his brown eyes twin pools of compassion. 'We'd appreciate it if you stayed around. We still have a few questions.'

But I was already guiding Alma to the exit. They'd have to wait.

They did, of course, but I didn't have anything to add when I returned. That was yesterday, hours ago, though not quite a full day. We've sat here in these chairs, in the family waiting area, allowing the television to do the talking between us, helping ourselves to syrupy coffee and Dixie cups of cold spring water. The only times we've stepped away have been to use the women's room, though never together. Each time, Alma returns a little more withered, her eyes averted, swollen and bloodshot through. I'm tired of the odor of pine antiseptic used to mop the floors.

'Bartholomew family?' A nurse is at the door, leaning against the doorjamb, her head peeking in.

'Right here.' Alma stands, her knuckles taut, her purse dangling in front of her.

'You can go in now.'

We walk down the hallway, and I can't help but wonder at the strength in Alma's legs and back; how it is she's able to stand erect in spite of the yoke of accusations and violence.

As we pass the elevator, the doors glide open and Mike is standing there. He seems to be from my distant past, not yesterday; too much has happened in the hours in between. Though his clothes are pressed, his hair neat, and he's shaved clean again, he manages to appear as wasted as I feel.

He goes to Alma first. 'How's he doing?'

'We're going to see him now.'

'With your permission, I'd like to see him after you.'

Mike holds her stare and she doesn't look away. Instead, she raises an eyebrow and tilts her chin. 'No questions.' It's a command not a plea.

'Kate McCarthy from my office is downstairs with a

couple of Whitman detectives – you met them yesterday,' Mike says. 'They don't know I'm here.'

Alma looks to me, but before I can speak, she nods.
'I'll see how he is.'

She walks away and I follow, but Mike catches my
arm.

'Clara.'

There are so many thoughts caught in the furrow of
his brow, his mouth, but I don't want to hear any of
them. I pull myself free.

'I should have assigned a detail to his house. I should
have known with a case like this, word would leak and
some vigilante would go after him.' He pauses. 'It's my
fault.'

I nod and turn to follow Alma, but before I get far, he
calls to me. 'I'm sorry.'

It's as though I've been stabbed myself, the words cutting, spinning me around. My hand seeks comfort in a
spiral of hair. 'You're *sorry*?'

His hands are shoved into his overcoat pockets, tensed
and balled, straining through the wool. 'I was wrong.
About Linus. I don't know what he was doing, making
those calls, but my gut tells me he didn't intend to hurt
anybody.'

He's staring at me, and it would be so easy to go to him
now. Fall against his chest, allow him to bear the weight
of my bones and troubles. I remember how strong his
arms were around me, the smell at the hollow between
his shoulders and neck. And I'm so very tired.

But I am not a fool.

If I were a different woman, I could tell Mike everything. That life is complex and messy, filled with cruelties beyond even his experiences. I could try to explain what it is to live among the dead, to bear witness to their last struggles for life, fighting for one more breath even when their lives weren't worth living at all. The way their vessels constricted within their eyes, their throats, the way a hand can be found still grasping toward another moment. Just one more. I've seen that yearning inside and out. Guts clenched, muscles flexed. I could describe the pearls of bruises that encircle lovely throats, the shredded spleens from shod feet, the slashes and entry wounds and multitude of crushed skulls that needed reinforcing for open caskets. I would tell Mike that never before or since have I witnessed such savagery as I did when Precious Doe was discovered. I don't know how it's possible for mere skin and bones to contain something as combustible, as wholly wicked, as the evil that prowls our world, seeking the most vulnerable among us. I would tell Mike that monsters really do exist. Most of all, I would plead with him to recognize that Linus is a good man. He must be.

'Linus didn't hurt anyone.' It's the best I can do.

Mike falls into one of the plastic chairs near the elevator. His back is bowed, his elbows at his knees. He stares at the floor as he speaks. It's a relief not to see his face.

'Every day in my job and in my life, I have to somehow make right other people's wrongs. And most times, there's so much bad in the world, in my world, sometimes it's hard to trust the good.' His voice is beaten and I can't help being reminded of when Linus brought him into the basement to say farewell to his wife and unborn child.

Mike stands before continuing. 'You and I believe Linus didn't kill Precious Doe, but my boss and the cops from Whitman are on their way up right now. He's the prime suspect.'

'He's innocent.'

He strides toward me, quick and sure. 'But he knows something, Clara. He made the calls. How does he know?'

I almost tell him then about the little girl and her dog Peanut, about the boyfriend, the untouchable Victor; but Alma interrupts.

'Clara.' She's down the hall standing just outside one of the rooms, her face resigned. 'Linus is asking for you.'

I go to her and behind me hear Mike say, 'How is he?'

Alma grasps my elbow, steering me aside before I go in. She's now the woman I knew before tonight, formidably composed, solidly forthright. 'The doctor said the best we can do is wait and see. It's been a shock to his system. Their biggest concern in people his age is cardiac arrest. At least he's off the respirator and can talk.'

I shake my head and feel my mind tumble. It's an

effort not to give in to the faint. When Alma's voice breaks through the fugue, I cling to it. 'We need to be prepared for the worst. I'm going to go call Reverend Greene.'

Mike and Alma continue speaking as I walk into Linus's room. A nurse, blond and pretty, is tucking a crisp white blanket under him. There are countless tubes buried in and snaking out of his body. One is pumping yet more blood into him. It's mesmerizing. His feet are somewhat propped, each encased in a blue plastic boot. Machines are at the ready, flashing, beeping their warnings: a platoon of sentries guarding his life.

And there is Linus, his eyes closed, his face hidden under an oxygen mask. Even though the nurse is talking, his breathing crackles above her voice. Though she tries to smile, her eyes droop with pity. 'You must be Clara. My name's Julie. He's resting now, but he's been asking for you.' She adjusts an IV line and then reaches for a cord clipped to his bed.

'This is his pain medication. He has an epidural, but if he wakes up and needs more, let me know. He'll get it directly through this IV. It might make him a little spacey, but we want to make sure he's comfortable.'

She sets the cord back and points to another below it. 'This is the call button; use it if he wakes in any distress. I'm right outside.' She pauses, reaching out to me and then pulling back. 'Please don't stay long, he's very critical.'

'Thank you.'

Her words are too much and I'm grateful for the relative silence when she leaves. Linus's hand is heavy in mine, huge and steady, the kind that's known work. I trace the ridges of his knuckles, the lines of his palm. In spite of his current state there is strength here, a kind of sturdiness I've always known but never really acknowledged, not even to myself. How many times has he swallowed my hand with this one when he gave thanks at supper, placed this hand upon my shoulder to praise my work? And always I pulled away.

'Clara?' His voice is muffled through the oxygen mask. He drags it down along his neck, wincing as he moves.

'Are you in pain?' He manages a nod. I don't call the nurse; instead I press the button, releasing more narcotics into his bloodstream. It doesn't take long before the tension eases from his face.

'You're okay,' he says, his words slow.

I nod, biting my cheek to stave off the tears.

'I thought they was lying when I didn't see you.'

'I've been here the whole time. Don't talk now, you need to rest.' I try to replace the oxygen mask, remembering the doctor's warnings, but he brushes it away.

'I've always loved you like you was my own.'

'Try to rest.'

'You need to know the truth.' He's caught by a spasm, his chest contracting with each hack. I fit the mask over his face, pushing aside his hand.

'How's he doing?' Mike is standing in the doorway. Just beyond him in the hall, Alma is talking to Kate and the other Whitman detectives. Alma shakes her head, her arms crossed in protest.

'I don't know,' I say.

Mike walks around to the other side of Linus's bed. He scans the array of equipment and turns his attention back to Linus, his hands braced against the metal railing. Linus motions to the mask. Mike pulls it free. I protest, but both ignore me.

Linus clears his throat, the phlegm catching and then gurgling again. He looks to Mike. 'I am the anonymous caller – don't go blaming Reverend Greene. He was protecting me from the slings and arrows. We trusted you to do what's right.'

Mike squeezes the rails of Linus's bed as he listens.

Between the crowd outside and the intensity of this room, I feel my chest clutch and pull. 'He needs to rest.'

Linus waves me off, clearing his throat again, and I feel my own catch. 'There are things that need saying before I die, Clara.'

'You are not dying!' My whisper is fierce, and I almost believe it's enough to frighten away the forces trying to claim him.

For a moment his voice is as it was, rich and textured, filled with life. 'Oh, I'm dying all right. They're all here waiting for me to show them the way home. They been waiting a long time now.'

'Linus.' Mike's voice rings through this peculiar air

that's settled around us. 'How did you know about Precious Doe?'

'Mike,' I say. 'He doesn't know what he's saying. He's on a lot of medication.'

Linus sputters. 'Trecie. Trecie told me everything. Told me more that night you was looking for her at Clara's. She was in the mourning room all along, with Angel.'

Mike nods and I try not to imagine Trecie's face transfixed by Angel's dead one. 'Why didn't you tell us, Linus?' Mike persists. 'We could have helped her.'

Linus doesn't answer, focused instead on some point beyond the foot of his bed. My mind is not my own, and I think of the other children hidden away behind Trecie's apartment door. No one knows how many; no one would miss one. Perhaps another one went missing three years ago and no one noticed.

'Linus,' Mike says, 'do you know who did this to you?'

Linus shakes his head and then begins to cough again, straining to sit up. 'They're here now. See them? Can't you see them right there?' He's pointing to the end of the bed as he calls to his specters. 'You're okay, the Lord's coming to take us all home.'

'Don't leave me! Alma!' I cry out for her and she hurries into the room, past Mike, pushing him aside.

'Linus?' Her hands press on either side of his face, pleading with him.

'It's okay, Alma, I'm going to see our Elton now.' He

smiles as tears slip away, forming ever-widening spots on either side of his pillow. Then his body convulses and his breaths come in wispy, reckless succession. As if from a distance, the machines begin to scream their warnings, their beeps turning to loud, flat wails.

'No!' I place my hands over the spot where his heart should beat, but there's nothing.

In the next moment, he grows quiet. In spite of the machines' noise, the room has an eerie silence about it. There's a stillness about Linus, too: the way the muscles in his face relax, how his arms and legs fall limp against the bed. His face, it's his face, one I know better than my own – though now it's a shell, in an instant the life within it gone. It's as if he's disappeared (*breathe, one-two-three*). My body reacts without my knowledge and my hands are suddenly on him, pushing and pushing against his chest. I feel a rib crack beneath me. 'Don't leave me!'

'Somebody help him!' Alma screams. She reaches for the nurse's call button, her thumb pressing again and again. A voice through an intercom mumbles a response, but Julie is already running into the room, whipping her stethoscope free from her neck. She immediately replaces Linus's oxygen mask and reaches for the nurse's button.

'I have a code blue.'

Alma and I are thrust against the back wall while Mike slips out the door, and instantly the room is flooded with bodies hovering over Linus. I turn away when one of them plunges a tube down his throat. As Alma recites the Lord's Prayer, I find myself looking around the room for the lost souls waiting for Linus to lead them home, wishing I could call him back.

CHAPTER TWENTY-THREE

The snow billows in soft tufts, blanketing the bed of crumpled leaves that already fill the basement window wells. There is a delicate rustling as the flakes settle into place and then nothing as they smother all other sounds. The late-afternoon sun waning in its sky is further dulled by thickening clouds, stray wisps of light filter through here and there. I expect others will be cheered by the prospect of a white Christmas.

It is frigid here in my workspace, surrounded by the frozen ground. With each exertion, my breath condenses before me.

I remove an ivory taper from the drawer and fit it onto my worktable. Its new wick takes several matches before catching, sparking in protest. The voices from Mozart's *Requiem* swell as the flame steadies and glows.

Just this once there is no mask, no gloves between my skin and the body. I turn to the sink and let the water run, waving my fingers through the stream every so often, feeling it eventually warm from the initial cold splash. I hold my hand under as it begins to truly heat, clouds of steam filling the basin. It's a thousand pin-pricks against the numbness.

I bring a stainless-steel bowl over to the sink and the cake of soap I stole from the master bathroom. It's a rich brown, yellowed around the edges where his hands wore away the best of it. It smells of cocoa butter and honey. It smells of Linus. I carry the bowl back to the worktable and begin working a lather against the washcloth.

The medical examiner, Richard, was careful to close his incisions with fine stitches to match Linus's flesh, a gesture of respect for his old friend. Of course an autopsy was required because of the nature of his death. There were many allowances, however. Mike and I were per-mitted to wheel his body through the hospital's warrens the dead are required to travel, underground tunnels hidden away from other patients and their families, all leading to dreary caves where hearses can slip in and out unseen. Mike covered my hand with his own where they met at the handle of the stretcher. Alma walked behind us, her chin aloft and face clear, Richard a discreet ten paces behind. Though it's forbidden to disturb a body in the care of the medical examiner, still she unzipped the body bag and kissed Linus's lips before we loaded him into the car. No one dared protest. I followed Richard the few miles to his office while Mike drove Alma home. I promised her I wouldn't leave Linus. It didn't take long.

The music pauses before the tentative strings of *Lacrymosa* flow into this room. My hands start at Linus's feet, swirling upward, leaving a trail of soap in their wake. His legs, then I trace the cloth along his stomach, starting at the center and waking in an ever-widening spiral. Where it's wet, his skin is darker, purely glistening. I dip the cloth back into the scalding water, rubbing what's left of the soap against it, and then cleanse his arms and the crevices of his neck. I hesitate before washing his face. His eyes are now forever closed to this world and the people in it. They will never catch me again, hold me there. It was as close to an embrace as I permitted. I study the crease of his lips, the way the bottom one protrudes just beyond the top. What would it have cost me to have allowed a kiss to the top of my head, to my cheek? The utter smoothness of his skin, like a baby's, all gone to me now.

I look at his hand and remember the one concession I made, how I reached for it in the car and held it in my own. How I felt something true there. It's all I have.

I'm gentle with the cloth, careful to keep his eyebrows aligned, his lashes separated. When I'm done, I pull a soft blue blanket up to his neck, tucking it under the width of his shoulders. It was in their linen closet; it smells of Alma's detergent. I couldn't allow her to see him covered in a common plastic sheet.

There's nothing left for me to do. Over the years, Linus spoke of his death often. His instructions were always clear: He wanted his face in a natural state. Once he's dressed, I'll transfer him to the casket and lay him out upstairs. It occurs to me that this will be one of the last moments I have alone with him.

'Linus.' I bend to his ear, my voice unnatural in this space. 'I know you're dead and can't hear me. But I want to say . . .'

I lift his hand, stiff from the formaldehyde. It moves only slightly, just enough for me to wrap my own around it. It's swollen and cold, unnatural, not at all the way I remember it. Now it's like those of all the other bodies I've prepared. I let it go before the memory of that touch overtakes the way I remember it in life.

I whisper the rest. There's more, but words are difficult things. They choke my throat and bind my chest. So instead I do what I wish I had done during Linus's life. I bow over his great chest and lay my head there. Soon my arms find their way around him, embracing this man who would have been my father if only I'd allowed it. If he had a lap, I'd climb onto it. I stay like that until my back aches, until the silence where his heartbeat should have been becomes unbearable.

Before I smooth the balm on his lips, I bend to kiss him. I could stand here, lose the day in his face, but Alma is waiting upstairs. She intends to dress him alone. Later, when it's time to bring him upstairs to the mourning room, I'll bring all of the irises (*faith, hope, wisdom*) from my greenhouse to make a bed for him in the casket. Only I will know the fleurs-de-lis are there.

Stepping outside, I phone Alma, but there's no answer, so I'll have to leave her a note, let her know her husband is ready. How does one word such a thing?

I walk the flight of stairs up to the mourning room.

When I open the door, Alma looks up from one of the leather wingbacks, her ankles crossed, a garment bag draped across her lap. Her back is rigid and her face clear.

'Is he ready?' Her voice is so firmly tethered to this world, solid and familiar.

'Yes.'

She stands, sighing as she does. 'I turned the ringer off. Reporters keep calling, one after another. I'm ignoring the doorbell for now too. Besides, this place will be filled the next few days. I don't think we can take on any new business just yet.'

'Of course,' I say. Still she doesn't move.

'It's a shame, you know? I have all this meat in the freezer. I was saving the rack of lamb for Sunday dinner; you know how it was his favorite. I don't know what I'm going to do with the mint jelly, either. Seems a waste, cooking for just one.' Alma stops, lost in thought. I catch a glimpse of the woman she'll become in the next few years: heavily lined, her mahogany skin grown ashen and slack. She's never appeared fragile before this. I think of how she held me at the hospital when my legs began to give and I wish I knew how to go to her. But I don't, of course I don't, and she regains herself anyway.

'Clara,' she says, steady again. 'We need to talk.'

There is no way to tell her no, so instead I stand several feet before her and wait.

'All of this is yours now.' She sweeps her free arm. 'This house, this business, everything.'

'Alma — '

'I'll continue living here, for as long as that will be.' Her expression is perfectly serene. 'I've lost all of my sisters over the years, and of course, my son. Now I've lost my husband—'

'Please don't.' This was never my plan. True, I don't have one, but I cannot be responsible for all that she's giving me. I don't know how.

'I don't expect you to take care of me, that's not what I'm saying.' She walks toward me. 'You're all the family I have left. Whether you know it or not, whether you like it or not, we're family *here*.' She grabs my hand and slams it against her heart. 'I need you to stay.'

I look away at first, but am pulled back. It's unbearable, how I ache to turn, but she won't let go. Again and again my eyes wander.

'Look at me, Clara.' I think of Linus lying one floor below us and summon all the will I have. I meet her and, when I do, feel a loosening within. Her heart pounds under my hand and her eyes are soft.

'I'll stay,' I finally say.

Her lips tremble toward a smile. She cups my chin, holds my gaze, and then brushes past me to the basement door, hugging the garment bag to her.

CHAPTER TWENTY-FOUR

Whorls unfurled themselves while I neglected my garden; ivory, crimson, pink confetti petals celebrating their debut. Though I was no longer mindful of their need to be showered twice daily and bathed for eight full hours under the solar heat lamps, still my flowers survived. Buoyant poppies (*consolation from beyond*) hover in a scarlet wave at the back of the room. There they mingle with gladioli (*ready-armed*), upright stalks heavy with periwinkle bells, caught in midair, ringing out proclamations of life and promise. Coneflowers huddle in the corner, lost among themselves.

Outside, the skies remain their foreboding gray while snow continues to fall, first drowning out the sun and now moon, yet still the flowers blossomed. My garden will be more dependent on me during the cold months. This past week has seen the weather turn from our crisp, glaring autumn to New England's brittle winter. Soon the ground will be too hard to bury the dead; the bodies will be stacked until spring, when the earth is yielding and tender again. It's life's eternal pledge to rejuvenate itself, but now that hope seems distant.

It would be unbearable to intern Linus's body in the basement all winter alongside those yet to come. I called the caretaker of Colebrook Cemetery yesterday while I waited outside the medical examiner's office and had him dig the plot before the snow fell.

I close my greenhouse door behind me. Reaching for the switch along the wall, I turn the dimmer low so that only those lights set into the steps and along my path glow a bare white.

I need to cleanse myself of the ugliness of the past few days, bathe in the beauty of my garden. My shoes slip off easily and with them, my woolen socks. The tiles are warm, almost hot against my skin. I drop my sweater on top of my things, pull free the elastic that restrains my hair, then walk down to meet my flowers. Each step is careful, deliberate; my joints are still thick from the cold basement, the rest of me numb from preparing Linus's body. As I unbutton my blouse, I think of Alma next door, struggling to pull on his shirt. I slip off my pants and know how it can be to drag trousers over inflexible limbs. But I must wash away these thoughts.

I'm here to savor the warmth, find some semblance of order that doesn't really exist. I reach between a grove of copper ambrosia (*love returned*) and find the faucet. With effort, the knob finally gives and the overhead sprinklers fill. Raising my face to catch the rain, I cup the head of a red-hot poker (*fierce in life*).

The water is cold, the air stifling, and together they prick my skin. My bra and panties and hair cling to me. I push back the strands covering my eyes and catch sight of something wondrous. The daisies are growing. I go to them, marvel at the ridged leaves of the infant flowers, so close to the earth in their terra-cotta pots, pressing, their stems still hidden beneath the soil. Beads of water pool and then run down them, and I can feel the same on me. The odor of wet dirt is familiar in too many ways.

I need time to think. Everything needs to stop so I can be here among my flowers and listen, allow my thoughts to wander. I lower myself onto the tile floor and feel its hardness penetrate me. Towers of aster loom; one catches the strap along my shoulder, caresses the length of my throat. Their marmalade scent and lavender faces soothe me. I rest my cheek against them.

It will be safe to cry here.

It's then I hear it: a knock at the back door leading out to the yard. The windows of my greenhouse rattle with it. My legs won't move, my eyes won't blink. And then I see him, pushing open the door.

'Clara?'

Mike doesn't notice me sitting here, hidden by my garden. I've faded into my surroundings, translucent as water; invisible like so many other times in my life.

He closes the door behind him, ignoring the showers overhead. His shoes slap at the puddles. 'Clara?'

His voice is louder now and there's a catch to it as he reaches under his suit coat. A snap and then his gun is out. He lowers himself behind a cluster of black-eyed Susans (*warm remembrance*) set upon a bench.

Both hands are wrapped around the gun as he sidles toward the door to my bedroom. This is a man I've never seen before: primal, capable of violence. Somehow it reassures me. He squats close to the ground as he approaches the two steps leading out of the greenhouse, his head swiveling as he moves. When he reaches for the door, I step out from my spot.

'Mike.'

In an instant he is upright and spun around, his gun locked on me. I can already feel a bullet burning a path through my chest. I wait for it, ready to fall.

'Jesus Christ!' Mike cries, lowering both hands before him. He doubles over, gasping. 'What the hell are you doing?'

I should feel naked, cover myself; I expect modesty to overcome me, the way my body has grown visible through the white cotton. Instead I'm suddenly alive. 'Why are you here?'

He holsters his gun and walks toward me, wiping the water from his face as he does. 'Your hearse was outside but you weren't at the funeral home, and when I rang the bell here, you didn't answer.'

I take a step. 'And?'

'I was worried, after what happened to Linus.' His eyes fall to my breasts and stomach, then lower. Streams that sluice within the lines around his eyes, the creases along his nose, shift with his expression. Droplets catch on his lips and then fall before he speaks again. 'I couldn't find you.'

I nod. He appears strong. His suit jacket darkens under the weight of water, his white shirt plastered to his chest reveals a rise of muscle across his stomach, a glance of bare flesh, and there's the hint of something more, something indistinguishable. I take another step.

'You're okay,' he whispers.

All I can do is shake my head. A part of me begs to cover my nakedness, hide the naked patches along my skull, create more, but, no, I won't go back. I continue toward him, watching his eyes dart around the room and then back to me.

Another step and the corner of his jacket grazes my navel. I arch my neck to meet his face.

'You're okay,' he whispers against my lips.

I continue shaking my head no, feeling my mouth brush his as I do. He reaches for my face and stills me. We could stop here. I could step away, walk to my room – he out the back door – and I could find comfort in my robe. Instead, I press myself into him.

I pull off his suit jacket, the sleeves turn inside out, and it drops to the floor. Of the thousands of buttons I've undone in my work, none have come so easily as those of his shirt. It's then I see it. A Celtic cross, lines of gold and red ink staining his flesh, an intricate expression of devotion. It lies across his chest, dropping as low as his waist. I press my fingers to it, to its north, south, east, and west, to its mind, body, heart, and soul. His stomach tenses under my touch. So thin. He lifts my chin with the barest caress and we regard each other. I imagine my gaze is as certain as his. When he breaks it to glance down and unclip his gun belt, it's as if the sun has gone down and my body wilts against his, straining for its warmth.

My hands are not my own; my hands would never reach for a man's belt, eager and impatient to loosen it, and then unfasten the pants button beneath it. When I feel his fingers on me, trailing up my back, fumbling before releasing the clasp of my bra, the urgency within me quickens. His breathing is jagged, but his fingers are smooth against my hips as they hook the sides of my panties. He slips them down my legs, kneeling before me, and I step out of them. He kisses my thighs, presses his face there, inhales deeply, and then stands again. He works his fingers through my hair, finding my shame, each of his fingers tracing the ridges of sores, his eyes never leaving mine. He pulls me closer.

Then my arms are around his neck and he lifts me onto the edge of my potting table. He is taut and flexed, hard under me. I curve myself around him, bury my nose in his hair. My mouth tastes the back of his neck: salt and sweat and life.

It's frantic, impatient; there's neither the time nor the desire to finesse a moment before it's over. When he lowers me to my feet, I feel the muscles of his arms shake. He collapses against me, each of us trembling. We stay like that with my ear pressed to his chest, until his heart no longer pounds, until it returns to a constant beat.

He lifts his head from mine, taking my face within both his hands. He tilts my mouth toward his, pausing to look at me first, probing, as if seeking a refuge within me.

And then we kiss.

CHAPTER TWENTY-FIVE

I dried his clothes while he slept. When they were done, I pressed his suit and then hung everything from the back of my bedroom door. He'll see them when he wakes. When I look quickly, it's as if there are two of him here.

He's stretched out, facedown, a naked calf resting outside of the blankets. My sheets have been pulled free from their snug hospital corners, my down comforter fluffed from his restless sleep. He spoke once as if from a dream, but the only word I could make out was 'sorry.'

After . . . well, after the greenhouse, we came here.

With my head against his shoulder, our limbs spun one round another, we found refuge in the dark. It wasn't until I started to fall toward sleep that he spoke.

'I asked her to get an abortion, but she wouldn't.' There was nothing to say, so I listened. 'You know I actually prayed she'd lose the baby? I did.'

Several minutes went by, his breathing was regular. *He's asleep,* I thought.

'Guess my prayers were answered.'

We didn't speak again, just held each other against the night. When he finally drifted off, I slipped away. I've sat in this chair most of the night, sliding between vivid dreams and surreal wakefulness, my thoughts turning again and again to Linus, until the tears finally came. There was enough time to bury the rest of myself before the sun rose.

It's been a comfort to watch Mike, to have had this one night. He'll be awake soon and it will be over; dawn is beginning to seep through. There's the gentle catch of his snore before he stretches and turns. The red and gold inks crisscross his belly, a patchwork of betrayal. No sense attaching myself to the moment; I don't have any expectations that there will be more like this.

I dressed hours earlier; there's much to be done. Linus's wake is in three days, on Christmas Eve, no less. Enough time to allow his family in Alabama to make arrangements to travel here and then stay on for the holiday. Alma said she couldn't imagine waking to a quiet house on Christmas morning. But I need to concern myself with now.

Without realizing it, I stand, take the few steps to Mike's side, and kneel there. He is truly asleep. I allow myself to smell his hair, that spot on his neck; how I ache to touch him. Instead I whisper.

'When I was in tenth grade, there was a boy who sat in front of me in math. I didn't know him, really. I knew he played hockey and that he liked geometry, but we didn't talk. Each time he passed back papers, he'd smile at me. Just to be nice – he didn't *like* me. Sometimes, when he came to class he'd say 'Hi, Clara' loud enough for the other kids to hear. Everyone liked him.'

Mike stirs and then his snores grow even again, his lips slightly parted, tender. It's safe.

'Once, while Mrs. Witham was at the chalkboard, he passed me a note. It said all of the kids were signing a petition, 'Clara Marsh Number One Slut,' but he refused to sign it. He even ripped it up. No one challenged him. All these years, I've saved his note.'

I watch Mike's eyes flutter and wait for them to open. Before they do, I take my seat and whisper, 'You remind me of him.'

He becomes restless, turns before he wakes, and then his focus is on me. 'Clara.'

He pushes himself up, but I refuse to linger over the paths my hands discovered along his body last night. His eyes are mere creases, his cheeks swollen with sleep, and his usually precise hair is wayward and lush. Mostly I avoid his mouth, the way it turns soft when he sees me.

I concentrate on my nightstand just beyond him, my gaze settling on *The Stone Diaries*. 'Mike, we have to go.'

'You're dressed? What time is it?' He turns to my nightstand, where the digital clock glows, and then to his clothes waiting for him. The shield that normally obscures his eyes descends. 'Yeah, I guess I'll be on my way.'

He stands, free of modesty, his back, his nakedness before me, but I refocus on the book. Its cover is of a limestone angel, her face in shadows and crowning her head, a laurel (*victory over passion*). Mike begins pulling on his pants with quick, jerky movements. His belt jangles with each tug.

'I have to tell you something, something I did,' I say. 'It's about Trecie.'

He stops and then turns. His voice is quiet when he speaks. 'What is it?'

I avert my eyes from his body, focusing on the matter at hand. It's a dilemma I have to face, a moment beyond whatever depths of courage I may have. I've already lost too much; I have to try. 'Three days ago, I met a little girl who I think could be Trecie's sister. The resemblance is so strong.'

His face relaxes and he lets escape a pent breath. He walks around the bed and kneels in front of my chair, taking my hand in his, smiling kindly as he speaks. 'Clara, there are a lot of little girls who look like Trecie. Brown hair and brown eyes are pretty common.'

'There's more.'

He releases my hand as I tell him of Mr. Kelly's Chihuahua, Peanut; the boyfriend; and what the pregnant neighbor told me, of the man who visits there, the untouchable. As I tell him all of this his expression changes, the warmth within his eyes bleeds out, and I grow cold, but still I talk.

When I finish, he stands and walks back to the hanger on the door and begins dressing again, his back to me.

'Mike.'

He doesn't answer, and I will myself to stand, to go to him and try again. Linus is dead and Trecie is in danger. Though I can sense the miles between us, I press toward him.

'Mike.'

'Why didn't you tell me?' His face is expressionless. He's pulled down his detective's facade, but I can see him there, beneath it, the layers of pain and betrayal rising to the surface. I wonder if my own mask has become as flimsy to him.

'I tried.' My voice is low and I can feel the rage of the past days begin to flow through me. 'And then you were on the other side of the interrogation table.'

He stares at me for a few seconds before reaching for his cell phone. And then I feel the air leave my body, stricken by a realization that should have been clear days ago. But so much has transpired in so little time. I needed to think, to listen to my thoughts.

'Who are you calling?' I ask.

'Kate. She and I are going to see the girl, see if she's connected to all of this.'

'No.' I grab the phone from him, snap it closed, and throw it onto the bed. 'You can't tell anyone.'

'What the hell are you doing?' He steps to the bed and snatches up the phone. He flips it open again and begins to dial.

'Mike, I think Victor is a cop.'

He doesn't acknowledge me, just continues holding the cell to his ear. I hear it ring on the other end. Once, twice, three times. I can't let anything more happen to Trecie.

'I won't tell you where the apartment is. I won't help you find her.'

He studies my face, my hair, and then closes the phone, running a hand across his mouth as he does. 'Clara, was that your hair I found in the greenhouse the night Trecie disappeared?'

There's nothing else to say; she needs me. 'I don't know. I don't think so.'

He runs his thumb along my jaw and nods. 'Okay. Look, I know you want to help these kids – '

'Mike, you and I will go there. You can talk to the girl, but only you. There's a chance we might find Trecie. We have to find her before we tell anyone.'

'Kate is my supervisor. I need to include her. We'll let Internal Affairs figure out whoever this Victor is, if he even is a cop.'

I want to tear at him, make him taste my fear. 'The neighbor said she called the police a few years ago and the officer who showed up kicked out the boyfriend. She said the new boyfriend is untouchable.'

He pats my arm. 'Kate and I will head over there, talk to the family. I know everyone on the department and there's no Victor. Ryan can go back to the SPCA, find out who adopted Charlie Kelly's dog, and Jorge can ask around the station about this Victor guy.'

'No.' He should understand.

'Clara, trust me.'

He reaches for me, but I push his arms away. 'Mike, who knew Linus was the anonymous caller?'

'Kate, myself, Jorge, Ryan, the detectives from Whitman. Everyone investigating the case.'

'Did anyone call the press?' I'm nauseated; the bile is clawing its way up my esophagus and into my throat, where it settles and burns.

'No.' Mike grimaces when he says this. 'They haven't made the link yet between him and the Precious Doe case. But it's only a matter of time before it's leaked.'

He must see it in me then, the realization I made minutes ago. He smacks his palms against his temples and begins pacing the room. 'Shit!'

His agitation quiets my sense of panic. He's with me now.

'Linus wasn't killed by some vigilante, Mike.'

He comes to me. He takes me by the arms and pulls me into him. 'I know.'

It doesn't matter if he hears me whisper the name into his chest, but he doesn't have to, because he knows. He knows. 'Victor.'

CHAPTER TWENTY-SIX

We're on the metal stairs. Mike's footsteps aren't muffled by the frayed carpeting that covers the steps and instead echo throughout the stairwell. My own are silent, tentative. When we reach the landing of the little girl's floor, I can't help but seek out the mouse hole. I'm not disappointed. There's a simple trap just outside the opening, its metal band clasped snugly over the brown rodent's neck. Its paws are stretched wide beside it and the black tail is strung long. If Mike notices, he doesn't say anything.

Before coming here, we stopped at Mike's house so he could change. Having driven by it many times before, I knew which modest Cape was his. He asked me in, but I waited in the car. It was enough to see the *The Sullivans* painted in trailing cursive on their mailbox. He didn't take long. When he returned, when he placed his hands on the steering wheel and twisted around to back out of the driveway, I noticed the band of white skin where his wedding ring had been. When he saw me staring at that spot, he brushed my cheek with his fingers and tried to smile.

Mike pulls open the landing door and we walk down what has become a familiar corridor for me. Though I can no longer smell Eileen Craig, there still exists an eeriness to this place: the pregnant woman's doorway festooned with aluminum garland and a large cutout of Santa Claus, defaced with black Magic Marker genitalia; just beyond, an abandoned plastic shopping bag ripe with near-empty cans of cat food; and farther down, the sound of a small dog yelping.

I motion to Mike when we reach the girl's apartment. There's the usual noise of the television, children's voices arguing in terse, quiet snatches, and, of course, the barking. He pauses to bow his head before raising a fist to knock.

The same girl answers, pressing her tiny body within the crack of the door. The pup is at her feet, cowering behind her legs.

Like the dog, I hide behind Mike, hoping the girl can't see me. He tenses and then strains his neck to peer into the room before looking down at the girl. 'Hey, there.'

She doesn't answer, just stares at him with blank eyes, an expression I've seen only on the most hardened adults. She appears not to notice the dog scratching at her calves.

'Is your mom home?' Mike keeps his voice soft and upbeat, but I notice the strain, as if he's trying to suppress a cough. The girl simply shakes her head. Any doubts I had, any second-guessing on the ride over, vanish when I look past Mike and catch the girl staring at me. Her nostrils flare as she bends to scoop the dog into her thin arms.

Mike reaches for his wallet and flashes his badge to her. 'My name is Mike. I'm a friend of Victor's. Can we come in?'

Everything about her grows slack before she opens the door wider and allows us to step in. There are the other children I've only heard before; three boys, all thin and hypnotized by the television, and a sister who can't be more than six. She has the same long hair as the older girl's, but her face is different: darker, with a broader nose and a pink, quarter-sized birthmark splotched across her left cheek. They don't turn when we enter. At the center of their semicircle is a large soda bottle filled with water and a plastic bowl, empty save for some popcorn kernels. On the kitchen counter, cereal boxes lie on their sides next to plates caked with hardened food; scattered throughout are several empty bottles of cough medicine.

Within the galley kitchen, I spot trash overflowing its container and piles more beside it on the floor. Several propane tanks, the knobs turned blue, are clumped in a corner where a refrigerator should be. My breath quickens when one of the boys whispers to a younger one, their long curls touching as they bend toward each other, and I can't help but think of how sunflowers grow, twisting themselves to face one another as they strain for light. The boys look to be three and four. All are so young, the third one still in diapers, their backs bowed and sagging, as if life has already withered them. There is no sign of Trecie.

I feel the panic begin to swell inside of me and turn to Mike. But he's become a cop again, his mouth smooth. He's smiling at the girl, though he flashes those eyes I've come to know. The little girl doesn't notice, her face hidden against the dog as she coos into his ear, 'E aprovado, Amendoim, ele é aprovado.'

'So is it just you and the other kids here?' He nods in their direction and takes the opportunity to scan the room. I follow his gaze and notice there are no pictures on the walls, and the only piece of furniture is a couch with a missing leg, dingy foam bursting through several holes in the arms. I spot a doorway leading to what I assume are the bedrooms. There are no signs of the holiday within these walls.

'Yes.'

Mike squats down in front of the girl. 'Mind if I pet your dog?'

She mumbles into the fur, her voice cracking as she does. 'Is she here to take Peanut?'

'No, Peanut's your dog. We came to talk to you. What's your name?'

She hugs the dog closer until he yelps and nips her hand. She drops him and watches as he scampers through the doorway toward the bedrooms. The girl stares after him before speaking.

'Adalia.'

There can be no more doubts; it's her, Trecie's sister. I can't stop myself. 'Where's Trecie?'

The girl freezes, her eyes wide and clear. Mike shushes me with a wave of his hand. 'Adalia. That's a pretty name.' He glances toward the television, where a frenetic cartoon races across the screen. 'Hey, why don't we all talk back there where it isn't so noisy?'

'Oh, right,' she says. 'You're one of Victor's friends.' She tenses then, her eyes flashing as her voice rises. She points to her sister. 'Inez stays here.'

'Sure,' says Mike. 'Whatever you want.'

In an instant, Adalia regains her stoic countenance. Her shoulders slump and whatever life was just in her eyes leaves them again. 'It's back here,' she says.

I can't imagine what it is we're about to walk into, and then I remember the pregnant woman telling me of the parade of men who come here trolling for drugs. My mind tries to comprehend this child, no more than ten, being a pawn of the adults in her life.

But when we turn the corner in the bedroom, there's no table with scales and Baggies neatly tied. There are no Bunsen burners or vials, pots of marijuana growing under heat lamps, no needles – all familiar scenes from pickups of clients who OD'd over the years. No, there's only a bare room with a soiled mattress, a grungy sheet kicked to the foot of it. A window with the shade pulled low. And then I see it, the mural in a child's crayon scrawl, the same one from the video.

Mike sees it too.

'Honey,' he says, 'where's your sister? Where's Trecie?'

Adalia doesn't answer. She merely stares off, and I'm reminded of the instant Linus died, when his body became a shell. I know where this girl has gone. I used to hide in the same place whenever Tom's friends visited me in the library.

When she speaks, her voice is as flat as her eyes. 'Just hurry.'

Mike appears ill, as if he smells something bitter and foul. He ducks out of the room, goes into the next bedroom, and then reappears in the hall, beckoning to me. I follow him toward the front door. The boys seem not to notice when we pass.

'There's a meth lab in the other bedroom, a real setup.' Mike's teeth grind as he speaks. 'There's no sign of Trecie. I've got to call Kate.'

'I know.' I check to see if Adalia's followed us, but only Inez and the boys are here.

'Adalia fits the description of the other girl in the videos, just older. Maybe there's another sister.'

I have no control over my hand. It's on the doorknob. Mike doesn't notice. He's busy reaching inside his jacket for his cell phone. My hand is turning the knob and my legs want to carry me from this place. I could run away, take Eileen Craig's identity. We could begin again in a city large enough where Eileen and I could become one, marry ourselves to a new life. Where no one needs me or believes that I can or should or could be someone I'm not.

Mike is holding the phone to his ear, though he's still speaking to me. 'Don't let anyone in or out, but don't touch anything, either,' Mike says. 'This is a crime scene.'

When the dog races around the corner, Mike bends to scoop him into his arms and thrusts him at me. Then he reaches behind me and bolts the door. Like the others in this apartment, I'm now locked in this world with no escape.

CHAPTER TWENTY-SEVEN

The dog's nails click against the hardwood as he races to the ceramic bowl. Alma's filled it with slops of defrosted beef stew. 'Leftovers from last week,' she said, the implication hanging between us. Last week everything was different. And now . . . I'm housing this dog until Mike knows if Adalia's foster parents will welcome a pet.

I came to Alma's kitchen knowing she would have food, something to tide Peanut over until I could get to the market. What I didn't expect, and should have, was her need to settle me with a meal too. She's already sat me at the kitchen table with a cup of Earl Grey. The only clue something is amiss is her dress; it's the same blue wrap she wore yesterday.

'Linus's brother and his family will arrive tomorrow. Reverend Greene said he'd pick them up at the airport.' Alma pokes at the pork chops in her skillet and then plunges the fork into a small pot of potatoes, its stock frothing over the edges. It's too much for lunch. 'I put fresh linens on the beds this morning, cleaned the guest bathroom. Is everything ready downstairs for the services?'

I nod, thinking of the flower arrangements that overflow the mourning rooms, so many some had to be moved here to their – to her – living quarters. Though Reverend Greene told Alma that whispers have begun to float above the prayers, the media have not yet made the link between his and Linus's connection to the Precious Doe case. It's only a matter of time.

When the phone rings, only Peanut flinches.

'Best to let the machine get that,' says Alma. Reporters continue to call and wait outside the house; every so often they knock at the door. We don't answer. A murder in Whitman is a rare enough occurrence that we can expect them to remain here through the funeral, perhaps longer.

'How long will you keep him?' Alma asks, eyeing Peanut as he noses the now-empty bowl against the wall. She drops a scrap of bacon into his bowl before crumbling the rest over the potatoes.

'Not long.' I don't tell her of Peanut's previous owner, Mr. Kelly, or how Adalia begged to keep her dog, cried and kicked as Mike thrust him into my arms, how he reassured her it was for only a little while, until the police and child protective services settled her and her siblings. I don't tell Alma how Adalia withdrew then, cocooned herself under layers of an impenetrable silence. Grieving her own loss, Alma's already heard too much about the state of Adalia and her siblings.

'Those poor children,' Alma says. Her back is to me as she reaches for two plates. 'Wouldn't it be nice if we could be their foster parents? I have all these rooms and now there's only me.'

She busies herself with cutlery and napkins as she speaks, never looking to me. 'Imagine? You could move your things in here, take the guest room, and they could share the other bedrooms.' I doubt she could bring herself to clear Elton's room.

She places a water glass at my seat and pauses over me, her voice taking on a frenetic tone. 'I could watch them while you worked, cook them proper meals. We could care for them together.'

Silence is my response.

She turns to the stove, stiffening her back as she mashes the potatoes. 'None of them said a word about the sister?'

How to explain the four catatonic children bound to the television, mute Adalia, and the pressing absence of Trecie? 'Nothing.'

I reach for my teacup, and as I swallow I begin to digest her words; there was something off about her tone, too precise and cloaked.

'Alma?' I watch her, concentrating, knowing that if I can translate her gestures, they will tell me more than she will intend to reveal. 'Did you know about Linus and Trecie? That she played here? Before, I mean?'

Her hand pauses over the pot. 'He was on a lot of painkillers when he spoke, Clara. A trauma like that can muddle a man's head.'

A tremor grows within me and I replace my cup before I scald my lap. 'That night we were looking for her, when we were all sitting at this table, did you know Trecie was here in this house? Linus must have told you.'

Alma strikes the whisk against the pot, sending flecks of mashed potato against the tile backsplash. 'I never saw the girl.'

I squat to clip on Peanut's leash; he flinches when I do. Feeling the breath leave my body, I become conscious of the earth spinning freely beneath my feet. When I stand, I steady myself against a chair. 'You knew. You knew about Linus, about everything. Why didn't you tell me?'

Alma whirls around, the whisk still in her hand, her lips curled in fury, and I'm suddenly reminded of my grandmother. 'Because it was unnatural. Because you wouldn't understand. You refuse to even try.' Her chest heaves as she speaks.

'Please.' But my voice is swallowed by the swell of horror gathering in my throat. Instead I fill myself with the sight of her; I need to see the woman I thought she was. I need to find her again. 'Alma, tell me.'

'They would have called my husband a freak, had him committed, and I would not have that. He was not, is not a freak. He was a man of God who saw the world differently. You know that. You know Linus was a good man.' Her body trembles and the whisk shakes in her raised hand. I search her eyes, but they're shrouded as if by rolling storm clouds.

'*Unnatural*? What are you saying?' The dog begins to whimper.

'Just stop it, Clara. Enough of this nonsense. You saw Trecie for yourself, where she's been, what she's been *doing* here. Open your eyes to what's been going on right in front of you.'

She can no longer stave off the tears, but I'm too ill for that. I race down the hall, pulling too hard on the leash. I hear the dog cry out as he tumbles down the last few steps. Finally we're out the back door. From above, I hear the kitchen window rush open and Alma calling out, her voice breaking, 'Linus is a good man!'

Hurrying across the parking lot to my cottage, dragging Peanut until I'm forced to bend and carry him, I know Alma isn't following, but still her words hound me. I fling my patio door open and slam it behind me, turning the bolt into its tunnel. When my cell phone rings from deep within my pocket, both Peanut and I startle.

It's Mike. 'How's the puppy?'

The little dog trembles against me, and I wonder at his life, how much trauma he's been privy to, the horrors he could detail. I tuck him under my chin and don't pull away when he licks my ear. 'Fine. Any word on Trecie?'

'No.' From the weight of his few words, it sounds as if each day were a decade in his life. 'Adalia's in with Kate and a psychiatrist from McLean Hospital now, but she's completely shut down.'

Though I continue to see Alma's face and hear her

words, I go through the motions of this conversation. If I think about either of these circumstances, each too horrible to fully realize, I will slip away and fade forever. 'And Inez, the boys?'

Mike sighs. 'From what the psychiatrist said, they've been isolated so long they've developed their own language. They learned some from television, but they can't hold a conversation with outsiders.'

There's a pause and I wait for something, some billow of hope to rise from the ashes. Instead Mike says, 'I was thinking of stopping by after work, bring over some takeout.'

But it's too late for me. Everything has come too late. 'I don't think so. Alma needs help getting ready for the wake.'

'Yeah, sure. Maybe tomorrow.'

I can't begin to contemplate a tomorrow. 'Good-bye, Mike.'

I hang up the phone and set the dog down. He scampers to a corner of the kitchen, looks to me, forlorn and uncertain, and then defecates on the floor.

While he squats, I walk to the hall and dig toward the back of the linen closet. There among the towels and soap, I keep my luggage. I pull out the pieces, three cheap black things, and feel for the Amtrak tags still taped around the handles. These are all the mementos I have marking my life in Slatersville. I finger them, reading the faded print, the date still legible, and think of a life I believed I could leave there.

It's time to start over, in a city this time, or maybe a farm out west, working with the invisibles who float between this world and another across the border. We won't speak the same language, be expected to share our lives or our selves. I can rent a shack near the orchards, a place of my own with only prairie dogs and hawks for company. It's time to be alone again. This time, I want it. One last wake. I owe Linus that, and then I'll move on, anew.

As if such a thing were possible.

CHAPTER TWENTY-EIGHT

Adalia's foster house is a neat split ranch with brown shingles and cranberry shutters. An evergreen wreath hangs on the front door with a crimson bow, a sprig of plastic holly tucked between the branches at a jaunty angle. A cheery blow-up snowman, its electrical cord buried under several inches of snow, waves to Peanut and me as I carry the dog along the salt-covered cement path. He whimpers when the wind kicks up, burrowing deeper under my coat.

Through the bow window, I can see Mike talking to a woman, both of them beside a Christmas tree adorned with multicolored lights. The woman is plump and blond, wearing a red sweater with bright patterns. I imagine that when I get closer, those colorful blotches will reveal themselves to be a Christmas tree with a bounty of presents spread beneath, all laced with real ribbons neatly tied. She spots me before I've a chance to ring the bell.

'Come in, come in!' She's not a pretty woman. Her cheeks are ruddy and fat; her eyes are magnified, wobbly behind thick lenses; and though her lips are cracked from the cold, it doesn't prevent a warm smile. She smells of talcum powder and bleach. As I wipe my boots on the landing of the split level, I spot Mike looking over the wrought-iron railing at me from the floor above.

'I see you brought the puppy,' says the woman. She reaches out to pet the dog huddled against my chest, but I turn aside.

Her smile falters a moment. 'My name is Janey Conyers. I'm Adalia's foster mother, at least for now.' She directs me up to the main floor. 'You know Detective Sullivan?'

I take the stairs ahead of the woman and stand before Mike. The living room is clean with a blue sofa and love seat, each positioned to face the brick fireplace and Christmas tree displayed before the window. The adjoining dining room is simple with blue and yellow check wallpaper and matching valances. Peanut pokes his head out of my coat when Mike reaches to scratch his head.

'Hey, thanks for coming over so quickly.'

I hug the dog to me and he nuzzles my collar. It was no surprise when he leaped onto my bed during the night, trying to sleep against me. Again and again, I put him back on the floor.

Mike's fingers graze my blouse as he strokes the little dog's back. I move so he can no longer reach. 'How is she?' I ask.

Mike starts to speak, but the woman interrupts. 'Poor lamb, she hasn't said a word or eaten a bite since she got here last night. My husband and I are working with children's services to see if we can get her brothers and sister here too. They've let us do that in the past. He's out now getting presents for the little ones. It's a blessing there's still two shopping days left.'

I ignore the woman and her cheerful optimism. 'Has she said anything about Trecie?'

Mike just shakes his head. 'We'll have to wait until her mother comes down from her high. We found her early this morning in an abandoned factory on Main Street.'

'Oh my Lord,' says Janey, stretching her Christmas sweater down along her thighs. 'What these poor children have been through. If I could just get her to eat something.' She casts a wistful look down the hallway toward the bedrooms.

Mike nods to the woman; his face is drawn and pale. Yet when he turns to me there is something more, something I've not yet seen: a smile for me. I wish I could return it. My mind flashes to him prowling my greenhouse, his gun pointing at me, and then what came after. I'll do what I can today and tomorrow to find Trecie, to see Linus through the wake – I owe them that much – but then I'm gone.

'How long before the mother can talk?' The dog sighs in my arms and shifts his snout deeper under my arm.

'Blood tests show she has heroin and methamphetamines in her system, so a few more hours before she'll be coherent enough to answer questions. She's known to the police; we picked her up about four years ago for possession and prostitution. Nothing since then. Neighbors said she'd leave the kids alone for days.'

'Oh my,' says Janey. She licks her lips and then asks Mike, 'What about pancakes? Do you think she'd eat pancakes?'

Mike places a hand on the woman's arm. 'I think she'd love it.'

'And ham patties, too,' says Janey. 'I was saving them for Christmas morning, but we have a lot to be thankful for this morning, don't we? I'll just be a minute.' Janey heads off toward the kitchen, taking all sense of hope with her.

'The mother isn't going to talk, is she?' I ask Mike.

He avoids me and instead looks out the window. 'In a few hours, she'll come down.'

'Mike.'

The furrow set within his brow tells me everything. 'We'll do our best.' He turns back to me. 'Don't worry, we'll figure this out.'

'Did you ask Ryan about the dog?'

'He said he dropped it off at the Brockton SPCA after leaving Charlie's house. I sent him back to the shelter yesterday and the director told him they destroyed the dog about a week later. Looks like the name is just a coincidence. Not a surprise, really.'

'And Jorge? Has he found the cop named Victor?'

Mike tries to reach for me, but I take a step back. 'Clara, we're doing everything we can. We're going to find Trecie.'

I squeeze the dog closer and he scratches at my arm until I loosen my hold. 'I want to talk to her. I want to talk to Adalia.'

'Clara, why don't you get some rest? You've had a rough week. Let us do our job. Maybe I could come over.'

'She'll talk to me.'

He crosses his arms and stares at me. 'I have to sit in on it.'

I hesitate, but there's no other way. I nod and together we walk down the narrow hallway. Mike knocks at the last door before turning the knob. Adalia is sitting on the bed, her legs tucked under, her back to us. If her life weren't so utterly shattered, I could imagine her being happy in this room. Though small, it has a white-frame bed decorated with a cheery pastel comforter. There's a matching desk and bureau, and on the wall, a poster of a kitten dangling from a tree branch, the words HANG IN THERE! scrawled beneath it.

Adalia remains still when we enter. Her hair is matted, though she's wearing newer clothes, a blue sweat suit. I suppose a shower would have been too traumatic given the past twenty-four hours.

Mike gestures to me and I make my way over to stand next to her. The only trace of life is when she spots Peanut, though I can't tell if it's fury or despair that crosses her face. The dog struggles against me when he sees her. My fingers clamp around him until there's no danger of him getting free.

'Hi, Adalia. Do you remember me?'

There can be no mistake now; her nostrils flare.

'Do you like cats?' I point to the cat poster and then return my hand to Peanut's head, stroking his velveteen ears. 'Or are you a dog person?'

She begins picking at a seam in the bedspread, tugging the thread free.

'I like dogs,' I say. 'I used to think I'd get a cat someday, but now I like dogs better.'

Her head whips up and looks back and forth between Peanut and me. Across the room, I see Mike shift his weight from one foot to the other. I swallow the vomit that rises in my throat.

'Peanut sure likes to cuddle. He slept with me last night, you know. I think he likes it at my house.'

Adalia's eyes begin to fill. It's a few seconds before I can speak again.

'Where's Trecie?'

She looks at me. One tear after another rolls down her cheeks until her lips tremble and her body begins to shake.

'Clara, that's enough.' Mike is too weak to do this, so I must.

'If you want your dog back, you have to tell me where Trecie is.'

Mike crosses the room to stand between Adalia and me. She's sobbing now, each wail piercing whatever life I have left. He points to the door, his voice a hoarse whisper. 'Get out!'

'Come on, Peanut.' I start for the door, but Adalia leaps from the bed.

'He took her away!'

'When?' I say, my hand cupping the dog's head. He begins to whine under my touch.

Adalia collapses on the bed, crying, her legs pulled in close. One hand worries at her ear, and she sucks the thumb of the other. Mike sits next to her, whispering 'It's okay, it's okay' over and over. But it's not, it never will be. When he looks at me, I don't look away.

'He beat her real bad and then he took her away. I don't know where,' Adalia says.

'Honey,' Mike says. 'Was it Victor?' She can only nod.

He pushes the hair from her face. 'When did this happen?'

Adalia doesn't answer. Her eyes have become glassy again, the way they did yesterday. Her mouth purses around the thumb and she begins to suck loudly. Her fingers have already rubbed raw the spot where her lobe meets the side of her head. I crouch beside her and open my coat. Peanut leaps the short distance from my arms to the bed and licks at the wetness of the girl's cheeks. She finally frees her hand from her ear and places it limply across the dog. He lies beside her, his snout just under her chin.

I head out of the room and fight the urge to run when I hear Mike's footsteps behind me. I make it to the foyer before he grabs my arm and spins me around, knocking me against the wall.

'What the hell was that?' I stare down, unable to stand the disappointment I can already hear in his voice. I try not to breathe either, to be reminded of his scent.

'Information.'

'Don't you get what this girl has been through? And to browbeat her like that? What the hell's the matter with you?'

I shake my arm free and open the front door. Gusts blow the edges of my coat and whip loose strands from my ponytail. The wind is especially piercing against the moist burns along my scalp. All fresh.

'I got what we needed to help find Trecie.'

Mike seizes my shoulders, forcing me to face him. 'At what price? That little girl is fragile. She needs help too.'

I take a step back, onto the front stoop. 'You can't help her. She's broken. Just like you. Just like me.'

'Clara, go home. Let the police take care of this.'

'You think you can fix everything, Mike, but you can't. You think by picking at things, pulling away the bad stuff, you're making a difference? It doesn't take it away, it's always there – the scars are always there.'

He doesn't follow me as I cross the yard, making fresh prints in the snow. But I can feel him watching. Before I can slide into the car, I hear Mrs. Conyers call to me, 'Clara, the pancakes are ready! Aren't you going to stay for breakfast?'

CHAPTER TWENTY-NINE

I drove around for hours. When I finally pull into the parking lot behind the funeral home, I'm momentarily blinded by the sun casting its last streaks of brilliance across the afternoon sky. At first I can't see his car, but then Reverend Greene comes into focus. He's opening his trunk as Linus's brother, Matthew, looks on.

'Hello, Clara.'

I'd forgotten how alike Matthew and Linus are, the same generous build and wide brown eyes. Though Matthew is five years younger, he lacks the vitality, the sheer wonder, Linus exuded, a certain innocence in the way he regarded the world and the people in it. Or so I thought.

'Matthew.' I nod, still unprepared to see him. It must pain him to look in the mirror, each pass a reflection of his loss. 'I'm sorry about your brother.'

'Thank you, Clara.' He sets his bag down on the frozen ground and takes my hand in both of his, just the way Linus used to do. 'I know it must be hard for you, too. You were like a daughter to him.'

Reverend Greene is standing just past Matthew, his hands filled with luggage, his face with pity. I wonder what the reverend's god would say about a man who stood at his pulpit week after week, demanding that his flock call out evil, loud and proud. And yet, when faced with it himself, the best this man could do was whisper from the shadows.

'Alma's making one of her dinners now,' says Matthew. 'Frieda and the kids are inside. They'd love to see you. I hope you'll join us.'

'I have to make the final arrangements. The wake's in two days,' I say, pulling my coat around me, against the wind.

Reverend Greene steps forward. 'Matthew, why don't you go on upstairs? I'll bring this up in a bit.'

As soon as Matthew is out of earshot, Reverend Greene begins to speak, a comforting touch on my shoulder.

I duck. 'Don't.'

He pulls back, nods. 'Clara, Alma told me what happened.'

'I have to go.' Just two more days and then I'll be free of them.

As I walk toward my cottage, Reverend Greene calls to me. 'You don't understand. Linus was helping that girl.'

It's too much. I think of Miss Talbot, her expression when she saw the boys pinning me against the library shelves; her complete and utter silence. How desperately

I needed her to cry out for me. I turn back. 'Helping? How, by lying to the police and to me? By letting a little girl continue to live in that hellhole with that monster? And you're no better.'

Reverend Greene is incredulous. 'That's not how it was. You know that!'

The wind freezes the sweat that forms on my brow, but I'm too hot to be chilled. 'I spoke to Trecie, I saw that room.' I choke, not wanting to say the rest. 'Alma said it was *unnatural*.'

Reverend Greene stares at me, his mouth open and his eyes even wider. 'May the Lord have mercy on your soul, is that what you think?'

I can feel the pull of my cottage, of my garden. I should just walk away, but stronger is the urge to stand my ground, for myself, for Trecie, and Doe, for all the children who were never loved enough. 'I don't know what to think.'

He takes a step toward me, reaching for my shoulder, but I push his hand away. Still, he tries. 'Each time that girl came to him, told him something new, he let me know straight away so I could call Mike. Linus didn't know everything, Clara. She only told bits and pieces at a time.'

'Why didn't Linus just call Mike himself? Why didn't he tell me?'

'Things were complicated, Clara. You don't understand.'

I start to leave, but he doesn't stop.

'Have you ever asked yourself why she didn't tell *you*?'

His words pummel me, leaving me breathless. I'm forced to confront him. 'What?'

His smile appears mournful and crushed. 'Have you? She told Linus it was because you didn't believe her.'

I clench my jaw, refuse to blink, pinch my palm; anything not to cry. 'She told me things.'

'Did she tell you she was trying to save her sister, the littlest one?'

I think of the youngest girl, Inez, how Adalia sought to protect her too. When Mike and I went to her apartment, Adalia insisted: 'Inez stays here.'

'You didn't know, did you?' Reverend Greene says.

My cottage is calling me. I have to water my garden, gather seeds to carry with me to my next life. 'I know enough.'

'No. You don't know.' He laughs, a soft, melancholy sound. 'You've got to have faith, Clara.'

He is staring at me, his eyes alight. I shake my head and begin backing away.

'Look to your heart, Clara, have faith – if not in something bigger than yourself, then in Linus. Trust in Linus.'

He finally stops, muttering to himself as he walks back to the suitcases. As he picks them up, he begins to sing, low and soft, a hymn from church. When he opens the door to Alma's, he doesn't look back. Still, I hear him, *'was blind, but now I see.'*

CHAPTER THIRTY

The moon is near full, illuminating shadows the street-lamps along Washington Street never touch. Passing under Alma's window, I see her there in the kitchen, her mouth moving, her face slightly animated as she washes something in the sink. When she stops speaking to the figures behind her (more family and friends in from out of town), I notice she drops the facade she's wearing for them, and for a moment I inhabit her grief.

But my legs keep moving me forward, toward the street. A few yards down and across is Colebrook Ceme-tery. I have to make sure the grave is ready for Linus's casket to fill it. That won't be until after the holiday, of course; barring inclement weather, he'll be laid to rest December 26. I'll stay for the wake on Christmas Eve, sure to be a townwide affair, but be gone before the funeral. My train leaves at dawn Christmas Day, just two days away. Feeling the cold burn through my boots, I allow myself an opportunity to consider what awaits me: constant warmth, the freedom to work outside, an entirely new category of flora. And, of course, the promise of peace. I'll forget this life and all its betrayals the way I've forgotten the last.

Tonight the only sound among the dead is the wind whistling through the outstretched limbs of a split oak. Linus's plot – bought alongside Alma's long ago – isn't far from the street. The gravediggers had the sense to move the backhoe out of sight, even storing the piles of disturbed earth in the dump truck and parking both behind the maintenance shed. It seems everyone loved Linus.

It's time to go; things are just as they should be. First, though, there's one good-bye I want to make. It won't take but a minute. I've brought the terra-cotta pot filled with young daisies. I know they'll die before morning, but the last I see of them, they'll be alive. Something will.

I don't need the moon to guide me; I could walk there in my sleep. In the beginning, many people would visit here. They'd leave teddy bears and hats, cards and photos of their trips to Disney World, as if Precious Doe could share in the memories of such a happy place. Soon their attentions petered off, as did the media's. It's as if mourning her were a trend now passed. The last item left, too many months ago to count, was a stuffed cat with yellow fur and green marble eyes. It looked well loved.

I should never have listened to Mike, should never have become involved. I buried her three years ago. It was easy for me to accept her death then when she was a stranger without any sense of a life lived. But now I know too much. Now it's as if she's reaching out to me through Trecie, begging for my help, but I've failed her. And Trecie. We all have. I wish Precious Doe could be dead again. There was some peace in that.

I'm within several yards when I see him. He's bent over Doe's grave, shining the beam of his flashlight on a small potted Christmas tree wedged into the snow. A glass ball is askew and he pushes it back into the tiny evergreen branch. As I pass the ground where his wife and child are buried, the moon illuminates another potted tree there. Tucked under its miniature branches is a wrapped box with red and green ribbons tied around it.

I think I've been quiet, my approach soundless, but Mike senses me. Without turning, he says, 'Do you think they know? Do you think any of them can see this and know?'

I want to tell him, *yes, of course, they'll love it.* I want to but can't.

Mike straightens, clicking off his flashlight. Shadows resume their posts and I wait until my eyes adjust to the moonlight before taking another step. I wonder how long he's been here, how long he knew I was walking toward this spot, a stop on my journey away from him.

'I was looking over the pictures we took from the tapes and it doesn't add up, you know?' Mike says, transfixed by Precious Doe's headstone, *blooming – tripping – flowing.* 'Most of the pictures are of Trecie, and we think the other girl is Adalia, right?' His voice is hollow, as if he's lost in a fugue far away from this place.

My steps are careful as I approach her grave. The pot is heavy in my hands; the muscles within my arms throb and my hands ache for my wool pockets. I crouch, my head alongside Mike's legs, and place the pot to the side of the little evergreen, the clump of daisies suddenly lifeless next to the cheerfulness of the tree.

'But I was looking at them and looking at Adalia in person, and I realized there has to be another girl. Adalia is nine; the girls in the photos and in the videos don't look more than six and seven. Inez isn't one of them, not with that birthmark on her face. But all three look so much alike. That's what you said, right? That you thought Trecie was about seven, eight?'

I stand, trying to get my footing on earth that continues to shift beneath me. Please, not another. 'Yes.'

'And Linus.' Mike's gaze remains steady on the headstone. 'He said in one of his anonymous tips that Precious Doe was connected to this, that she was in the videos.'

'Yes.' My hands want to find the comfort of my pockets but somehow can't move.

'But the ages don't add up. The M.E. determined Doe was approximately seven when she was killed, so either we have a bigger problem involving more girls or Linus was wrong—'

'Mike, stop—' I can't bear any more of this. I can't live within other people's lives.

'Or maybe the girl in the video isn't Trecie. Something just isn't right.'

He seizes my arms, squeezing too hard, his face twisted in thought – he's still lost in his head. 'Come back to my car with me. I have some photos there.'

'I can't.'

'Please, just once more. I promise.'

He must feel the shudder that rolls through my body, because his eyes suddenly snap back to the present. His face and hands relax, and he embraces my cheeks within his hands. 'I know, I know.'

It's when his thumb slips along my cheekbone, caressing the rise there, that I relent. It's the last thing I'll do before I rest. One picture. I nod and he releases me.

He's hard to keep up with, his legs so long and his stride purposeful. I'm breathless when we finally reach the green Crown Vic. He opens the trunk and rummages through the same cardboard box I've come to dread.

'I had some blown up to see if we could identify a scar, birthmark, anything about this guy, but all we have is his hand and part of his forearm.' Mike's voice isn't weary the way I've come to expect. Instead it's quick and jumpy, energized by some spark.

He pulls out a couple of photos and passes them to me. In the semilight, they're grainy and blurred, but still I know the older girl is Trecie. 'It's her.'

In the next moment, Mike's flashlight is on them and I can see more clearly. The two girls, yes, Trecie, and a younger version of Adalia. So there's another sister, another victim. And then I notice the man's hand. The ragged nails, the cuticles around them inflamed, minute scabs rimming the middle finger. The hand is splayed, bony white, and I think of that time I saw a man eating chicken wings.

My knees begin to buckle and the photos flutter to the ground. Mike's hands are instantly on me. He guides me to the passenger side of the car, opening the door and lifting me in one motion. Then he kneels beside me. 'I'm sorry. I've put you through enough.'

'No,' I try to say, but my breath is gone, smothered and wispy. He's rubbing my back, reassuring me 'It's okay.' I didn't guess there would be such comfort in those words, in the strength of his hand pressing against me. 'It's him,' I manage.

Mike becomes motionless, his hand limp. 'What?'

'The hand. Look at the nails, it's him.'

The only sound other than the wind is of my teeth clacking against themselves. Mike doesn't notice; he's returned to the fugue, staring at the photos. After several seconds, his voice catches me and I jump.

'Vic-tor-y.' He draws out the word in a hushed whisper.

He lunges across me, leaning his body against mine, his hand seeking out something on the driver's side. Beneath the scent of cold is Mike's own, and for the briefest of moments, I allow myself to rest my cheek against the back of his shoulder. When he straightens, I see his cell phone in his hand.

'Hey, Andrew, are you on the desk?'

I hear the hint of a voice on the other end, but nothing more.

'Can you look up a 911 call for me? It was about four years ago.'

A pause.

'I think it would have been a domestic. The address is 452 Clarendon Street.'

Mike nods. 'Yeah, that's right, the Vanity Faire. Apartment 316.'

It seems time has slowed as he waits for Andrew and the computer to call to the present voices from the past. His eyes never leave the photo.

'You got it?' His other hand finds the spot just above my knee and squeezes. 'Who responded to that call?'

When Mike's eyes find mine, I already know what he'll say. 'Ryan.'

CHAPTER THIRTY-ONE

It's near midnight and we are two days past winter solstice, the longest night of the year; it's the day before Christmas Eve, before Linus's wake. In ancient days, it was a time to celebrate life's renewal and hope. If I could muster the spirit, perhaps I'd view my leaving as a sort of rebirth, a new life. First, I'll need to let go of this one.

Mike's house is like the others on this side street, a white Cape among the blues and grays. His is the only one without Christmas lights or even a simple wreath nailed to the front door. If he weren't framed in the bow window, a single floor lamp backlighting the living room, one could be forgiven for thinking the house abandoned.

I intended only to drive by, a final silent farewell before I leave. When I noticed that the sole streetlight across from his house was out and there wasn't another in sight, I thought it safe to park here, for just a minute or two. Even if he doesn't see the hearse through the pitch, a neighbor could, one who might call Mike to ask who on their street had died.

He's talking on the phone, a carton of milk seemingly forgotten in his hand. Behind him, above the fireplace, hangs a portrait. I imagine it's of him with Jenny, their baby safe within her womb. A family portrait. A television's blue light flashes from an unseen corner, the rise of a chair and love seat just visible: room enough for three.

He walks the length of the living room, pivots, and then walks back again. He stops when it's his turn to speak. He raises his hand above his head, appearing to shout into the phone, shaking the carton until he throws it against a wall I can't see, just the splatter that leaves dark streaks along a corner. Mike's standing directly in front of the window now, leaning his forehead against a single rectangular pane, the phone still pressed to his ear. He must think he's alone in the darkness or, like so many who've lost loved ones, that he's invisible.

But I see him. I've always seen him. There may even have been days when I thought I could see deep within him. Until the other night, I never expected he would see me too.

I look beyond Mike and try to imagine what his life was like when this house contained life. How it must have smelled when Jenny was there to cook his dinners, her belly filled with their future, then after, the scent of colostrum and fresh laundry if life had been kind and their child had been allowed to be born. How their lives would have been. Every last corner of his whole filled with laughter, the swell of an infant wailing in the night, the murmur of his and Jenny's lovemaking. I wonder if he whispered to her, something tender and casual, or if theirs was a passionate bed, never dragged down by monotony.

I close my eyes and imagine what the rest of that house might have been like: a yellow kitchen dotted with whimsical ceramic roosters; a small sitting room with just enough space for a desk and a bookcase lined with true-crime hardbacks and the occasional Maeve Binchy novel; a nursery with fluffy pink blankets and a cerulean ceiling with painted clouds drifting high above a crib. There must still be pots and pans in that kitchen. If life were forgiving, I could learn to fill them with recipes from Alma. Perhaps there's room on those sitting room shelves for my *Sibleys* and Woolf. A bare corner for my ficus. If life were kinder still, Trecie would be tucked safe within there, Adalia, Inez, and their brothers, too – a second chance for us all. What would it be to have that life, to know constancy and devotion? To walk through that door, fall upon that sofa, and into his arms? To read side by side or watch a movie, and when it grew late, to slip into bed, one of our own, and lie together without barriers. There would be no clothing, no words, no reticence. . . .

Just the chasm of the past.

I have nothing to fill that nursery; innocence cannot grow within me again. There's not enough of me to satisfy the nooks of Mike's life the way Jenny did. Nothing can save those children. There's no place in that house for them. For me. He may see me today, want me to share his dinners and bed, but I expect he'd soon see through me, come to feel my hollowness and realize I'm too small to fill his void.

I catch my reflection in the rearview mirror. My skin is a thin film over my skull, my chin and cheekbones too prominent. My eyes are so dark that a trick of the shadows makes them appear to be vacant sockets. Oh, and my hair. How skillful I long imagined myself to be, clever with parts, the way I teased curls over the bald spots, obscuring them all with a ponytail. I touch the scars now. So many. They're all there for anyone to see; only I was blind to them until now. The metaphor is not lost on me.

I flip the mirror up and then start the hearse's engine. Mike jerks his head. As if he can see through the dark, he meets my gaze and presses his palm against the pane. Before pulling away, I raise my own hand to the driver's-side window and for one last time imagine the possibilities.

CHAPTER THIRTY-TWO

The window wells of my basement workspace are filled with snow. The sun's morning light manages to crack through the crystal fissures, splashing prismatic colors across the glass.

I can hear them above me; my ceiling groans with the combined weight of what seems to be nearly all the residents of both Whitman and Brockton, on Christmas Eve no less. Alma wanted to get an early start, knowing that most would be celebrating later today. She didn't want to assume the entire day; they will have the late afternoon to put this behind them, to enjoy the holiday cheer. To make it easier for all, she cooked for two days, filling three buffet tables with various holiday platters, and at the center of each, her grandmother's crystal punch bowls. That's her way. She'll keep the funeral home open late into the evening to welcome stragglers, those who have nowhere else to go and who are eager for a bite of the holiday. I know Linus would have been touched at the showing.

Before I wheeled his body up to the mourning room,

I wavered between the irises (*faith, hope, wisdom*) and a bouquet of hydrangea (*heartlessness*). It reminded me of the stories Linus liked to tell of Job, of how the man's trust in his god was tested again and again. This morning I had my own crisis of faith; I believe I chose justly.

I find my book of flowers in the cabinet, nestled beside the ivory tapers and my Mozart. I need only the book. My fingers run the length of the candles, and for a breath I think I can't leave this place behind, this work, these people. But then the memory of Mike's call, a shrill ring in the darkness before dawn as I lay awake wondering if Trecie was alive or dead, reminds me of what I already know: I can't stay here surrounded by doubt, knowing that people who breed pain will never know it themselves.

Mike called to say Ryan is gone. It wasn't Andrew's fault, not really. He let Kate and Jorge know, just like Mike asked, but then Andrew thought he was being helpful when he called Ryan, too. Everyone knew how eager Ryan was to catch Trecie's attacker. He had been a part of the investigative team after all. It never occurred to Andrew he was alerting the monster that the townspeople were on their way.

Mike told me how Kate went to Trecie and Adalia's mother, still in custody, but recovered from her high, and showed her Ryan's picture. She agreed to make a positive identification if the DA would ask the judge for leniency on her behalf. She refused to say more.

Mike's voice may have cracked when he told me about his visit to Adalia. He didn't want to show her the picture, he said. She finally had her siblings there, and her foster mother said she was starting to eat a bit. So I think it killed Mike a little more to have to do it. He got what he needed, though. As Ryan would say, *victory*.

Ryan's gone, so, really, he is the victor. There will be no punishment for him. He and Tom and Mr. Kelly and Mr. MacDonnell, they all wisely chose silent victims.

Mike said they searched Ryan's house and found a stash of movies hidden in the attic rafters. And meth. How his wife must have protested.

He also said Ryan's the prime suspect in Linus's murder. The DNA is being processed now. Mike assured me there's no evidence at this point that they were co-conspirators. He believes the motive for the killing was Ryan's fear that Linus knew more from Trecie, not that Linus was somehow involved with Ryan. Mike didn't say if that's what the rest of the investigative team believes. He didn't have to. They stopped by Alma's last night with more questions for us. I never let on what Alma said, either. It's over. Case closed.

What's pressing me forward, away from here, is what Mike left unsaid. That the police think Ryan probably killed Trecie, too. So I'll leave now before I learn anything more about these lives. I'll leave before Mike can drive here and tell me they've found another body in the woods, another little girl. If I'm not here when he comes, then he can't tell me. She can still be alive. They'll find Ryan or they won't, it doesn't matter now.

There are hours left before Linus's wake ends; no one will notice my absence. I can hear the back door opening and slamming shut every few minutes, voices calling out to one another. I should go upstairs, stand beside Alma one last time, but she has Matthew and I haven't the stomach.

My cell phone rings, hesitates, and then chirps again. The signal is weak in the basement beneath the layers of soil and concrete.

'Cla—,' Mike says. 'We're—way—there—out—'

Through the crackle of a bad connection I can sense his determination. No, I don't want to hear any more. It's time to move on. I turn the phone off and leave it on my worktable.

Conversations float down the stairs, quiet laughter and a bronchial cough. And then there's another sound. Footsteps. A gentle brush of shoe against grit against cement stairs. No wayward mourner has ever found himself here. But Trecie has.

I forget my book and hurry over to the door. My feet move and I don't know how I've crossed this dreary workroom so quickly, except I don't want her to see any more horrors in her life. She doesn't need to smell the formaldehyde, see the stainless-steel table at the back of the room angled above the sink, the scalpel and tubes on the utility cart, the trocar with its menacing spearlike tip hanging next to the sink. I crack the door and a part of me wants to pray, to believe, to hope for what I need most. A miracle, Trecie standing before me.

But when I look out the narrow opening into the hallway, I see only darkness. The light is out, and when I flick the switch on the wall it refuses to go on. I begin to close the door when a hand, scabbed and ragged, shoves it open, throwing me backward onto the cement floor.

Ryan is standing there, his outline framed by darkness. He glares at me before closing the door behind him. His movements are slow as his eyes hold mine – four, five seconds – and then he begins to sidle toward me. I scramble to my feet. It's hard to tear my eyes away from his, the way his tongue glides over his lips as if he were a lion ready to pounce. When the fluorescent light catches something shiny in his left hand, I shift my gaze and become fixated by the knife there.

It's nearly the length of my forearm, curved with an ugly serrated edge. It appears to be smiling. The blade has a high sheen, mesmerizing, as it bobs in tempo with Ryan's stealthy walk.

I don't move until he lunges.

I lurch backward and fall against my utility cart, sending it crashing. My candles and tools scatter across the floor.

Ryan's laughter bounces around the room, as if he already surrounds me. 'Who's the cat and who's the mouse now, Clara? You thought you and Linus could psych me out?'

My hand feels behind me for something solid to push up on. I need to face him. Instead I touch something familiar, the cylindrical handle of my scalpel. Its blade is humbled by the hunting knife Ryan wields, but it's sharp and it's all I have.

When he lunges again – he's taunting me, he barely comes close – I reach out and slice his arm with the scalpel. He pulls back – not far – and scans his wound. He stops smiling, his jaw bulges, and his chest heaves a primal cry.

It's not much, but it gives me a chance to stand. I don't want to be afraid of him, I don't want to feel my bladder seize and throat close. I want to be fierce, to fight for Trecie and me, and in some way, Mike. But I can't. Terror has drowned me.

He knows it. His flash of anger has been replaced with that awful smile again.

'So, how'd you know, anyways?'

I'm distracted by his pupils, one fully dilated, the other a pinprick. His nostrils flex and contract, a thin rivulet of blood streaming from one. Meth high. He licks it away with his tongue.

'Where's Trecie?' Even to my own ears, my voice is tinny and weak. 'What have you done with her?'

'Fuck you!' He steps closer and I can smell his metallic breath. 'I was like a father to her, I loved her for real.' He wipes at his nose. 'Who told you? Linus?'

I don't answer, I'm blind with panic. He becomes a flash of blade and malevolence, his arm thrust high above his head and then slashing down. He's too fast, too comfortable with confrontations, and it's a moment before I feel the jagged burn within my shoulder. When I look there I grow dizzy at the sight of so much of my own blood. I watch in horror as the scalpel clatters to the floor.

'Tell me,' he says.

'Trecie,' I whisper. The sound of my voice startles me.

'You *know* Trecie's dead! Who else?'

'No!' I cry at his words. My knees are too stiff to bend, but my feet continue to shuffle backward. Each movement presses my sopping shirt against my side. The sensation is somehow worse than the wail of pain emanating from my shoulder. Still, I'd rather listen to that than whatever else Ryan has to say. I won't believe him.

He continues toward me as he talks. 'I started to give her little sister some attention and the brat threw a fit. That's what's wrong with kids today, disrespecting their elders. I didn't mean to kill her. It was an accident.' He stops and then smiles again. 'But Linus, yup, that I meant to do. Now you.'

There's no place left to go. Like all those afternoons in the library, my back is once more pushed against the wall. I can't believe this is how I'll die. That the last I'll ever take in of this world will be the odor of formaldehyde, the sight of the worktable, and the man who killed Trecie and Linus.

Each step Ryan takes toward me is slowed by my fear, every few inches of his approach seems to last for hours. I don't mean to notice the drool that collects at the corners of his mouth, my blood blackening the shaft of his blade, dripping down his wrist; I think it's odd that I can no longer hear or smell or taste anything, that my vision beyond Ryan is blurred.

It isn't until he's within inches of me that I think – no, I don't think – I *feel* the hook of the trocar pressing into my back. My hands move, I don't tell them to, they simply do, to reach behind me for the metal handle. It's a primitive thing, like a spear with jagged teeth used for shredding flesh. The tip of my right middle finger scrapes the many needlelike teeth at the end of it, and for a moment I relish the sting.

Then he's upon me. He's bent low over my face, too close, his hands on either side of me, pressing me against the wall. I can feel his thighs pinning my hips, his lips close to mine, parted as if for a kiss. I hate him.

Ryan begins to giggle, soft and hollow. 'Vic-tor-y.'

He bends still more. His lips reach mine and I bite down hard on his tongue.

Before I hear him wail, there's a sense of movement, something I don't see or hear, but know, his hand moving from its place on the wall beside my head, the knife scraping against the cinder blocks, a second, just a second, then a flash of something beside me.

I move too. One hand, I don't know which, swings the trocar around and the other hand meets it there, both grasping the handle. Like I've done hundreds, thousands of times before, I plunge it deep within the abdominal wall and up, higher and harder than I ever have, though never into a living person. There's a sudden explosion of blood from his gut and mouth, his nose. In an instant his body grows limp and the weight of him hangs upon the trocar. It's hard to let go of the handle, I don't want to give him another chance to hurt me, but his mass at the end of it makes it heavy. When I do, he slumps to the floor with his legs at queer angles. I'm oddly thankful for the drains. I move along the wall, keeping my eyes on him as he writhes. He reaches for me, his hand flailing against my leg, but I edge faster away from him.

Blood follows me. It smears itself along the path I make against the wall. I put more distance between Ryan and me: a foot, two, a yard. And then I feel it. Without looking, I know his knife is in me, deep within my side. There it is, the black plastic hilt of it all that's visible now, the blade having disappeared, my white shirt (*was it white?*) now drenched, ruined.

I slide down the wall, my knees bending before me. I know enough to fall on my right side, away from the knife. Beside me are the scattered remnants of my candles, tools, my flower book. It's spine down, pages flung wide and fluttering each time I exhale against it. My nails scrape along the floor as I move my hand to still the flapping. The photograph it's open to is of a meadow, a vast expanse of green scattered with white starlike flowers.

No one knows I'm here.

This room is colder than I've ever known it to be, even colder on the floor. Now that I know it's there, I can feel the knife pushing inside of me with each breath (*one-two-three*). I try for small ones, they hurt less, but even that becomes too much. I hear Ryan moan from across the room. He's still there.

When I open my eyes (*when did I close them, for how long?*), I regard the painting, Linus's painting of the shepherd, until the golden nimbus blurs. Now I know I'm truly alone.

And cold. I'm so very, very cold.

CHAPTER THIRTY-THREE

I open my eyes again (*how long this time?*) and a terrific shudder wrenches me full awake. Ryan is there and still, eerily quiet, until his chest rises slightly and there's a bubbling from his gut. My tools are strewn about, the book too, its spine now cracked. I need to leave this place. His eyes are open, staring in my direction, a river of blood dripping into the floor drain. He blinks, his mouth moves, but there's no sound.

Given the chance, he will kill me. A jolt of adrenaline resolves the pain in my chest; it's effortless to first sit, then stand. It needs to circulate through my bloodstream long enough for me to walk the short distance through the hallway and up one flight of stairs. My feet move one in front of the other, propelling me toward the door. I can't hear my shoes drag along the tiles or the reluctant give of the door's hinges; I'm listening only for Ryan's movements, too afraid to check. I make my way toward the mourners at Linus's wake, toward help and a quick visit to the emergency room. Really, there's no pain to speak of; I suspect a few stitches is all I'll need. In spite of what's happened, for Alma's sake, I hope she doesn't see this. She's been through enough.

In the hallway it's completely pitch, so black the light from the prep room can't follow. I feel my way along the walls, careful to press hard against the concrete surface in case the adrenaline begins to wane. It's too far to the door leading outside, and I'm certain I've passed the stairs already. Then my hand finds the knob and I push it open.

The glare is blinding, purely white. The morning sun reflects off the snow, snow that covers the ground, the cars, everything. I continue walking, feeling my way. People will still be arriving, someone to catch me, because I'm certain to fall. There was so much blood. Another step and I'm there.

But I'm not.

I'm not in the parking lot of Bartholomew Funeral Home. There's no cottage; my arch with its scraggle of hibernating wisteria is not beyond here. Surrounding me instead is a field thick with Kentucky bluegrass, patches of yellow starlike flowers growing in luxurious bouquets. Miles away are mountains tinged azure, rolling high into cadmium peaks, falling deep into valleys of goldenrod. And before them, a softly lapping ocean. Ships sail there, billowing dots of scarlet, emerald, amethyst canvases knotted to masts, set against an impossibly blue sky. A September blue sky. There aren't enough words.

Closer is a river with people strolling near its edge, while others sit watching it flow. The water itself isn't clear or white or a translucent blue, no, it's a constant flash of every color I've ever seen and some I haven't. I can hear it gurgle against its banks. And music, too. Mozart? Something familiar. A willow tree, grander than any other, dips its roots into the water, its branches an explosion of reedy stems, the older sister to the one at Colebrook Cemetery. A trailing arbutus (*faithful love*) winds from the uppermost tip, circling down along to the tree's exposed roots, its pink-and-white flowers dotted with the river's spray. A boy, no more than seven, with a nest of auburn ringlets, stumbles and falls into the rush of foam. Before anyone can catch him, though no one tries, no one even startles, he's whisked under and away. I race to the river's bank, but it's impossible to see much beneath the surface, only those curls, and then nothing.

A young Asian woman wearing a white ao dai, an orange and black cat entwining itself around her legs, smiles and applauds and then turns to me after the child passes. 'Hello, Clara.'

Before I can think, ask how she knows my name, the words spill from my mouth. 'That boy—'

'Yes,' she says, her smile faltering, 'it's like that sometimes.'

'No one tried to save him.'

'He can save himself,' she says, and the cat's suddenly within her arms. 'Oh, Thuy, where are your manners! Clara, I am Thuy.'

Thuy (I *know* her; how?) turns back to the others, who appear not to have noticed the loss of the child.

Conversations I can't hear swirl around us. Laughter tinkling from within a forest of dogwood and crabapple, a riot of pink and mottled green leaves, commands my attention. A man and woman run from there, my age I think, across a white paddle bridge to another cluster of trees, Japanese maple and cherry, followed by a Lab and a golden retriever both romping and barking; all gather under a shower of blossoms. Fields of wildflowers, a maze of hedge and burning bush, lie between here and there. Not far away, the sky ripples with snowflakes gliding in every direction, released by fantastic clouds. When I look closely, it's as if there's a kaleidoscope in each flake.

I know what this is; I've read about such conditions. It's a neurological phenomenon, oxygen deprivation from too much blood loss. A simple chemical reaction. I feel for the hilt of the knife in my side but find nothing. A dream, then, an artful hallucination. I need to get upstairs to Alma, to a hospital, though I'd rather rest here just a moment more. Yes, a dream, I know this. Still.

'Clara,' says Thuy, the cat now gone. 'There isn't much time.'

I feel for a scab along my crown, a spot of comfort. There is none. But there's hair, my own, only now it doesn't feel at all coarse and ugly. All the wounds have been smoothed away, replaced with something luxurious. I try to settle my mind, make order of the incomprehensible. Thuy is all that appears clear now;

the rest of this place begins to blur as if seen through a sheet of water.

It's then I realize I'm not breathing. There's no ache in my side, no hunger or thirst, no desire to lay my head down, close my eyes, and drift away. What an effort it all was! Such a relief to be without the constant struggle to live, to forgo everything that accompanies life's exertions. No more being trapped in a cycle of endless consumption – nourishment, air, space – yet never being filled.

I want to tell her of my discovery, but there's no time, none at all. Thuy reaches for my wrist but never quite touches. Instead, it's as if her hand has blended within my own, blurring the boundaries of skin. We are the same, a flutter, and suddenly we cross the field, standing before an overgrown jungle dotted with bloodred flowers the size of watermelons, all lit from within. A path unfolds along the ocean of grass that grows in waves between here and there, flattened by invisible feet.

'They're coming,' Thuy says.

I turn to ask Thuy *who*, but she's gone. Just then a woman begins to appear in the field. I don't recognize her at first. She's young, younger than I, her hair long and brown, her lips a rich garnet. More beautiful than I remember. She's holding a baby in her arms, the one from my dream, naked and plump.

'Baby Doll,' the young woman says, extending her arm to me, stretching without reaching, the other hand still cupping the infant. I smell the woman now, her scent as recognizable as my own. She's sunshine and milk, wool and comfort.

From far away I hear my voice. 'Mommy?'

She nods and extends the infant to me. I take in the soft rise of gold of the child's hair, the crevice of her neck, the curve of her bottom, the thick folds along her thighs, her eyes and mouth and fat belly. If only I could touch them in this watery dream. 'My baby.'

'Clara,' my mother says. The euphoria within me passes when an older woman appears beside them. 'You remember your grandmother, don't you?'

I do, of course I do. When she looks to me, my grandmother begins to cry. At first I assume they're simple tears, but then I see their rigidity, the way they catch and twinkle in the light. They're hypnotic, mesmerizing the way fire is. Captured within each tear is an ocean of regret.

'What's happening?' I want it to stop. My grandmother appears stripped raw and I want to look away, but I can't.

'Now she knows your pain,' my mother says.

When I look into my grandmother's face I remember, I don't want to, but I do. What it was like to live in her house, how it felt to be a child who was nothing more than a pustule. I do remember.

'Make her stop,' I say.

But my mother simply shakes her head, taking my daughter from me. 'I can't.'

My grandmother, with her ragged face and swollen

eyes, becomes hypnotic, pulling me into a swirl of light and blackness, sucking me deep into her vortex. She shows me the horrors of her life, how she came to be the woman I knew. In the next instant, we're back beside my mother and daughter in this blissful field. I can hear the river again. Over there, a canopy of magnolia blossoms shades a man leaning against its trunk. Though his back is toward me, I notice he's nearly the same width as the tree, and tall. When he turns, I know him, I almost do. I'm sure I know him. I start to ask my mother, but my grandmother is still bowed over. 'Please, forgive me – '

'Only if you can,' my mother says, swaying with the baby against her.

I think back to my childhood of welts and bruises. If only I had known my grandmother came to me at night and caressed my head. How she longed to love me.

'I forgive you.' Once the words are out, I feel something hard in my chest. It pushes, scraping my insides as it works itself up and out. It's in my mouth and I spit it into my palm. A black stone with a razor's edge, so heavy both of my arms strain to hold it.

'Let it go,' my mother says. 'It will only weigh you down.'

When I drop it, the rock becomes a white puff, a seedling. A warm breeze flows through me and I feel another empty corner of myself fill. In an instant the seedling is carried away. I watch it lurch and sway on the breeze until it plunges into the river, finding its place among the many colors. It glows purely white a moment and then it's gone, carried off by the rush of water.

When my grandmother turns to me, her face is clear, free of the strain and grief and bitterness. 'Clara.'

I start to answer, but something sharp tucks into my side and I gasp instead. And then it's gone.

'Mother, can we go now?' I have everything I need. Almost. Almost will have to do; it always has.

She shakes her head. Under the arbor of magnolia branches, alongside that man (*I know him*) is a queue of hundreds. Most stand, their arms filled with flowers. My mother leads the way, the baby still in her arms, my grandmother beside them. I follow. Together we approach the others, and when we're close enough I recognize the individual faces within the crowd. I know them all. Another gasp of air fills my insides, catching me off balance, and I reach to steady myself on my grandmother's arm.

The first in line is a young girl with loose blond curls. She bounces forward and I recognize her delicate mouth and cornflower blue eyes. Even for three Mary Katherine was tiny when she died. She hands me a bouquet of chamomile (*nobility in adversity*), kisses my cheek, and then skips away.

More yet, their faces kind and eager. Soon I'm standing on an island of flowers, dense and fragrant. None wither. They're given to me by Brooks and Tommy, Juan and Martha, Greg and Melanie. Flowers stretch for miles across the fields, climbing the trees and trailing still farther until they claim the stars and dot the ocean. All are entwined. Another burst of air flows through me, so much so that I remember what it is to feel real pain. I inhale deeply and when I do, I'm taken with the fragrances that surround us. I can smell again.

There's a woman whom I knew both in life and in death, and then after again in the photo Mike kept on his desk. Though Jenny's extending her flowers, alstroemeria, I think I should ask for her forgiveness, for Mike. But I'm not sorry. Jenny nearly touches my arm. 'You love him, you miss him.'

How can I? Here I have everyone beside me. Nearly so. Here there's no fear, only twinges of phantom pain, and mostly comfort. But I nod – I do miss him. I know Jenny loved him without regret. I wish I could say the same.

Another burst of air whips down my throat, expanding and then contracting, knocking me down hard. I roll a bit, a cramp forming deep within my core. Lying on my belly, weak, my vision wavering, I see him, the man who's been standing under the magnolia tree all the while. He walks toward me, his huge lumbering self. Even here he exudes a warmth the others find irresistible. They retreat, though, and my vision narrows to only him.

I can barely lift my cheek from the ground with the terrible pain settling into my chest and shoulder, sharp and heavy. He stands over me and I want to touch him, but it's as if a wall of glass lies between us.

'Clara,' he says.

All I can feel is a yearning, a need to hold his hand, to crawl into his lap and lay my head against him. Burrow myself a niche there the way a child would, my nose pressed into the musk of him, knowing he'll keep me safe: *I'll take care of you.* He told me he would. Yet I didn't believe.

When I twist my head to see Linus more clearly, I feel each wring of my ligaments, every vertebra bend and crack. I hold on to the pain, wallow in it, blinded, and when I see again, there's a girl standing beside him.

Trecie. She steps between Linus and me, and I understand now. I finally know.

'Linus,' I say, and he lifts me to my feet.

Trecie tugs on my arm and points to the fields of wildflowers beyond this one. 'Like your house.'

Then she bends and I feel a tickle against my ankles and along my calves. She pulls some flowers free, but they grow too thick to leave a bare patch. She hands a bunch to me.

'I waited for you.' Her voice is muffled, her face buried within my side. Such a lovely dream.

'Waited?'

She tilts her chin to meet my eyes. 'We're finally here.'

I weave my fingers through her hair, still I try to give her comfort. I start to speak, but it's as if my mouth is smothered, something pushing itself into it and inside of me, and then lightning explodes along my side.

'Are we dead?' I ask Linus.

A terrific shudder overtakes me and in an instant I'm returned to my basement workspace. My vision is blurred, but over there are the tools strewn about, the book of flowers now against the far wall next to Ryan, who's shifted. And above me, Mike. I can smell the formaldehyde and hairspray, the blood. Ryan's and mine. I taste my own. I taste Mike, too. There's a whoosh from deep within when he releases the contents of his lungs into my mouth. He's pressing his lips against mine, the breath that he took forced into me. *One-two-three*, I hear him count it out; every second's an hour. His fear is mine. He places his hands, fingers laced one over the other, onto my heart, but he doesn't bother to count. Instead the sounds coming from him are guttural, primal, until there's clarity, *Breathe, Clara!* Through his touch, I feel the give of my chest, the slackness of my mouth, and the power of his willing me to live. I feel everything. This I know is real.

A hurricane blows within, and I'm gone from him, back to this beautiful dream, to Linus and Trecie. We're in an infinite field of sweet-smelling asphodels, in the distance, the river. There's nothing else, no one else. When I right myself, a throb begins to form in my shoulder and along my side. It's almost enough to distract me from this moment.

'He's calling you back,' Linus says. 'He's working real hard to save you. You're going to have to make a choice. Not much time left, not much at all.'

'I don't want to leave you again, but . . .' The ache in

my shoulder, running the length of my side, is ablaze.

Linus lowers his voice until it's soft and rolling, thunder on the horizon. 'Clara, you're dead. Problem is you never lived. All those flowers . . . what have you ever allowed to take root?'

I look at Trecie.

'True, you tried.' He places a hand on Trecie's shoulder. 'It happens sometimes. It's a terrible thing, naturally, but on occasion some get lost along the way. Maybe they're just stuck in that netherworld waiting on someone, or on some kind of justice. With Trecie here, it was a little bit of both, wasn't it?'

She nods, her eyes meeting mine. I don't understand what he's saying. She shifts toward me, pressing her head against my waist. I can feel her.

'Trecie?' I say, pulling her closer.

'No one was ever that nice to me,' she says. 'You tucked me in with all those pretty flowers. I didn't want to leave you. You loved me.'

Suddenly her arms are filled with daisies, stems straining into buds, then unfolding into blossoms. Trecie keeps her head low against my belly. My own hands fall there. I already know what I'll find, but still I seek it. When I push the hair back, the hair that had once been shorn away, it's there: a perfect pink star.

'Precious,' I say. 'Precious Doe.'

Another gust, but this time it's as if Mike's lips are pressed to mine. I can no longer see Linus and Trecie, this place. I feel only Mike, his breath inside of me, the pressure of his hands against my heart.

The river is somehow closer now. I've crossed the field without moving and now I'm here, lying on its banks, too tired, too pained to raise myself. The others have come with me. My mother stands above me, holding my baby tantalizingly close, my grandmother by her side, Thuy, too. And there's Linus, Trecie beside him, her hand tucked into his great one. I can no longer see the others.

My mother kneels beside me and I remember how it was, what it was to be adored.

'Please,' she whispers. My daughter strains toward me and I reach for her, but her skin is slick.

Now Trecie, too. Her hand in mine, but it's too heavy to hold.

The sound of wind rushing within me is so great, I barely hear Linus say, 'It's time to decide, Clara.'

My toe dips into the river – it's terribly cold and yet it tugs at me. It slams against its banks, and contained inside the roar I hear something else, a voice, Mike's. It's calling to me, pleading. The pain within my shoulder and side is dulled, replaced by a greater ache. I want him. 'I want to live.'

Linus sets Trecie down beside me. She whispers to me – I can't hear her, but I know what she says. Then Linus spreads his palm against the expanse of my head. 'Ah, and you didn't have a chance to meet my boy. Next time.'

His fingers, the only warmth left, push me then. My

body starts to slip into the river and before the current jerks me under and away, I see Linus standing there, tossing in a bouquet of irises.

I'm whipped by a fierce current, knocked against the sandy floor. There's the smack of the river's bottom against my skull, it's ice moving through my veins. All at once I need to breathe, but can't. The pressure inside my chest explodes against my lungs. Pain is everywhere. I'm carried along deeper, faster, and I'm so very, very cold.

I try to grab the bank, but instead I touch the arm of a man rushing past me. He smiles just before the current whips him around a bend. There are more people all around me, each being whisked along his own route.

The sound of water pounds within me, it pushes and jerks. Crashing. A flash of brilliant light and then I smash against something hard.

From nearby I hear *Mike, let us take over.*

We're losing her, a different voice calls.

Another, *Still no pulse.*

Then one I know whispers in my ear. 'Don't leave me.'

It's as if I'm lost in a well, its blackness enveloping me. Straining toward the surface there's light, a blurring of colors and figures, the tang of blood and the nasal-prick of alcohol. Every limb burns, the bag that covers my mouth and nose pierces me with air, the hands that crush again and again against my chest, the jab in the bend of my elbow; leaden pain.

It's almost too much until I hear Mike's voice again.

'Come back to me.'

It's soft and pleading, fearful and true. I want to hold fast to that sound, tuck myself into it and bind my life to its promise. His hands are at my temples, caressing my skin with long smooth strokes, his lips against my ear. He is with me. He is with me.

'Clara . . .'

A word, a single word imbued with a tone, an earnestness that implies everything.

And so I choose to breathe.

ACKNOWLEDGMENTS

Though the commonly held perception is that the writer's life is a solitary one, I don't imagine that's quite possible. My own journey has provided me with touchstones and rocks, those who've inspired – either knowingly or not – and those who've supported me every step along the path.

To the members of The Writers' Group: Lynne Griffin, Lisa Marnell, and Hannah Roveto – extraordinary writers all. None of this would ever have happened without each of you. You are my boulders.

My uncle Richard D. MacKinnon, funeral director of MacKinnon Funeral Home in Whitman, Massachusetts; Boston firefighter; and a man of unwavering faith and honor. You make me believe.

Marshfield Police Detective Steve Marcolini, an honest-to-God hero, who lent his experience working on the front lines combating child predators.

Officer Michael MacKinnon, who instructed me in every facet of police work and shared some stories of his own. Not only are you the kind of big brother a sister dreams of, you've dedicated your life to protecting the rest of our community.

To Brockton Police Officer Al Gazerro for sharing his expertise about the department. Each member of your force is a credit to the great city of Brockton.

Scott Murray, whose work with children helped to shape this story.

Every writer should have the bedrock of a writing community and mine is found in Boston's only independent writing center, Grub Street. Special thanks go to Eve Bridburg, Chris Castellani, Whitney Scharer, Sonya Larson, and some of the instructors who've astonished me: Arthur Golden, Hallie Ephron, Lara JK Wilson, Michael Lowenthal, and Scott Heim.

Years ago, when I assumed writing a book was a quixotic chore, I heard Jonathan Franzen on Terry Gross's *Fresh Air* say that writing *The Corrections* counted as among the happiest days of his life. Unwittingly, both encouraged me to try, and that very day I started. Edith Pearlman's *Self-Reliance* inspired me to be bold, and Susan Landry taught me by example how to write. Thank you.

To every editor who ever gave me a chance, especially Clara Germani, Beverly Beckham, Dr. Danielle Ofri, JoAnn Fitzpatrick, Sarah Snyder, Irene Driscoll, Linda Shepherd, Viki Merrick, Jay Allison, and Cathy Hoang.

To those who pointed me in the right direction when I thought I'd lost my way: Heather Grant Murray, Hank

Phillippi Ryan, Kristy Kiernan, Gail Konop Baker, Michelle L'Italien Harris, Julie Zydel, and my high school English teacher, Roberta Erickson.

And to the greatest agent a writer could want, Emma Sweeney. Thank you for not giving up on me even when I considered giving up on myself.

My editor, Sally Kim, is both brilliant and humble, capable of coaxing out the best from every story. Words are not enough.

Years ago, I interviewed my publisher, Shaye Areheart, for a story that never ran. Though she doesn't recall it, I never forgot. It is quite literally a dream come true to work with you, but to have the support of the entire SAB and Crown team is more than even I imagined. Thanks to each of you.

My UK editor, Sara O'Keeffe, offered such wonderful insight and suggestions that made for a better story. Many thanks.

Every child should have parents like Robert and Mary MacKinnon. Thanks for giving me the greatest gifts a child could ever hope for, unconditional love and support.

To my beloved children, Alex, Ian, and Devon Crittenden, for the gifts of time, patience, and love. As much as you believe in me, I believe in you a thousand times more.

And, finally, to my husband, my love, Jules. You were right.

TETHERED

READING GROUP NOTES

In Brief

Clara couldn't remember much about her mother. Not truly remember. She'd been so young when the accident had happened, her mother was a blur to her – a blur in a summer dress. She could vividly remember her mother's wake though. Her grandmother bringing her near the casket, but not to look, not to see her mother. Just to kneel and pray. Rushing to escape, she'd collided with Mr Mulrey the undertaker, and pleaded to go home, to escape – she wanted her mother. So Mr Mulrey showed her, urged her not to be afraid, and ushered her to the coffin. It was the first time she'd seen her mother since the accident, and she looked lovely. Asking her mother to take her home, Mr Mulrey explained that her mother was dead. The comfort she felt was not from the god who'd taken her mother away, but from the undertaker who'd given her back. Perhaps that explained her life now.

As Clara prepared the body of the old woman for the wake, she restored her like her mother had been restored – to how people did and would remember her. As she neared the end of her tasks, she began to think of the cup of tea she would have when she returned to the cottage she rented from the owners of the funeral home, Linus and Alma. Linus was so good with people, as good as she was awkward. He always knew what to say, and she never did. Blending invisibly into the background was her aim, while Linus greeted and immediately put at ease. She had chosen the flowers she would place with the old woman – a secret care that she gave, always choosing the flowers that said the right thing. She knew the old woman wouldn't mind the dark as she turned off the lights and made her way upstairs.

Just as she was opening the door to the welcome natural light, she noticed something out of the corner of her eye – there was a little girl in the foyer.

The girl had an aura of neglect about her, but eventually said that Linus allowed her to play there. It seemed unlikely, but why would a little girl want to play in a funeral home? Then there was her name – Trecie, short for Patrice. It was only her name, but it was the same name as the doll that Clara had placed in the casket with her mother all those years ago. Still – it was just a name. Clara was uncertain what to do, and then her beeper went off – the medical examiner had a body for her. As the longed-for cup of tea faded further into the future, Clara went to Linus's office.

Linus seemed distracted, but confirmed that it was okay for the girl to be there. As Clara prepared once again to leave, although with a less pleasant destination this time, she told Trecie it was time to go home. Then Trecie pulled her hair into a ponytail. 'When you were a girl, did you wear your hair down?' she asked. It's just an innocent question Clara insisted to herself – she can't know anything . . .

Who is Trecie? And what does she have to do with Precious Doe, the unidentified murdered girl who so touched the community's heart, and who Detective Mike Sullivan is determined to identify?

About the Author

Amy MacKinnon is a former congressional aide and freelance writer. She lives outside Boston, Massachusetts with her husband, their three young children, two cats, and their English bulldog, Babe.

THE STORY BEHIND
TETHERED

Each year, my family gathered at my uncle's brick Tudor house for Christmas dinner. It was an elegant affair, my uncle and aunt generous hosts. Surrounded by several generations' worth of holiday décor, my aunt would lay their dining-room table with rosy hams and a Rockwellian turkey, fruit pies that glistened, and all manner of chocolate treats. As a mother of three young children, I treasured the chance to sit, surrounded by those I loved best. We'd eat while reminiscing over the past, sharing our news from the present, and, occasionally, our hopes for the future.

One year, after loosening our belts, my uncle told us of the renovations he had recently completed to his downstairs business. *'Would you like to see?'* he asked. There wasn't a polite way to say no. It was then my uncle showed us the refurbished rooms of his funeral parlour. In all the years we'd shared Christmas dinner, it never occurred to me that we celebrated the joy of the season one floor above the dead.

The rooms of the funeral home were gorgeous, though no sign of holiday cheer could be found in any of them. Still, it was a comforting place. All of the moldings were intricately carved and then polished to a high sheen; chairs were covered in sombre, tasteful fabric; tissue boxes were positioned on every available surface. My uncle explained it was a difficult time for death: the earth was hard, darkness fell early, and, of course, it was Christmas. But, he said, it's also a welcome time. In a season when we celebrate the birth of hope, what better time to venture into eternity? Though I wasn't a person of faith myself, my uncle's words were spoken with such confidence, such utter serenity; it was hard not to believe them.

When we finished the tour, I turned to my uncle and asked, '*But where do you prepare the bodies?*' While everyone else retreated back to the festivities, my uncle led me down a warren of halls to a lower level; finally, we came to an ancient door. He gave it a firm push and it opened to reveal his basement workspace. It was so unlike the rooms we'd just left. Here, concrete walls were stripped bare, and two stainless steel tables were angled, the feet tilted toward porcelain sinks.

Shelves were stacked with jugs of formaldehyde and gels; others contained substances I didn't recognize. The floor was dotted with drains for easy clean-up.

There was one bit of colour against the nearest wall, a spot of comfort to help my uncle through some of his more trying cases, no doubt. It was a portrait of Jesus overlooking the most oft-used table. Pointing to it, my uncle said, '*I put that there to remind me I'm never alone with the dead.*' Without faith, I wondered if I could do such a job, if anyone could. In the weeks that followed, I couldn't forget the image of my uncle, gazing towards that painting.

She came to me soon after, pervading my thoughts and dreams, more real to me than nearly any other person I encountered during the course of a day: a woman undertaker who didn't believe in God. She told me her story in bits and pieces; from the beginning it was clear that hers was a life of trauma. It took months to complete the first few pages, and still I didn't know her name.

One day my husband and I stopped at an antique shop, hoping to find a bargain. It was then I told him of this woman who haunted me. She'd only recently shared her name. '*It's Clara,*' I said, '*Clara Marsh.*' I hoped it meant something; that I could move forward with her story. Inside the store, we went our separate ways, he in search of rugs, while I sought out something far more elusive, something I couldn't name. It was then I saw it, propped on a pedestal table, against a candlestick. There before me was a yellowed envelope with a one-cent stamp pasted in the upper right-hand corner, the recipient's name across the front in Palmer's cursive: *Clara Marsh*.

It was a sign. Surely, it was a sign.

Amy MacKinnon

FOR DISCUSSION

'I've always known I'm alone with the dead.' The author let us know this early in the novel. What does it tell us about Clara?

'Humans – all animals, really – are born to seek life and avoid death.' Why doesn't Clara?

The author gives us a strong sense of Clara – how does she achieve that?

Look at the ways that hair is used in the novel.

'Shame no one ever takes the time anymore.' Is there a sense in the novel that the past was better?

'There's no justice in death.' Is there not?

'Silence is not a crime.' Isn't it?

'Life is suffering.' What does this tell us of Clara?

'When we concentrate on the breath, we're aware only of that moment. And that's all we ever have, really, is a moment. And when we no longer breathe, we no longer exist.' Is Clara right?

'Stereotypes are born of truth.' Is this true, do you think?

'Before life, they were tethered by an umbilical cord; after, by hope.' Is this a true reflection of mothers and daughters?

'Not all lies are born of deceit.' How is the truth dealt with in Tethered?

'But it's the curse of the young to be hopeful.' Is it a curse?

Invisibility is important in *Tethered*. How?

SUGGESTED FURTHER READING

The Lovely Bones
by Alice Sebold

The Secret Scripture
by Sebastian Barry

When Will There Be Good News?
by Kate Atkinson

Sharp Objects
by Gillian Flynn

*The Curious Incident
of the Dog in the Night-Time*
by Mark Haddon